CHRISTOPHER BUSH
THE CASE OF THE CORPORAL'S LEAVE

CHRISTOPHER BUSH was born Charlie Christmas Bush in Norfolk in 1885. His father was a farm labourer and his mother a milliner. In the early years of his childhood he lived with his aunt and uncle in London before returning to Norfolk aged seven, later winning a scholarship to Thetford Grammar School.

As an adult, Bush worked as a schoolmaster for 27 years, pausing only to fight in World War One, until retiring aged 46 in 1931 to be a full-time novelist. His first novel featuring the eccentric Ludovic Travers was published in 1926, and was followed by 62 additional Travers mysteries. These are all to be republished by Dean Street Press.

Christopher Bush fought again in World War Two, and was elected a member of the prestigious Detection Club. He died in 1973.

CHRISTOPHER BUSH

THE CASE OF THE CORPORAL'S LEAVE

With an introduction
by Curtis Evans

DEAN STREET PRESS

Published by Dean Street Press 2018

First published in 1945 by Cassell & Co., Ltd.

Cover by DSP

ISBN 978 1 912574 23 0

www.deanstreetpress.co.uk

INTRODUCTION

Winding down the War and Taking a New Turn

Christopher Bush's Ludovic Travers Mysteries, 1943 to 1946

Having sent his series sleuth Ludovic "Ludo" Travers, in the third and fourth years of the Second World War, around England to meet murder at a variety of newly-created army installations—a prisoner-of-war camp (*The Case of the Murdered Major*, 1941), a guard base (*The Case of the Kidnapped Colonel*, 1942) and an instructor school (*The Case of the Fighting Soldier*, 1942)--Christopher Bush finally released Travers from military engagements in *The Case of the Magic Mirror* (1943), a unique retrospective affair which takes place before the outbreak of the Second World War. In the remaining four Travers wartime mysteries--*The Case of the Running Mouse* (1944), *The Case of the Platinum Blonde* (1944), *The Case of the Corporal's Leave* (1945) and *The Case of the Missing Men* (1946)--Bush frees his sleuth to investigate private criminal problems. Although the war is mentioned in these novels, it plays far less of a role in events, doubtlessly giving contemporary readers a sense that the world conflagration which at one point had threatened to consume the British Empire was winding down for good. Yet even without the "novelty" of the war as a major plot element, these Christopher Bush mysteries offer readers some of the most intriguing conundrums in the Ludo Travers detection canon.

Curtis Evans

TO

AUDREY GRAY

A SMALL GESTURE TO SUPPLEMENT
MUCH GRATITUDE

Chapter I
FRANCIS KENRAY

IT WASN'T I who discovered the body. I want to make that perfectly clear, if only for the benefit of a couple of club acquaintances of mine.

In the course of an argument one of them flippantly remarked that I was scared of going out in the black-out for fear I should trip over a corpse. His pal added a bit of facetiousness to the effect that nowadays whenever I spat I spat blood. Perhaps I took both them and myself a bit too seriously when I expostulated that in the course of fifteen years' association with the Yard, and wholly on cases to do with murder, I'd discovered only two corpses of my very own, and that seemed a mighty poor record. I also added that I didn't spit.

But I think those two fellows were taking themselves a bit seriously too. Nothing is easier, as I know to my cost, than to start some argumentative hare and in a matter of moments to be defending that utterly imaginative animal as if it had been for years a cherished household pet. So I wonder now just what they would have thought if I had told them in all seriousness that not only had I discovered two corpses, but had also provided one of my own: that, in fact, I had committed what was tantamount to murder. What I do know is that they'd never have believed me. And yet I did commit that murder, though it will not be till this particular story's almost over that you learn how and why.

The body, as I have said, was not discovered by me, nor by the Yard if it comes to that. It was found by a man named Grampy who works for the Ministry of Supply, and I hasten to spike the guns of my facetious friend by adding that I don't mean the Ministry for supplying Corpses to the Yard. But my association with the affair which I arbitrarily christen the Case of the Corporal's Leave, began before there was a corpse at all.

The last thing I want to do is to be long-winded, but I think there are things you should know about the whole set-up, including myself. I was invalided out of the Army in the autumn of 1943 and was at once at a loose end, with my wife still doing nursing service up North and all the time in the world on my hands. Then George Wharton— Superintendent Wharton to you—stepped fortuitously in. I'd been associated with George for fifteen years, as I've already said, and now he was proposing that instead of being a haphazard sort of specialist consultant— gross flattery that on his part—I should do a whole-time job. The Yard was desperately short of men and had in addition a hundred new responsibilities, so there'd be plenty to keep me occupied. He added several more blandishments, though I was far too gratified to let him know that I regarded them as such. Then with an air of sacrifice and reluctance I accepted the offer. The terms were pretty generous, though that was no great gratification, except that I could confidentially tell myself with a burst of adulation that the Powers-that-Be—as George cryptically alludes to them— wouldn't pay good money if they didn't want me pretty badly. And the work sounded interesting enough: Special Branch jobs principally, and likely to take me all over the country. A Yard car at my disposal too, and petrol in reason. By the time I'd had the job for a couple of months I was hoping it might be a permanency. Not that I didn't work. In some ways I'd never worked so hard in my life.

On that morning of early January 1944 I went to the Yard to report on an assignment I'd been given in Wales, and it was about nine o'clock when I walked into George's room. He was in one of his heavy, preoccupied moods, and I didn't know then what was on his mind. But I mention the matter of moods because George is a man of many, and very few of them are governed by circumstance. A Superintendent of his versatility and standing is concerned with every stratum of society, and it is his boast that he can be all things to all men. A great character actor was certainly lost when George threw in his lot with the Law, and even to-day, if he went on the halls, I think he'd bring down the house. George, as a hawker of vacuum cleaners, or the man who calls for the Prudential, would be in the same class as Will Fyffe. But if I've given the impression that George is a mountebank, let me hasten to qualify and deny. No man can be more magisterial and dignified when he has that mind, and as for his general competence, no man gets as high in the Yard hierarchy without unquestionable reason.

George often impresses on me in my moments of mistrust or dubiety that my great asset is that nobody could look less like a detective. I suppose he is right though I never feel particularly cheered by the reminder. I am six-foot three, if you'd like to know, and thin as a rake, and the tooth-brush moustache I've clung to as a relic of Army life, is counter-balanced by horn-rimmed spectacles, and the whole effect, I'm told, is that of a Professor whom someone has been trying to turn into a Commando. But George ought to know, for no man looks less like a sleuth than himself. He may be bulky and over six-foot, but the hunched effect he can give to his shoulders puts him out of the police category in the twinkling of an eye. Then there is his vast walrus moustache which he wipes on occasions with spacious sweeps of a voluminous red handkerchief. There are his antiquated spectacles which he speciously dons to give the appearance of a very human, and probably henpecked, family man, and over the tops of which he peers with looks that vary from mild surprise or mental pain to something like a leer or squint. Then there is his repertoire of tricks, used as circumstances seem to warrant: wheedlings, pained expostulations, outbursts of wrath, blandness, self-deprecations and every brand of humbug and camouflage. And all are accompanied by what he deems suitable gestures and noises: chucklings, indignant snorts and contemptuous pursings of the lips. And from my point of view, since I've known George intimately for fifteen years, the amusing thing is that he still brings that extensive repertoire of humbug to bear on me, who can read him like the largest-sized print. Perhaps that's why I'm so fond of George, for life is rarely dull when he's anywhere around. And don't forget that the George I've described is the one seen through my eyes. The Yard thinks sufficient of him to have nicknamed him with both admiration and endearment "The Old General", and what the criminal classes think of him could be expressed only in a language so lurid that no publisher would allow its printing.

But George was inclined to be dull that morning, with never a quip or one of his elephantine attempts at leg-pulling. In a quarter of an hour he had vetted my report and was graciously pleased to say it hadn't been a bad job, and then he pushed back his chair and pulled out his pipe.

"Something on your mind, George?" I said. "Or aren't you feeling too fit?"

He began an indignant snort, then transferred it elsewhere.

"Ought to have been at Chelmsford this morning," he said "and here I am, cooped up and waiting for a telephone message."

"Anything important?"

He gave a real snort at that.

"Only someone missing. A hell of a thing for me to have to occupy my mind on." He spread his palms indignantly. "As if people weren't missing every day! There's the proper machinery, isn't there? That's what I told that bloke at the India Office. He's missing, I said, and the machinery's been set going. We couldn't do any more if it was the Prime Minister."

"The India Office?" I asked with polite surprise, and just at that moment the buzzer went. George swooped.

"Who?" he asked snappily. "Who?"

"Oh," he said, and his voice became milder. "About that, is he? . . . I see. A Mr. Francis Kenray. . . . Right-ho. Send him up."

"You'd better nip in there," he told me, and nodded to the door that led to the tiny lavatory. "This ought to be interesting. To do with that missing Big Bug I was telling you about."

I grabbed my overcoat, hat and gloves and nipped into that lavatory and I slipped the catch. Standing on the seat you can see through the fanlight and every word in George's room can be heard. George's reference to a Big Bug was interesting enough. Phrases like that are part of his stock-in-trade of camouflage. The Big Bugs, he will say with an air of contempt, or the Powers-that-Be, or One of the Nobs, and yet there is no bigger snob alive than George. Any old school tie will send him all of a dither, except thank heaven, my own.

The man who was shown into his room was just above medium height and strongly built. His age was the middle fifties and the first impression I gathered was of ease of bearing. Francis Kenray was definitely not rattled, and indeed he looked like a man whose quiet poise it would be hard to upset. But for his rather untidy moustache I should have guessed him to be a lawyer, and though his voice had no particular quality, it was as quiet and unperturbed as his bearing.

"Mr. Francis Kenray?" asked Wharton, putting on a pose that I might call mildly magisterial.

"That's right," Kenray said. "You're Superintendent Wharton?"

"At your service, sir," Wharton told him unctuously. "Take a seat, Mr. Kenray, and let's hear what's worrying you."

"It's about Sir William Pelle," Kenray began, after a pause. "I believe you know something about it already."

"Well, maybe," said Wharton non-committally. I could imagine the smile that accompanied the next remark. "All the same, sir, I'd rather like to hear it all again. From your own angle, if you follow me."

"Well, there's nothing much to say, really," began Kenray. While he was speaking it struck me how absolutely motionless he sat, as if afraid even to make a gesture, like a Scotsman at Christie's.

"I should have met Sir William at his place last night and most unaccountably he didn't turn up. His secretary got in touch with the local police and I believe they got in touch with you. Then this morning I rang the secretary and gathered there was no news so I thought I'd better come here personally and—"

"Exactly, exactly," said Wharton. "And now do me a favour, Mr. Kenray. Suppose I know never a thing about all this. Start at the very beginning. Who *is* Sir William Pelle? Where does he live? Why did you have to see him? You get the idea?"

Wharton leaned back and Kenray evidently had the idea for he began in the right place. Sir William Pelle was a retired Indian Civil Servant who had a house at Pangley. I'm disguising the names of all the places involved and for very excellent reasons, as you may see. Pangley is exactly half an hour from Charing Cross by fast train. Kenray himself was living at Hurstham, on the same line, and seven minutes short of Pangley. The so-called fast trains from Charing Cross make only three stops before Pangley: at Waterloo, London Bridge and then Hurstham. Both Pangley and Hurstham are large residential suburbs with old, substantial houses and big areas of new property built between the wars.

"It was to do with that Bengal famine appeal," Kenray said. "Various items of jewellery kept coming in: some valuable and some not so valuable. Sir William took over the secretaryship of the gift side of the appeal and opened a little office in Cunningham Street, just off the Haymarket."

"I know it," Wharton told him.

"No. 7, it is," Kenray went on, and then for the first time he seemed to pause as if at a loss. It was a moment or two before he went on, and either some trick of the light deceived me or I caught a quick, dry smile.

"If you'll pardon my saying so, Superintendent, Sir William was a very self-willed, opinionated man. He used to deposit the jewellery by dribs and drabs, as they say, at his town bank, and last night he was collecting it and taking it down to Pangley."

"How much? I mean, what was it worth?"

"I can't say." He permitted himself the faintest gesture: just the least shrug of the shoulders. "Probably thirty thousand pounds. Maybe twice that. I couldn't say. But it would all go in a small attaché-case."

"Jewellery is making big money at the moment," Wharton remarked.

"Very big," Kenray told him. "But what you want to know is where I come in. I'm an antique dealer. My main shop and office is in Lower Regent Street and I've also a little place in Hatton Garden. Jewellery's my particular line." Again he permitted himself a gesture; this time another shrug of the shoulders and a deprecatory smile. "When I was a younger man I wrote a book about it. That's why Sir William called me in, or was advised to call me in. I do a lot of work for Christie's and Sotheby's, by the way. And that's why I was supposed to go on to his place at Pangley last night—to inspect the whole collection of jewellery, and give a rough valuation and advise as to sale. Eight o'clock I was supposed to be there—"

"Just a minute," broke in Wharton. "Why couldn't you have seen the jewellery at Sir William Pelle's office in Cunningham Street?"

"Exactly," said Kenray. "I told Sir William that. I said it would save time and trouble, and I was a busy man. But no. It had to be at his place and at eight o'clock."

"He didn't even ask you to dinner?" asked Wharton with an attempt at humour.

"As a matter of fact he didn't," Kenray said. "And another thing. I was absolutely horrified when I heard he was taking all that stuff down in an attaché-case, and I told him so."

"What did he say?"

"He said, 'Good gad, sir, we're living in England, aren't we? And what do you think I am? A child or something?'"

"Pure Poona, eh?"

"Well, Sir William was rather like that," Kenray said mildly enough. "A little man, and very fiery and peppery. Livery, perhaps I should have said."

"But it wasn't your headache?"

"It certainly wasn't," Kenray said. "I told him it was his affair and I'd be seeing him at about eight o'clock. And I did. That is, I went to the house and found the whole place in a hubbub. Sir William hadn't arrived. He'd said he was coming on the usual four-five from town and then at about three-thirty or so he rang up to say he'd be taking the four-fifty. But he didn't come on it, and he hadn't arrived when I got there. I waited till ten o'clock and then the secretary and I went to the railway station—only five minutes' walk—and saw the stationmaster and the ticket collector. Nobody remembered Sir William getting off a train. In fact, they said if he had got off he wouldn't have been noticed. The collector didn't know him and if he had he'd never have noticed him except by accident. People just come surging out of the doors by those early evening trains. Swarm out by the hundred."

"I know," said Wharton, feelingly. "And what did you do then?"

"Went back home," Kenray said. "The secretary, so he told me this morning, got in touch with the Pangley police and they, I believe, got in touch with you."

Wharton heaved a sigh and then pursed his lips.

"Just one little thing," he said, and after what had apparently been due reflection. "Your own movements last night. You went home to Hurstham and then on to Pangley later?"

"I didn't," Kenray told him promptly. "My eyes aren't any too good, nor my heart either, for that matter."

I'd been wondering about that purple colouring of his and if he lifted his elbow, but that mention of a heart put me right.

"What I mean is this," he was going on. "I could have had a car from my own place to the station and another from Pangley station to Sir William's place, but I was doing the job for nothing and I didn't see why I should be out of pocket. As a matter of fact Sir William did arrange to have a taxi waiting for me. He walked always. It's about five minutes, as I was telling you. One of these unspoilt country lanes his way."

"But what about that train he 'phoned he was coming by? The four-fifty? It would have been pitch-dark when he got to Pangley by that. What I mean is this. He had a taxi to meet you. Why didn't he order one to meet himself? Or did he?"

"Not so far as I know," Kenray said. Then the dry smile came again. "He had the car for me because I insisted on it. He said the walk would do me good and I told him bluntly that I wasn't giving it a chance."

Wharton simulated a chuckle.

"Well," he said, "it certainly looks as if he didn't order any taxi to meet himself. But about you, Mr. Kenray. I gather your whole arrangements for the evening were disturbed."

"Not too much," Kenray said, and with the same mildness. "I usually go home by the four-fifty, though if it's a wet, dark night I make it the four-five. What I actually did was this. I had some arrears of work to clear off at the shop. My sister runs that, by the way. I got in at about five and I was a bit tired. Had the whole day at a sale and wasn't feeling any too good. My sister had tea ready for me and then I had a little nap in the office. Then we had a bit of dinner at about half-past six and then my sister—she's got eyes like a cat—went with me to Charing Cross where I caught the seven-twenty, as I'd arranged with Sir William."

"I get you," Wharton said. "You had only the one journey instead of two, so to speak, and a very sensible arrangement too, if I may say so. But your sister. She travelled with you?"

"Travelled?" said Kenray, rather perplexed.

"Doesn't she live at Hurstham with you?"

"No, no, no," Kenray told him. "She did for a time during the blitz but normally she lives at the shop. There's a nice little flat above it. My man has a cubby-hole there too. Useful for fire-watching."

There didn't seem anything else to ask or say and Wharton heaved another sigh.

"Well, as I told the India Office this very morning, Mr. Kenray, there's nothing we can do in addition to what's being done. The whole machinery's been set in motion and if he's to be found, then you can take it from me that he'll be found." He leaned forward. "But strictly between ourselves. You're a man of the world, like myself, and what passes between us is nobody's business."

A pause for effect and he put his question.

"Sir William couldn't possibly have hopped it— skedaddled or whatever you like to call it—with that nice little collection of jewellery?"

"Out of the question," Kenray said bluntly.

"But why?" insisted Wharton.

"Well, he'd been an important public servant in India. The authorities wouldn't have asked him to take over this particular branch of the Bengal Appeal Fund if they hadn't had a pretty high regard for him." Then he thought of something else. "Besides, where could he go to? Take myself. I go occasionally to the States, but it's under strict Government licence and priority, and only because I'm selling stones and jewellery to bring dollars to the Treasury."

"I'd overlooked that," Wharton told him. "But loss of memory. What about that?"

"I couldn't say. Certainly he was a very nervy man. I think I mentioned that before."

"Wealthy, was he?"

"Hard to judge," Kenray told him. "I'd say he had enough and no more. He's got a nice little place at Pangley, but nothing out of the way. I gathered he'd been hard hit by the war."

"Who hasn't?" asked Wharton feelingly. "Married, was he?"

"A widower," Kenray said. "One son, now out East. In the Indian Civil, I believe."

That seemed all, at least Wharton leaned well back in his chair. I thought he was getting to his feet to indicate that the interview was over, but suddenly he leaned forward again.

"Just a couple of questions, Mr. Kenray, and I hope you won't take offence. Just why should you, personally, who seem to be only indirectly involved, have decided to come to me?"

Kenray made never a movement. There was such a silence in the room that, when he spoke, his voice sounded unnaturally loud.

"One's a personal reason, and I'd rather it wasn't mentioned. My sister—stepsister, really—is a widow. A year or so ago her only son, my nephew, was killed over Dieppe, and she contributed, anonymously, a rather valuable piece of jewellery to this Bengal Fund as a tribute to his memory. There was a proviso that the proceeds of its sale were to be devoted to something special in my nephew's name."

"A valuable piece of jewellery, then?"

"I think it would have made a thousand pounds," Kenray said calmly. "My sister's more than a knowledgeable woman. She picked it up years ago and was holding it for the boy's wife—I mean, if and when he married."

"A fine young fellow, was he?"

"They don't make many like him," Kenray told him quietly.

"I'm sorry," Wharton said lamely. "And you're married yourself, Mr. Kenray?"

"I'm a widower," Kenray said. "My wife died a year ago. But about that second reason I had for coming here. I'd like to lay my cards on the table."

"Why not?" asked Wharton, and spread his palms in a generous gesture.

"Well then," went on Kenray. "Not only was I naturally anxious about this gift of my sister's, but last night, when I got to thinking over things, I decided they didn't look any too good for me. I had to look at everything from every angle. Frankly, what I had in mind was that Sir William might have been murdered for the sake of the jewellery."

"Yes?" said Wharton, and waited.

"Well, from what I might call my end, I was the only one who knew he was going home last night with the jewellery in that attaché-case of his."

Wharton chuckled hugely.

"But my dear sir! Suppose things are as bad as you thought, why in heaven's name should a man of your standing be suspected of being implicated?"

"Why not?" Kenray asked him bluntly. "Surely you'd have had to question everybody, however remotely concerned. And as far as I'm concerned, to put it very mildly, I have to spend the whole of to-day at Christie's. It's, an important sale of jewellery and I mustn't miss it. I want to be there, not here being questioned by you. Very nicely questioned, I ought to say in fairness to yourself."

"Very generous of you," Wharton told him, but I could tell from his tone that Kenray's frankness had been very much of a facer. "Another five minutes, Mr. Kenray, and you can be on your way. And I'm very grateful that you came. But about no one knowing from your end. This stepsister of yours. Did you mention anything to her?"

"She knew practically everything," Kenray said, and, to me, very surprisingly. "She's my partner in the business and, to tell the truth, there's branches of it she knows more about than I do."

"Exactly. But what did you tell her?"

"Well, she knew I'd been called in as adviser and she knew, of course, that I was going to Pangley to see Sir William last night. But she didn't necessarily know the essential thing—that he was bringing all that stuff along in his attaché-case."

"Ah!" said Wharton. "That clears that then. But what about Sir William's end. Garrulous, was he?"

"Well . . . yes," admitted Kenray dryly.

"To whom would he be likely to talk? At his office, for instance?"

And then, before Kenray could reply, the buzzer went.

Chapter II
NEW ASSIGNMENT

I COULDN'T GATHER anything of what Wharton was saying, for his voice at the very outset gave a dramatic hush, though that at least should have told me that he was listening to what he called One of the Big Bugs. No sooner had he finished than he was confirming at least that much. Back in his chair he leaned and heaved a sigh as if the cares of the world were suddenly on his already stooping shoulders.

"Well, you're lucky being able to get out, Mr. Kenray," he said with a kind of jocular plaintiveness. "I look like being tied to this desk till something happens." His tone changed subtly. "That was the India Office. They seem to know all about you."

"I've had dealings with them before," said Kenray unconcernedly.

"I said you'd been good enough to come along," Wharton went on. "And, by the way, all this is very hush-hush. Whatever happens, not a word is to get out. They don't want any scandal. I know nothing. You know nothing. Nobody knows anything. You get me?"

I could imagine the leer that accompanied the question. Kenray merely remarked in his non-committal way that he understood.

"Well," went on George, evidently finding him a tricky one to handle. "I think that's about all."

"You were asking about his office," Kenray reminded him.

"Of course. What sort of a place is it?"

"Just a couple or three rooms," Kenray said. "Almost an accommodation address, if you know what I mean. There's a sort of young lady secretary—name of . . ."

He produced a notebook and turned the pages.

"Oh, yes. A Miss Chaddon. Lent, I think, by one of the Ministries. That's all there seemed to be."

"Then if he did chatter at the office, she's the only one he could have chattered to."

"Looks like it."

Wharton grunted; grunted again, and, finding himself at a loss for ideas, got to his feet, hand held out.

"Well, I mustn't detain you any longer."

I drew back from the fanlight for Kenray was facing me as he rose, but soon I heard the voices moving away. The door opened and closed and the voices ceased, so I gathered up my belongings and prepared to wait for Wharton. It was five minutes before he was back and he was carrying a small clip of papers.

"Shan't keep you a minute," he said and began looking them through. I caught sight of the *Who's Who* on his desk and reached for it.

There was a goodish bit about Sir William Pelle—a third of a column perhaps, and I haven't the least intention to bother you with all that. Besides, I want to put down only what was of subsequent importance, and you might do worse than take a tip from me and regard the following extracts in that light.

SIR WILLIAM HENRY PELLE. Born 1881, Father. Claudius Pelle of the firm of Pelle and Letouret, Fine Art Dealers, Rue de Rivoli, Paris. Educated Winchester, and Balliol Coll. Oxford. Indian Civil Service 1907. Member Malanagram Commission, 1917. Chairman Mysore Inquiry, 1926. K.C.S.I., 1928. Author of *Peasant Proprietorship*, 1934. *Problems of Legislature*, 1937. Married, 1912, Eleanor, daughter of Sir Leyland Frame, Administrator Ta-jnore Province. Son. William Leyland Pelle, born 1913.

I didn't know then, of course, what was important and what was not, but I do remember that I thought that Kenray, like my-self, must have gathered some at least of his information about Pelle from a volume of *Who's Who*. Wharton wasn't particularly interested, and I was pretty sure he'd already looked him up. What he was interested in was Pelle's description as just fur-nished by the Chief Inspector who was handling the inquiry. That secretary, Miss Chaddon, had provided most of it and that other secretary, a Roger Mavin, at the Pangley end, had fur-nished the rest.

"Why a Pangley secretary?" I wanted to know.

"Because he was writing his autobiography," Wharton told me none too patiently. "Never mind about secretaries. You get that description clear."

It was on the tip of my tongue to ask why, but I thought it better not to. Pelle, the description said, was aged sixty-four and five-foot six in his shoes. Thin grey hair, complexion pink, moustache white, and clipped. Very sparely built and weight only about eight stone and a half. Eyes blue. Slightly receding chin. When left office was wearing warm brown tweed suit, heavy dark-grey overcoat, brown felt hat and brown shoes. His attaché-case bore his initials and though worn was stout and in good order. No stick or gloves. No glasses, but carried a mon-ocle, rarely used, in breast pocket with narrow black ribbon round neck.

"By the way," George said when I handed that description back. "It wasn't a bad move, was it, on the part of the Old Gent to have you listening in there?"

By the Old Gent he meant himself. That's one of his little deprecatory tricks for patting—or should I say thumping—him-self on the back.

"Why?" I said.

"Why?" He stared, then tried to look pained. "This Kenray doesn't know you, does he? Never seen you."

"I still don't see it."

He clicked his tongue exasperatedly.

"One of these days you *will* see something and then I shall have a fit."

"Something to look forward to, at any rate," I said. "But why shouldn't Kenray have met me in here? Have I signs of incipient measles on me, or what?"

"Why shouldn't he have seen you!" He snorted derisively. "Nothing fishy about that yarn of his, was there? Comes here off his own bat and gives the excuse that he'd rather get the questioning done before we've had time to look round."

"I see," I said. "You think he's decided that attack is the best form of defence. If so, I don't agree. He seemed to me a likeable man and an honest one, and a man of standing an importance in his own profession."

He was going to make some blazing retort and then, for some specious reason of his own, thought better of it. His gesture was almost a cringe.

"Never wash out a suspect till you're dead plumb sure, and then give him another look over before you make up your mind."

"If you like I'll say the rest of your little piece for you." I said. "You were doing this job when cradle marks still ornamented my backside. One of these days I may make a detective—"

"You will have your little joke," he told me, and I was only just in time to dodge the nudge in the ribs. "But seriously," and his face straightened accordingly, "I'd like you to look into one or two things." A note of plaintiveness crept in. "I'm tied up here for a bit and Gawd knows when I'll get out. You have a look round."

"At what?"

In the presence of such dumbness he was finding it hard to keep himself in hand.

"At what? What a question to ask! Kenray's at Christie's, isn't he? Who's in charge of his shop? That stepsister of his. There's your chance to find out a few things."

It was an assignment that I hated like hell and my face must have shown it.

"Why not Pelle's office?" I said.

His tone became a wheedle.

"You just humour the Old Gent for once. You're the one man who can go into that shop and talk the lingo. Then you can go to Pelle's office later. Ring me every now and again so that I can pass anything on."

"Have it your own way," I told him, and, I hope, graciously, though what George would pass on to me when I rang him up would be, as long experience had taught me, absolutely damn-all. I was to 'phone so that George could learn what was happening to me, and not the other way round.

"That's the spirit," he said, and actually held my overcoat for me. "Might do worse than have you take over this case. It's right up your alley."

"That's fine, George," I said, and I didn't even smile.

I had managed to get back to my old flat at St. Martin's Chambers, and as I moved off that way I was in a rather cynical mood. The whole business of inquiry seemed to me to be so utterly footling. Sir William Pelle was missing and that was that. The full machinery for tracing missing persons was in operation and nothing else, it seemed to me, was needed or helpful. Why then should Wharton be diving off the deep end and foreseeing murder and sudden death? Any British citizen was entitled to the aid and protection of the law, but why this extra hullabaloo about Pelle? Still, as I told myself, maybe George, if he didn't have prescience, did at least have some inside knowledge, which knowledge he was as usual, and for inscrutable purposes of his own, keeping for the moment to himself.

And, after all, what had I to grumble at? As I said when I left him, he was the boss and my job was to do what I was told. I told him that I'd do my best, and rounded my offer with a sly allusion that seemed to tickle his sense of humour. He chuckled like blazes at that questionable quip and said it was good and he'd have to remember it, but I still think the chuckles were stimulated and the point a bit too subtle.

And there's one good thing about police work—there's no clap-trap about loyalty to this and that. The only loyalty is to the job in hand. The last thing on earth I was likely to say was, "My God, I mustn't let Wharton down!" My job, I repeat, was to find in the haystack of Kenray's shop some clue to the needle of Pelle's disappearance, and that job, nebulous enough in terms and scope, I would do my best to do. But I could tell myself with an inward chuckle that I was going to do it in my own way. Wharton isn't the only one with a special stock and brand of humbug.

When I first worked with him I was squeamish about all sorts of things, but a year or so in his company made me a skilled and remorseless liar in the cause of truth. It follows naturally that if George believed in humbug, hypocrisy and concealment, I, as a respectful pupil, developed brands of my own. In fact, I have to-day no qualms about keeping back from George just what I think the time isn't ripe for him to know, nor do I always keep strictly to the truth in describing how I have arrived at this and that. I often wonder if he sees through my little tricks as well as I see through his own. But it's all very amusing, as I hinted before, and the curious and gratifying fact remains that we generally wind up a job not only satisfactorily but in some sort of double harness.

And about this latest assignment, I was proposing to work in my own way. I hadn't told George, for instance, that I had ways and means of getting inside information about Kenray, and from a vantage-point far removed from the shop. That's why, as soon as I reached my flat, I tried to get hold of Luddly. He's at the Victoria and Albert Museum, and something to do with ancient and medieval jewellery. I forget his official title but it's something out of the *Arabian Nights* like Keeper of the Jewel House.

"Who's speaking?" a voice said.

"Travers. Ludovic Travers."

"Hang on, will you, sir," the voice told me, and for best part of five minutes I duly hung on. Then I heard Luddly's voice. There were various gossipings and mutual inquiries and then I asked most guardedly about Kenray.

"I know him very well," he said. "The best man in London, and a most excellent fellow generally."

"Implicitly reliable?"

"Absolutely. He's got more murky secrets under his hat than any man I know. Do you know him, by the way?"

"I don't."

"Well, you'll find him very quiet and unpretentious. Like that shop of his. That's just off Lower Regent Street, if you should want it. His sister runs it, by the way."

"Name of Kenray?"

"No, no. Allbeck, her name is. Grace Allbeck. I've known her for years. The most charming woman. Perfectly delightful. My missus is very fond of her."

"Good, I must drop in some time."

"Poor soul, she's had a pretty thin time," Luddly went on. "Lost her husband in the last war and her only son—only child in fact—in this. Topping fellow he was too."

"Well, thanks very much, Luddly," I said. "I'll keep all that under my hat."

A few more words about fixing up a lunch rendezvous some time and we rang off. What he had told me didn't seem to make things any easier. That Kenray was a man of standing and integrity seemed certain, and there seemed, too, no earthly reason why I should now go to his shop. Except, of course, that Wharton had made that much a definite assignment.

I had a hunt through my wife's jewellery and found the piece I wanted. Then I walked through to Leicester Square and so to Lower Regent Street. The shop, which was just into Rodney Place, was certainly an unpretentious one, but it had more than a touch of class. The door of the side entrance was painted green and in addition to the bell-push had quite a charming knocker. In the first of the two smallish windows were two fine bow figures against a background of coloured velvet and flanked by two *famille verte* bowls in which were tiny sprays of yellow jasmine. A delightful effect, I thought, and showing definitely a feminine hand. As for the other window, the centre part of which had a steel grille, that held no more than a dozen pieces of jade and antique jewellery, but each piece, though that sort of thing is out of my special orbit, looked the perfection of its kind.

I walked on a few yards to get myself into a suitable frame of mind before making an entry and to view the shop from a distance. Above it was the single word

KENRAY

the reticence of which seemed to be the shop's sole flamboyance. And just then the door opened and a man came out. That is, he didn't come full out. He emerged and then turned, and he seemed to me to be shaking his fist at someone in the shop! Then I had a good view of him as he backed away and turned, his head still shaking angrily. Then what should he do, and though it was a perfectly fine morning, but open an umbrella, stoop forward against it as though leaning into the wind, and move on with a perfect disregard of what might be in his way. At Lower Regent Street he turned left and I lost sight of him. But I knew him well enough. He was Bertram Dane.

Dane isn't his real name. What happened to him later you will subsequently know, and so I'm running no risk of a libel action by his heirs and assigns, if any. All the same, what little I say about him is implicitly true.

Dane was the last of the eccentrics, the queer characters who flourished as late as Edwardian times and who adorned, or otherwise, the halls of the Savage and other clubs. Not that Dane was gregarious, far from it. He had a miser's reputation even if he was the owner of the finest collection of antique and medieval rings in Europe. He was immensely wealthy, for his father had been a mid-Victorian cotton king. Dane himself, by the way, was, as I reckoned, just in the seventies.

As for his eccentricities, he wore clothes that must have come down to him from his father and been worn by himself continually since. Do you know what is supposed to be the most tragic and mournful line of verse ever written? It is this, and a translation from the Chinese:

Drearily drips the rain from the hat which I stole from a scarecrow.

I don't believe that comes from the Chinese at all. I think Dane wrote it.

One other eccentricity should be mentioned. He had a house built for his collection just before the last war, and in St. John's Wood. But the lower story of the house he had no intention of using, except for a special back entry. He lived in the other two stories and offered the lower one to the police as a kind of club and canteen, and he must have had prior knowledge that the offer would be accepted. The last I heard about it was that it was a police and wardens' post combined. But you see the point? Never a penny to pay for special police protection! Surrounded at night with his priceless collection of jewellery and sleeping sound in his bed.

But what I was wondering was what had been happening inside Kenray's shop that morning and what had made the old man so obviously infuriated. In fact, the wish to know and my backward turn were one, and I was entering the shop almost before I was aware of it. The first thing I saw was a woman, standing with her back to me across the rather small room and facing a narrow passage that probably led to a showroom. There was no bell on the door and the strip of matting deadened my steps, and so engrossed did she appear to be that she had evidently heard no sound. Somehow I knew she must be Kenray's sister. She was tallish—about five-foot nine—and lithely built, and I remember I was faintly puzzled for I had anticipated someone rather elderly, and there was a woman still in the prime of her life. Her brown hair had only the faintest fleck of white and it curled round the white neck and above the collar of the sage-green jumper. I knew there was a smartness about her simple dress which it was beyond me to analyse.

Suddenly she stooped, her arms about a largish wooden box. It must have been heavy, for she had to rest it for a moment against the side of the low counter before she raised it to the top. I was moving forward, and at the sound of my feet she turned. At once I knew she was Kenray's sister. There was a definite likeness, even if I now judged her age to be the mid-forties.

"Sorry," I said. "I'm afraid you didn't hear me come in. May I help you with that box?"

I didn't know why but her eyes seemed to be searching me closely. Then she smiled.

"It was foolish of me," she said. "I oughtn't to have tried to move it. I'm not so strong—really."

I smiled too, and I didn't know why. Perhaps because the voice had such charm. Perhaps at the thought that one so lithely strong and so attractive in herself should think it necessary to proclaim her essential femininity.

But a man suddenly appeared in the passage. He was wearing a green baize apron and his cap was on as if he had just entered from the street. He was shortish, red-faced and looked a robust seventy, and he had a straggly moustache not much smaller than Wharton's.

He caught sight of me, and flicked a forefinger to his cap. "Mornin', sir."

Before I could give him a good morning he was going straight on.

"Now what about them boxes, Miss Grace?"

"I thought you were out, Tom," she said.

"So I was but I'm back now." He caught my eye and almost gave me a wink as he said that.

"Take them to the office and remove the lids," she told him. "Then you'd better go to dinner."

In that bare half-minute I had a good chance to study her. Knowing Luddly, I knew it must have been some paragon of a woman who had called forth those eulogies of his, and I was not disappointed. I told you that her voice had a peculiar charm, and the quality of breeding, but there was far more to it than that. Into her face I probably read far too much, and there were things that Luddly had mentioned that doubtless coloured my thoughts, and yet all that was far from explaining just how I felt, nor have I power of words to make my feelings clear.

I do know that when she first faced me her face was flushed from lifting that box, and the warm colouring and that startled stare of surprise somehow set the years back so that I knew that once she must have had what I can only lamely call a bewildering loveliness. Now as I saw her more closely it seemed that I could read on her face the experience of a lifetime, and much of tragedy, though of tragedy serenely borne. Everything about her had character and sureness of poise. Even that startled moment had been no more than a moment, and her stare was not perhaps the hardness I'd at first thought it, but a directness that was disconcerting.

Tom moved off with the box, arms well round it and feet well apart, and it seemed as much as he could manage. Grace Allbeck turned back and on her face was a faint inquiring smile.

"Your man's a countryman?" I remarked politely.

Her smile went and once more she seemed to be making a quick mental search of me.

"He's a Londoner," she said. "He's been with us a very long time now. But why should you think him a countryman?"

"I really can't say," I told her. "Perhaps it was that flick of the forelock he gave me. I'm a countryman myself."

There was a moment or two of awkward silence. As I fumbled in my breast pocket I was damn' sure nevertheless that Tom was a countryman. True he had a faint London accent, but I was a Dutchman if it wasn't set against a background of East Anglia.

"This piece of jewellery," I said. "I happened to be passing this shop and wondered if you'd be interested. My wife is thinking of selling it so as to contribute to war bonds and things."

She had beautiful hands and long, sensitive fingers and at once she was smiling again as she took it and held it against the light. Then she inspected it with a strong glass.

"Interesting, is it?" I said.

"Yes, quite," she told me. "Could you tell me how it came into your possession?"

"It was given to my wife by some Indian potentate or other in return for some favour when she was out there. You may remember her, Bernice Haire, the actress."

"But of course," she said. "But it was a good many years ago when I last saw her. Is she acting now?"

"Only in a hospital," I said. "But her idea was that it was native Indian work."

"It's Persian," she said. "Sixteenth century."

"Really? And the gold is twenty-four carat?"

"Oh, no," she said. "But that doesn't affect its value. You see this greenish tinge when I hold it like this? That shows it's an alloy of gold and silver."

"How very interesting!" I said, and it was. "Must have taken someone years to cut all that delicate tracery out of the metal."

"But it wasn't made like that," she said. "It was made in a wax mould. The melted alloy was simply poured in." And, as she handed it back to me, "I should be delighted to buy it if your wife decided to sell."

"What's it worth," I said, and tried to be casual.

"I can give you fifty guineas for it," she said, and as calmly as if it had been five shillings.

"Then I think my wife will certainly sell," I said. "Will you keep it here till I hear from her?" That might give me an excellent excuse to return, if necessary, to the shop.

"I'd rather you kept it," she told me.

"Yes, but I might go hawking it round. You know, trying to get a better price."

She smiled. "That's very quixotic of you. But you wouldn't get a better price. I will take your name and address if you care to leave it."

"I'm only a stone's throw away," I said. "Travers— L. Travers—St. Martin's Chambers."

She wrote it down and it conveyed nothing to her whatever. Then, as there seemed little further to say or do, I smiled and turned. She was following me to the door, and then I turned again.

"By the way, just as I was coming here I saw an old acquaintance of mine coming out. At least I think it was. Bertram Dane."

Her lips parted and I could see I had startled her in some curious way. But I hadn't. It was only that she had suddenly remembered something. With an, "Excuse me just a moment," she was making for the passage.

"Tom," she called.

"Yes, Miss Grace," came the muffled voice.

"Go easy with that lid! And don't forget there's another box here."

"All right, Miss Grace."

"We have to be so careful," she told me when she came back. "But what was it you were asking me?"

"Nothing important," I said. "I only thought I saw old Bertram Dane going out of here."

She laughed gently. "I'm afraid you mustn't tempt me into stories about patrons. We often see Mr. Dane in here."

"Did you ever see his collection?"

"Once," she said. "Quite a long time ago."

"He's a queer fish," I said. "I hadn't seen him for years till this morning. That's what made me so—well, so impertinently curious."

"Isn't it natural to be curious?"

"A dangerous hobby sometimes," I said. "But thank you again for telling me all those interesting things. My wife will be thrilled."

The door closed gently behind me and I had that queer feeling of stepping into a vacuum that one gets paradoxically when stepping from a confined space and comparative gloom into sun and free air. Also I suddenly felt hungry. And I remembered a little restaurant on the far side of Rodney Square.

When I'd taken the trouble to walk all that way round, I found that restaurant gone. Then I thought I'd go to my club and lunch there, and ring up Wharton. But as I came in sight of Kenray's shop again I saw a man emerge from the side door. His apron was off and he was wearing his overcoat and bowler.

"Then you can go to your dinner," was what Grace Allbeck had told him. 'Tom' she had called him, and he had called her 'Miss Grace' and if he wasn't some sort of family retainer, then I was woefully out.

That was why I told myself I might do worse than try to lunch with Tom.

Chapter III
NOTHING AT ALL

TOM CROSSED OVER to the Haymarket and down Mortimer Street. Fifty yards along where Charters Street crosses it, he turned into a pub, the Eagle. I was close on his heels and before I'd taken a couple of steps inside was having to clean my glasses so thick was that saloon bar with the dampness of human breath and tobacco smoke. When I put the glasses on again Tom was being hailed by a small group of men in the far corner.

I ordered a pint of bitter and managed to elbow my way towards him. I needn't have worried. So loud were his group talking that I could have heard each word from yards beyond where I took my stand, and that was with a good view of his back.

"You have a look at 'em," one man said, and Tom held out his hand to another man who gave him a small paper bag. What Tom pulled out was a shallot.

"Not a bad sample," was his verdict. "I've seen worse than them. Put them in about the end of February and see they have somethin' to eat and you ought to get a rare good crop."

"They'll be in long before February," their owner said. "The first time it's fine, end o' this month, in they ruddy well go."

"All that's out o' date," Tom told him contemptuously, and waved a hand round. "Look at last year now. Mine didn't go in till the first week in March. And I'll tell you for why. Ground were, too sodden, that's why. My brother-in-law, he say, 'You're too late with them shallots', he say. 'Wait you and see!' I say, and what happened. The best crop I ever had. And I had 'em all inside afore July was half out."

There was a babble of argument at that but Tom didn't stay for it. He was edging his way towards a door on his left and I went through it close behind him. That lunch room was packed and I couldn't see a sign of a vacant table. But Tom was still going forward and making for a single table in the far corner with a turned-up chair. He had taken his seat before I let him catch sight of me, and pretty forlorn I looked, standing there holding my half-consumed pint and looking round for a pew.

He gave me a second look before he spoke.

"Didn't I see you in the shop, sir?"

With apparent difficulty I remembered.

"You'll be lucky if you find a seat here now," he told me. Then: "Tell you what. I can make room for you here, sir."

He was signalling to a young waitress who came straight over and then found a spare chair. For over twenty years he'd had his midday meal at that pub, so he told me. I asked him to have a drink with me. He thanked me and said he was having his usual, which turned out to be a half-pint, brought with his meal. The meal itself wasn't the worst I've ever eaten, if a pretty long way from the best. The beer wasn't bad for a war-time brew and it was that that we talked about first. Then I asked him what part of Norfolk, or Suffolk he came from. You never saw a man so surprised. Then he chuckled.

"Miss Grace was tellin' you about me, was she, sir?"

"Not at all," I said. "An East Anglian never drops all his lingo, or his accent."

"Well, you weren't far out, sir," he told me. "Cromer's my home, though I've been up here for thirty year or more."

"Then you now call yourself a Cockney?"

"What me, sir?" He shook his grizzled head. "I'm Norfolk, I am, sir, and I don't care who know it. A Norfolk Dumplin', that's me. And them lot out there knew it what you see me with. Tellin' me about shallots! I grew shallots afore half o' them knew what shallots was."

"I'll bet you did," I said. "Got an allotment in the suburbs have you."

"Well, not exactly," he said. "My brother-in-law has though. Him that married my sister. She live near Woolwich and I sorta keep an eye on his allotment. Matter of fact I was over there only yesterday."

"Good," I said. "What's your name, by the way?"

"Fulcher," he said. "Tom Fulcher."

"A good Norfolk name," I told him, and added that his employers must think a lot of him. And that started him off. I think it was only rarely that he had a listener as good —or as eminently apt, if I may say so—as myself, but he certainly told me all I wanted to know. And it wasn't altogether that he was merely garrulous. There were far more things to it than that: a nostalgia, for instance; a pride in Cromer's achievements during the war, and that old pathetic attempt we all make to recapture the days so irrecoverably gone,

I'm not going to allow you to be bored by Tom Fulcher, but I'd like to make something perfectly clear. After the first ten minutes of the Kenray family I began to be bored myself and then I had an idea which tickled me immensely. All that Tom was telling me had no bearing on Pelle, but it had a decided bearing on the assignment which Wharton had given me, which was to find out—or so I read it—all I could about Francis Kenray. What I could do then, and with a cynical satisfaction, was to present him with a perfect genealogy of the Kenrays as the result of the morning's work. "Here you are, George," I would say. "You wanted facts and here they are. Family tree included free. All the latest. All part of the Travers service."

A fine old family, the Kenrays, according to Tom. The one for whom he first worked was an auctioneer, and there were two sons, Francis and Harry. Old Mr. Kenray was an antique collector and all the family had it in their blood. Tom modestly said he had it in his own.

When that Mr. Kenray was still young and the two boys only boys, Mrs. Kenray was left a widow. A handsome woman, Tom said, and within two years she married the Rev. John Crowner, rector of Great Pentry, about five miles from Cromer. A year later she gave birth to Grace.

There was a manager for the auctioneer's business and later Harry took it over. Much later Harry died after a motoring accident and the business was sold. Francis, who had gone to school at Norwich, later joined a London firm of antique dealers. He had inherited money in trust from his father and later on he bought the business he now had. And since it was at that same time that the Cromer business was sold, Tom Fulcher was induced to join Francis in London, a step he had never regretted, for a finer man to work with just didn't exist.

"What about Mrs. Allbeck?" I said. "She seems a very charming lady?"

"Lady's right, sir," he told me with an asseverating sideways nod or two of the head. "A real lady she is, sir." He smiled to himself. "Not that she don't snap my head off sometimes, but that don't amount to nothin'. A lady, sir, that's what she is."

Then he began to tell me for why, as the Norfolk phrase has it. She was the apple of her father's eye and no money was spared on her education. The handsomest girl you ever saw, and I didn't need Tom's evidence to assure me of that. A bit of an adventurous one too, though you wouldn't think it to look at her now. Had a will of her own and you just couldn't drive her or lead her either, for that matter, if she wasn't so willed. Went to a slap-up school in Norwich and then to a finishing school abroad. Only eighteen when she wrote home that she might be getting married.

"And why not?" Tom asked me. "They used to marry young in them days, and a good thing too. Scared the life out o' the old rector though. Then we heard as how she was goin' to study paintin' out there, or somethin' and the next thing I heard was that she was home. Shocking ill she was with one o' them breakdowns. Howsomever she got over it and then she married Mr. Allbeck. A painter, he was, and then damned if he didn't join up when the last war broke out and if he didn't get killed, right at the end of it. In what they called the Artists' Rifles, he was, and there she was left. Then young Master Hugh was born. You've heard about him, sir?" he asked me.

I said I'd heard somewhere that he'd been killed.

"Shot down over Dieppe," he told me. "Got the D.F.C. afore that. A squadron-leader, he was." He shook his old head again. "One o' the nicest young gentlemen you'd ever want to meet, sir. Always ready for a joke, too, like his mother used to be. A bad day for us all when he went."

"Must have broken his mother's heart."

"It did that, sir. She didn't show it much but you could see, if you know what I mean. Changed her a bit, even when she began to get used to it. Never used to get out of patience with me till that happened. Not that she do now . . . not much."

And that was that. I've told it in five minutes but he took half an hour. I sat on after he'd gone, jotting down relevant facts and dates for George's benefit, but I knew from that half-hour that my own first impressions of Francis Kenray had been right. Whatever jiggery-pokery there had been about the disappearance of Pelle—to use a pet phrase of Wharton's—Francis Kenray had had no hand in it.

I stood for a moment or two on the pavement outside that pub before I made up my mind what to do. Then I walked to Piccadilly Station and rang up George. He said nothing had happened at his end except annoying inquiries from the Big Bugs, and I told him I had nothing either, or nothing rather that wouldn't keep. Just before I rang off I said I was just off to Pelle's office in Cunningham Street, after which I'd ring him again.

Kenray's description of that office was pretty exact. It consisted of a couple of rooms, the smaller of which had been fitted up as a cloakroom for the use of the lady secretary. The larger room wasn't much more than a cubbyhole though it had a desk, a side-table and a filing cabinet.

I want you to have a good look at Doris Chaddon. I wasn't too far out when at my first sight of her I placed her as a Mayfair young thing who'd secured a cushy job. Her father turned out to be one of the most eminent bores of my acquaintance, though I didn't tell her that, and her family tree was stiff with Blimps and those who are said to be *at* such and such a Ministry.

Her clothes had that quality about them that I had noticed in Grace Allbeck's. A fine-looking girl too, about twenty or so, and poised to the point of cool aggressiveness.

"Yes?" she said, pert as you please, when I stepped inside.

I pulled out my credentials and laid them on that side-table in front of her. If Pelle's desk hadn't been locked I knew she'd have posed at that.

"But we've already seen the police," she said.

"Who's *we*?" I asked her amusedly.

"Well, I have," she told me, just a little bit knocked off her perch.

I gave her my most delightful smile.

"Then I'm frightfully sorry but you'll have to go through it all again."

"But I told them everything!"

"Including your name?"

"I'm Doris Chaddon," she said, the least bit annoyed.

"Then I'm just as bored with all this as you are, Miss Chaddon," I said.

She smiled faintly at that, then decided not to be amused.

"I'm not bored," she said. "I'm very worried."

"I know," I said, and helped myself to a seat. Then I asked her if she was any relation of old Hackford Chaddon, and that broke the ice as I've indicated.

"What was it like being here with Sir William?" I asked; and roguishly, "Pretty good job, what?"

"Well, I didn't tell that to the police," she said, "but it wasn't a bad job."

"What on earth did you find to do with yourself?"

"Oh, sometimes there'd be a letter of acknowledgment to write if a gift came in," she told me airily. "Or a bit of filing. Or sometimes Sir William would have a letter of his own."

"A regular racket," I said, and added quickly that I was in it too. Then I asked what Sir William did with himself and it appeared that he used to drop in every morning—except Saturdays—at about ten-thirty; do what there was to do and then brisk off to his club. Later he'd look in again or simply ring up. The really hectic days were when jewellery came in. That was great fun, she said. Letters of thanks, entries in the files, and Sir William bustling off to the bank's strong-room. Terrific excitement."

"But over in time for lunch?"

She laughed. We were getting on fine.

"Oh, rather. Always over by lunch."

"Didn't he ever take you out with him?"

Her face clouded momentarily at that and she gave me a quick look. She saw I hadn't meant what I might have meant.

"Only about once," she said, "and that was very formal. A sort of present for typing some letters for him."

"Easy to get on with, was he?"

"At first I thought I couldn't possibly stay," she said. "He was so fussy and overbearing." She shrugged her shoulders. "Then I got used to him. And, of course, he knew a lot of my people, and that made things different."

"Well, well," I said, and heaved a sigh. "It's a job I'd like to have had. You had lunch, by the way?"

"Working rather quickly, aren't you?" she told me and not altogether reprovingly.

"My dear young lady, I'm old enough to be your father."

"I know," she said. "That's always the opening gambit."

"A pity," I said, and added that I meant the lunch. "But since I'm here and have to show something for my time, what about telling me, in strict confidence, anything that you didn't tell the police."

"But you *are* the police!"

"Don't you believe it," I said. "That was all eyewash. You know how it is. Anything that's done nowadays has to go through about fifty various ministries."

"I know. Dreadful, isn't it. Such a waste of money and time."

She took one of my excellent cigarettes and as soon as I'd flicked off the lighter, asked what I wanted to know. "Tell me about yesterday," I said, and added that I'd bet her a new hat that Sir William had been as fussy as a hen with a brood of ducks.

"You'd win," she said. "He was absolutely priceless."

I won't trouble you with her rather funny account of the afternoon. One thing, however, that I did gather was that she knew all about taking the jewellery in the attaché-case, and that she'd known his intentions well before that afternoon. So there was another pretty problem. To whom might she have chattered?

"What was his reason for doing anything so risky?" I asked her.

"He said it was like that *Purloined Letter* story of Edgar Allan Poe," she told me. "Nobody could suspect he had all that jewellery in that ordinary little case."

"Well, there's something in that," I said. "You got a list handy, by the way?"

She said the police had the only copy retained in the office. Sir William had taken two copies with him, and I guessed that one of them had been intended for Kenray.

"What did he actually do himself during the afternoon?" I wanted to know.

"Well, first he went to the bank," she said. "It's quite close, just in Tabard Street, and he collected the jewellery. That had to be before the bank closed at three. I said I'd make the usual cup of tea. There's a gas-ring in there and we often have a cup about that time when he's in. Then while I was making the tea there was a telephone call."

"Pardon me, but that would be just after three?"

"Yes, just after three. I was inside there and couldn't hear much but he seemed to be rather angry at first. Then he calmed down, I actually heard him say, 'Well, if that's the case I'll be delighted to come.' Then when I came in with the tea he said he wasn't going home by his usual train, but the four-fifty, and would I go out and get some cakes and we'd have a regular tea. There wasn't any real hurry so I took a bus to Fuller's."

"And that was all?"

"Well, yes. We had tea here and he left at about five to four. I did ask him if he'd care to leave the case here and call back for it later, but he said certainly not. Almost snapped my head off."

"You left with him?"

"Oh, yes. I always did when he came here in the afternoons. I would go down first and he would lock up after me. I had my own key, of course, for the mornings."

"But you didn't have to get here very early?" I suggested with a knowing smile.

"Not too early," she told me with a smile that was equally knowing.

"And do you have a charwoman?"

"Oh, no. There's nothing to do, actually. I usually have a quick clean-up myself."

"I suppose you haven't the foggiest notion who it was that 'phoned Sir William?"

"Not the foggiest," she told me, but the rather hard look in her eyes told me that there was something behind the prompt answer.

"Not even if it was a man or a woman?"

"No idea whatever," she said, and got to her feet as if to avoid that particular questioning. I rose too.

"Well, I must be getting along," I said. "But what's your own idea about this disappearance? Had the old boy anything on his mind?"

"Not he," she said, and laughed. "He was always most frightfully pleased with himself."

"Might his memory have gone?"

"That's really too priceless," she said. "The poor dear hadn't any memory. He always had to write everything down, and then he'd lose the paper he'd written it on. You won't repeat any of this?"

"God forbid," I said hastily, and then heaved a sigh. "Well, I'll be pushing along. May see you again some time. Any new ideas about lunch in the near future?"

"We'll see," she told me flirtatiously.

"I might have some inside dope to pass on," I said as I jotted down the telephone number. "Sorry to bribe you like that, but we old men have to do something about things."

"But you're not a bit old," she told me hopefully. "I mean, as some. If you'd take those glasses off I think you'd be frightfully good-looking."

"I may give you a ring in the morning," I said blushingly as I opened the door.

"Don't make it too early," she warned me, and on that note of mutual understanding we parted.

*　*　*　*　*

What was the actual beginning of my change of view I do not know, but before I'd reached my flat I was feeling vastly different about the curious disappearance of Sir William Pelle. What my feelings actually were would be hard to say, but they were a mixture of alarm, cynicism, amusement and wrath. Things as I now saw them were like this.

Some dear old pal of Sir William had suggested him for that sinecure—and admittedly unpaid—job of handling the gift side of a charity appeal. Sir William himself had probably rejoiced to be a man of affairs once more, and in a contact, however vague, with India. The same or some other dear old pal had provided him with Hackford Chaddon's daughter, and the daughter herself with a job that was more of a rest cure. Funds were available for office expenses and office furniture was loaned, and after that a nice unhurried time was had by all.

As for the business side of things, that made me shiver. The Chaddon girl certainly saw each piece of jewellery and broadcast details among her friends, and whatever the possible warnings Sir William might have uttered, she would also have spread the news about taking that jewellery to Pangley in an attaché-case. Thirty thousand pounds' worth at least, and the only thing needed for a change of ownership was to give the old boy a jab in the belly in the dark and grab the bag.

It is a nervous trick of mine when at a mental loss or at a moment of discovery to fumble at my glasses or even unhook them and unconsciously begin a careful wiping. I did that then, and on the steps of St. Martin's. By the time I knew what I was doing, I definitely had an idea, and it was one that made me more alarmed than ever. A punch in the belly, I had been thinking, and in the dark, and then a clutch at the attaché-case and Bob's your uncle, as the comedians say. And there was the key phrase that set me thinking. *In the dark.* I said it to myself again, and it was a kind of Open Sesame, with a door swinging back and ideas flowing in. And was I glad that Doris Chaddon had seemed not averse to the idea of a free lunch!

I expect you've seen the lines my thoughts must have taken, and if you have, then you'll have seen something else. I have said

I was alarmed, and so I was, and it was that alarm that washed out completely such flippancies as presenting George with the family tree of the Kenrays. The less I told George, in fact, the better. If I said I thought I was on to something, and progress could only be made by taking some fair nitwit to lunch, then George would contrive to handle that side of the inquiry himself. One of his main boasts is that women are like putty in his hands, though I prefer to call them fists. Besides, why should I tell George anything till I was dead plumb sure?

As soon as I was in the flat I rang him, and he was still in.

"Any news, George?" I began.

"Yes," he said. "We know he did take that four-fifty from Charing Cross."

That was real news, and I told him so.

"Why are you sure?" I said.

"That'll keep," he told me in that infuriating way he sometimes has. "What about you? Picked up anything?"

"The answer's straight from ITMA," I said.

"ITMA?" Then he exploded. "What the hell's that got to do with it?"

I gave my best rendering of Signor So-So.

"Nothing at all," I said. "Nothing at all."

Before he could tell me I was a hell of a fine detective, I hung up. What I wanted to do was to write to my wife, and then wander round to the Yard, but by the time I had opened my desk the 'phone was ringing. It was George again.

"Who cut us off?" he was asking indignantly.

"Lord knows," I said.

"Where are you going to be from now on?" was what he wanted to know, and I told him. Then he was asking again if I hadn't found anything at the Kenray place.

"Nothing that won't keep," I told him in his own language.

After that I got on with the letter to my wife. Not altogether a personal letter as you may be thinking, but Government business in Government time. What I told her about, and very guardedly, was that brooch affair and what it was worth. I knew she always considered it too ornate to wear except with fancy dress, and my advice to her was to sell, even though she had no need of the money. Though I've found it profitable and safe to be frank with my wife about the great majority of things, I didn't see any good reason for telling her my own reasons for wanting to sell. But out of that feeling of general alarm about Pelle I had visualized a situation where Wharton—accompanied doubtless by myself—would have to make a routine questioning of Kenray at his shop, and I wanted to prove to Grace Allbeck that I had been genuine in my first reasons for calling there, and altogether without guile.

And if you ask why I should be so squeamish, then I'm afraid I can't exactly say. Perhaps the true answer is that I hated the idea of a woman like Grace Allbeck assessing me as merely a tout of the police. Personal snobbery, you say? Maybe. I prefer to call it the conserving of the last remnants of respectability left to me after years of contact with Wharton.

In any case I didn't get the chance to do much self-analysis for no sooner was that letter written than the 'phone bell went again. Wharton's voice was urgent.

"That you, Travers?"

"Who else?" I said.

"I want you to get a move on," he told me. "Just grab your hat and coat and be at the south side of Westminster Bridge in— What's the time now?"

"Half-past three," I said.

"That's what I make it," he said. "Then be there in ten minutes from now. That all right?"

"I'll be there," I said. "But what's up, George? Discovered anything?"

"Yes," he said. "Pelle's body."

And then he rang off.

Chapter IV
ON THE SPOT

I sat with George in the back of the car. As soon as I saw he wasn't driving I knew we were bound for somewhere that would involve a journey home in the black-out. The first question I asked was where were we going.

"To New Cross," George said, "or rather, a mile or so on. Some sort of marshalling yard."

"Body found on the line, was it?"

"In a railway truck, so they told me."

"Good Lord! How on earth did it get there?"

"Maybe some ganger or other didn't like to see the line all untidy," George told me with heavy humour. "But what do you think I'm going down there for? To find things out, that's why."

"You said he definitely took the four-fifty," I began, and trying to anticipate. "By the way, how did you know that for certain?"

It was Carrow, I gathered—the Chief Inspector in charge of routine—who had found that much out. People enter a train in driblets after the first rush of a queue, whereas at the exits they come as a flood. That's why Carrow tried the Charing Cross end, and the man who'd been on duty at the particular platform gate. The man remembered Sir William well, though he didn't known him by name. A regular little bantam cock of a man was his description of him, and before he knew who he actually was, and he owned that he'd described him like that because of a verbal scrap he'd once had with him over the wrong half of a ticket. Sir William travelled third class, and that train was packed to the very roof.

"Then how the devil could he have got chucked out?" I demanded of George. "He couldn't even have fallen out of a door, or someone would have pulled the cord."

"Maybe they were all too glad to have a bit of extra room," George told me sardonically. "Maybe several more got pushed off or squeezed out." He snorted. "When we get to New Cross we'll know all about it, won't we?"

"I know," I said. "He went to the lavatory and someone entered behind him and bolted the door." Then I was shaking my head. "No. It couldn't be that. You can't get a body through a lavatory window."

"Listen," George said, and his voice had an infinite weariness. "I'm an old man and I haven't much longer on this earth. Would you do me a favour and let me end my days in peace?"

"Anything to oblige," I told him flippantly.

"Then stop that damned theorizing. Theories!" He snorted again. "Where'd they get us to?"

I might have said that that depended on whether they were his or mine. I possess, or am cursed with, a ramshackle, flibbertigibbet, crossword sort of brain, portions of which dart from odd corners, foray for a second or so and then pounce. I hate, even if I surreptitiously admire, the chess kind of brain that plans for an hour ahead and takes into account the permutational movements of a score of pieces. And when I put myself quick questions, I dislike and suspect obvious answers, and the tricks of both crossword compilers and criminals have taught me that. George, not without his moments of wit, once said that the fact that there are two sides to every question is for me merely an excuse to find a third.

But while George is always scornful of my theorizing, he is never too proud to profit—if with a difference. I claim that a third of my theories turn out right and I claim too, that that's an exceptional average. George ignores the third and argues on the basis of the other two. As soon as my one third looks like being a winner, George, in some subtle and imperceptible way, begins appropriating it and by the time it has proved a winner, that theory has been George's from the very outset. Another of his little tricks is much in the same vein. When things go right, George talks about 'me', which is himself. When they go wrong, then it's sometimes blatantly 'you', or, if he can't wriggle out of all responsibility, he makes it 'we'.

"You and your theorizing!" he went on. "You tell me what happened to-day. What was Kenray's place like?"

I gave him a guarded version but I sealed and delivered it with the final assertion that Kenray was a man beyond all possible suspicion. I told what Luddly had said and added Tom Fulcher's revelations.

"What's his financial status?" George wanted to know.

"My God, George, you expect something from a casual visit!" I told him. "How should I know what his status is? All the same I'd bet both he and his sister are more than well-off by any standards. And they have something more valuable than money—a high reputation."

He merely grunted.

"But in terms of money," I went on. "She could afford to give to charity, and merely because her dead son had once been a pilot in India, something worth a thousand pounds."

Over George's face came that smile which always reminds me of the one that might have come over the face of a lion that suddenly discerned a particularly succulent Christian.

"She might have given it, but it might have been his. And I wouldn't mind giving you a thousand quid—if I had it—if I'd only got to crack you on the skull and take it back again."

"That's an idea," I said, for it struck me as ingenious. "Kenray donates a valuable piece of jewellery because he knows he's going to get it back. That means we've got to look into his alibi."

There you have it, you see—my flibbertigibbet, dart-hither-and-thither sort of brain. Already, in the presence of a new theory, I was ignoring my own claims that Kenray couldn't have been the killer.

"Pelle *was* murdered, I take it?" I asked George.

"He was murdered all right," George told me grimly. "What did you find out at his office, by the way?"

I gave him what I hoped was a humorous account, and he was as blasphemous as I'd hoped. The Chaddon girl might have blabbed to half London, he said, and that old fool Pelle too. And advertising the fact that he was taking thirty thousand quids' worth of stuff in an attaché-case!

"Tell me something, George," I said. "You're better up in the law than I am. Suppose Pelle hadn't been murdered as well as robbed. If someone snatched the bag and got clear, what would his responsibility have been?"

The car swerved as it took the left-hand fork at the Marquis of Granby and that rather upset his snort.

"Responsibility? After what you've told me, he'd have been lucky to have got off without a charge of criminal negligence."

"He'd have had to pay up?"

"Of course he would!" George snapped at me. "If he was a man of honour, he'd have paid up straightaway."

"And if he hadn't the money?"

"That was his funeral," George said. "But what's the use of going into that? He's dead, isn't he?"

I said no more for several reasons. One was that we were turning into a side street and I knew we were getting close to our destination. And I didn't say that even if he was dead, then his estate might have to pay, for that might have induced George to ask me more about Pelle's office and the last thing I wanted to do was to give him the faintest hint of that really promising theory that had come to me earlier that afternoon. Then the car turned sharp right and there was the marshalling yard. A man was standing by the open gates and George introduced him as Carrow. A dour, pertinacious cove he looked to me, and with plenty on his mind.

We walked round and even under trucks and across what seemed miles of track and then all at once came on a solitary truck near which stood a small group of people. One was a porter and another an assistant traffic manager, and there was a youngish man in spectacles. There were also a plain-clothes sergeant and a couple of his men.

"This is it, sir," Carrow said, and waved a hand at the truck.

As far as I was concerned it was very much of an anti-climax for there was nothing to be seen, for that truck was covered by the usual tarpaulin. But the situation must have been rehearsed, for as the inspector finished speaking, the sergeant moved forward and drew back a corner, and there was something that was probably Pelle.

"A very high wind last night, sir," Carrow told Wharton. "This corner rope got snapped, as you see. Otherwise we mightn't have discovered the body till the truck was unloaded."

Wharton didn't see, but he nodded. Then in his mildest voice he was telling the onlookers to get back a few yards if they didn't mind, and when he wanted one of them, perhaps he'd be good enough to come forward.

"How much do they know?" he asked Carrow when the sergeant was moving them off.

"Not a thing, sir."

"No idea who he is?"

"No, sir. Except Mr. Mavin."

"Which one's he?"

"The young gentleman in the glasses, sir. Sir William's secretary. I got him here for formal identification."

"Make sure he doesn't talk to the others," Wharton said.

"He's been warned, sir," Carrow told him. "And there's a man there."

There was also a man with us who hadn't been introduced. Wharton was giving him an inquiring look when Carrow anticipated. It was the police doctor. Wharton gave him a shake of the hand and a genial smile, and then was asking to be given a leg-up. I got one too, and Carrow drew the tarpaulin well back.

From the quick descriptions I'd overheard I should have recognized Pelle at once. Wharton gave a grunt.

"Proper little bantam, isn't he."

I had long learned not to wince at Wharton's reactions to corpses. To him, and to Carrow for that matter, they were like radishes—twopence a bunch. And Pelle did look fierce and bristling in his miniature way as he lay there, body slightly curled and eyes glaring full at us.

"Body been moved at all?" Wharton asked.

"Not to make any difference," Carrow said. "And we've had him photographed."

"Damn these castings!" exploded Wharton as he nearly wrenched an ankle in moving forward. They were heavy steel castings rather like those that hold railway metals to the sleepers, only ten times the size and burnished and the whole floor of the truck was covered by their two layers, with the tarpaulin to protect them against rust. Pelle had certainly ended up on a hard enough bed.

"The body was placed here," pronounced Wharton.

"That's right, sir," said Carrow. "It couldn't have been chucked in. The tarpaulin would have stopped that."

"Actual cause of death?" asked Wharton with a lifting of eyebrows at the doctor.

"Blow on the back of the skull, just here," the doctor said. "An abnormally thin skull, I'd say."

Wharton grunted then stooped gingerly over the body. A grasp of the shoulders and he turned it on its face.

"Hallo!" he said, "What's this?"

This was a patch of white that was thickest at the corpse's rump and showed less plainly up the back of the overcoat. Wharton felt it.

"Sticky," he said, and then put his fingers to his tongue. "It's sugar!"

Carrow craned up to look and then had a taste.

"Sugar it is, sir."

"Very curious indeed," Wharton said slowly. "Still, it shouldn't make things any harder. What about time of death?"

"We've got that to a nicety," Carrow said, "or rather, we can get it. He had some tea and cakes at just after half-past three yesterday afternoon, so the stomach content ought to give the right answer."

"Pardon me," I said, "but did you learn that from Miss Chaddon?"

"That's right," said Carrow, and looked a bit surprised. George gave me a glare, but that didn't worry me. I wanted to know just what that young lady had told the police and Wharton wasn't going to stop my finding out.

"Clear his pockets out," Wharton said, "and I'll take whatever there is. Make a duplicate list. Have all his clothes tested and especially his overcoat and his boots. How did the body come to be found, by the way?"

Carrow, busy at three jobs at once, said it had been seen by a Horace Edward Grampy, an official of the Ministry of Supply and from whom a written statement had been obtained. He was travelling that morning from Sevenoaks to town by the ten-thirty and as his train halted outside Batmore Junction with the signals against it, a goods train crawled by on the near side. The wind, still blustery, drew back the tarpaulin flap and showed what he thought was a body.

"Thought?" demanded Wharton indignantly.

"He didn't see it till it was almost by him," Carrow said. "Also, by the time his train was on the move again, the goods had turned off into a siding. Then when he got to his office he thought it over and gave them a ring at New Cross. By that time it was nearly midday."

"How was he able to see into this truck?" asked Wharton. "It was closed, wasn't it?"

"It's all in his statement, sir," Carrow told him imperturbably. "The goods was on a lower line that comes to the same level about half a mile on, so he could see right down on it."

Wharton cast an eye up at the sky. Dusk was none too far off and his tone took on an impatience.

"I'd better have a talk with some of those people. Who actually found the body?"

The traffic man and the porter were called over but it was at the far side of the truck and out of sight of the body that Wharton did his interviewing. The traffic man was the only one who really mattered, and Wharton honoured him by taking down his answers. As I'd hate to bore you with a quarter of an hour of talk, here is a summary of what Wharton learned.

1. That particular goods train and the four-fifty from town were never within miles of each other.

2. With regard to the four-fifty, the number of passengers getting out at Hurstham would not make any appreciable difference to the crowding in the carriages, since they would be filled by those standing in the corridors. In

other words, Pelle could not have been killed on the train and his body thrown out.

3. Pelle did not go to sleep and overshoot Pangley Station. The next stop was Sevenoaks, the terminus, and inquiries had been made there.

"In other words," said Wharton, "he"—that was how he alluded to Pelle throughout—"took the four-fifty and got off at Pangley alive and well. The train was on time?"

"Dead on time," he was told. "There was no fog and we *have* to keep on time with these locals."

But what mattered most was the movements of the particular truck in which he had been found. They were as follows.

That truck was shunted on the goods train at Sevenoaks in the afternoon. The train then moved on to Manwood Junction and there was a good deal of shunting there till about ten at night, when the train moved on then to Bat-more. More shunting and then it moved on to New Cross Yards.

"Devil of a slow business, wasn't it?" asked Wharton.

"None of it priority stuff," he was told. "Night shunting is a slow job, sir, in the black-out, especially when it's as dark as it was last night. None of the stuff on the train was all that important."

"Well, we're more than grateful to you," Wharton said. "Now do something else for me. Write down all you've told me. Add any other times that goods train had to stop because of signals, shall we say. Keep a copy yourself and let me and Inspector Carrow each have one. And keep it all under your hat. Not a word to a soul."

"A lot of use telling him that," George told me when he'd gone. "One good thing though. The papers won't be allowed to print a thing."

"A fine specimen of bureaucrat," I said. "And you always talking about democracy."

But George was beckoning to the young man in the spectacles and the three of us converged on the truck front.

"Mr. Mavin, isn't it?" George said, and held out his hand.

I was having a good inspection of Mavin. He looked as if the Services had turned him down on account of physique, but he had quite a pleasant baritone voice, if a bit precious. He looked at close quarters much older than I had thought at first, and was, in fact, just thirty. Very definitely Oxford was my opinion.

"How'd you get here, Mr. Mavin?" Wharton asked after he'd shaken hands and introduced me.

"A car fetched me," Mavin said.

"Then you might as well come back with us," Wharton told him. "We ought to be off in a minute or two."

Carrow had just finished noting down the contents of a small wallet, and in a couple of minutes everything was in a linen bag.

"You might as well get him away now," Wharton told the doctor. "Let me have a full report as soon as you can. At Pangley for the next hour or two and then at the Yard."

Wharton and Mavin set off together. Carrow's two men carried the body on a stretcher and I brought up the rear with the inspector himself. It was he who asked me if I had been doing anything on the case and I gave him a carefully edited outline.

"What did your people get out of that Miss Chaddon?" I asked him.

I gathered that his information was highly edited too, though he did mention the telephone call that had made Pelle take a later train.

"Did you think she knew whom that call was from?" I asked him bluntly.

"Why?" he asked me quickly. "Did you think she knew—"

"I hoped she knew," I told him, and then changed the subject. "Did you get anything important out of Mavin?"

"Not a thing," he said. "Except that he knew that Miss Chaddon."

"Did he indeed!" I said, and wished I'd kept my mouth shut. "But what's he do for a living usually."

"An author, so he told me."

"Don't remember his name," I said, and by then we were getting near the yard gate again.

* * * * *

"Pangley Station," Wharton told the driver and was motioning Mavin to get in behind with himself. I sat alongside the driver, but I could hear each word that was said.

"How'd you come to get this job with Sir William?" was Wharton's first question.

"He knew my people," Mavin said, "and me too— indirectly. His son and I were at Winchester together."

The same old racket, I was thinking, not that a secretaryship with Sir William was a plum of the literary market.

"Chiefly about India, this autobiography?"

"Yes," Mavin said, and rather diffidently.

"You know the country?"

"In a way—yes," Mavin said. "I was born there."

"Must have been an interesting job," Wharton said, and I was prepared to hear him say unblushingly he was a literary man himself. "And what was Sir William like to work with? Everything's in the strictest confidence, by the way."

"I suppose he was about the same as most," Mavin said philosophically. "A bit peppery now and again."

"I can guess," said Wharton with a world of sympathy. "A bit trying at times. And what's your own particular line? Novels, or what?"

So Wharton knew Mavin was an author. I thought, and I wondered what else he knew that he hadn't seen fit to hand over.

"I've tried several things," Mavin said, and evidently wanted it left at that.

"Who are your publishers, Mr. Mavin?" I leaned back and asked, if only to tell Wharton I was still there.

"I've had several in my time," he told me, and again was disinclined to say more.

"And who are you with now?"

At the moment, he said, he wasn't with anybody, by which I gathered he had no contract. That job with Sir William had taken all his time.

"How long have you had it?" asked Wharton.

Mavin thought for a moment and then said it was just over a year. That struck me as the devil of a while for a full-time secretary to spend in compiling a book like that. But by then we were passing the first pink bungalows on the outskirts of Pangley and the night was practically on us. Soon we were crawling through darkened streets and at last up a slight incline. A train roared above us as we went under an archway, and there we were at Pangley Station.

Chapter V
CALL IT A DAY

WHARTON HUSTLED the two of us out and then looked at his watch.

"Just on time," he said, and I expected him to add that the Old Gent had been smarter than we'd suspected. Then he produced a torch.

"What are your eyes like, Mr. Mavin?"

"Not too good in the dark," Mavin said.

"Then you'd better keep close to me," Wharton told him. "You've got to show us the way to the house."

He told the driver to bring the car on about twenty yards behind us. When he halted, the car was to halt. I was wondering why we were still waiting and in a matter of seconds I knew why. It was the four-fifty from town that had just come in, and now people were pouring out of the door beyond which we stood. Hundreds there seemed to be, though probably no more than scores, and only when they had thinned did Wharton make a move. His torch flickered across the hard gravel of the station yard and Mavin and I were at his heels.

On our left ran the railway and a goods train chugged by quite close to us. On the right was a bank that ran upwards to some woods. Then about a hundred yards on we came to a fork. Wharton halted and listened. Most of the crowd had moved down to the left and one could hear their feet and their voices. To the right was scarcely a sound.

"The buses are just down there," Mavin said, indicating the left. "We go this way."

Now we were in a widish lane with no more than fourteen feet of metalling. At each side were wide grass verges whose edges were churned to deep furrows by traffic. The hedges were tall and unkempt, and then suddenly the hedge on the right was trimmed, and there was a large double villa. Again Wharton halted and listened and this time there was never a sound ahead of us.

A hundred yards on and we came to another fork. The left was a main continuation, Mavin said, and ultimately came out south of Sevenoaks. Our way was to the right, and this time we were in a lane as rustic as you'd hope to find. There was a scant twelve foot of metalling and the wide verges were grooved and muddy where passing vehicles had churned them up.

"Why's there all this traffic here?" asked Wharton.

"There's a military depot about five miles on," Mavin said. "A lot of searchlight and gun posts all round too."

The lane narrowed erratically and curved to the right. A hundred and fifty yards from the last fork was a cottage, and on our left. Wharton sprayed light over its neat gate and along its brick path to the front door.

"Who lives there?" he whispered to Mavin.

"Sutton," whispered Mavin back. "He's the gardener and handyman."

Wharton sniffed. In the air was a heavy autumnal kind of smell compounded of damp soil and rotting leaves. Dew was dripping from the branches that overhung the narrow track. Wharton gave a grunt that might have meant anything and then moved on again, and all the time his torch was on the grass verges. Another hundred yards on, and again on our left, was a white gate. Wharton's torch showed the name—'Kalpoor'.

"Here we are then," he said. "How long would it have taken us if we'd come straight here?"

"Sir William said he once did it in four minutes," Mavin said, and in his tone was a faint scepticism.

"You think he trotted," was Wharton's comment.

"Well, I usually do it in just under six minutes," Mavin said, and Wharton seemed satisfied enough.

Mavin pushed the gate open and we waited till the car came through. A narrowish drive of some fifty yards turned left to the front of a Victorian, red-brick house, with twin bay windows and a small pillared porch. Mavin's key opened the door and he switched on the hall light.

"What exactly did you wish to see?" he asked Wharton.

"Sir William's room, I think. The one where he worked."

Mavin opened a door on our left, switched on the light and ushered us in. A cheerful fire was burning in the grate of an ornate fireplace. Plenty of books were in various cases, and portraits, doubtless ancestral, were on the walls. There was a mahogany desk at which Sir William himself worked and a side-table, filing cabinet by its side, which Mavin always used. On another table was the telephone. The brown hide chairs looked comfortable and nicely worn, and in the air was the faint smell of cigar smoke. Wharton had a sniff at it and then deposited his linen bag on the open flap of the desk.

"Snug little place," he said, and was taking off his overcoat. Then he took out his notebook and flicked over the leaves. Mavin stood by aimlessly, pork-pie hat in hand.

"Hm!" went Wharton, and began adjusting his antiquated spectacles. "Your household staff here is a cook-housekeeper and one other maid."

"There used to be two maids," Mavin said. "One got called up and we haven't been able to replace her. Sutton has to help, of course."

"And he was in his cottage last night from five o'clock onwards," Wharton said, eyes on the notebook.

"I believe so," Mavin said. "I mean, I believe he told the police so." He seemed a bit out of his depth for next he was stammering that he didn't mean that Sutton had told an untruth. It was only that he hadn't been present when Sutton was questioned.

"Exactly," said Wharton graciously. "And the two women were in the kitchen all the time, or as near as makes no difference."

He closed the book, satisfied doubtless with the impression of omniscience. Then he peered mildly at Mavin over his spectacle tops.

"And where were you from five-twenty onwards?"

"I?" asked Mavin, a bit taken aback. He smiled lamely. "Well, actually I was here. I always waited for Sir William here. He'd told me over the 'phone that he'd be in by the five-twenty."

"And when he didn't turn up?"

Mavin shrugged his shoulders.

"I rang for the kitchen and countermanded tea, and then I went up to my own room. I knew I had half an hour before the next train in."

"And when he didn't come?"

"Well, I began to panic a bit. Because of Mr. Kenray coming, if you follow what I mean." Wharton was saying nothing and he went stammeringly on. "What I mean is it wasn't till he didn't come by the seven-twenty that I was really alarmed. You see, we should have been having dinner by then. And then Mr. Kenray came and finally I rang the local police."

"That's clear enough," was Wharton's comment on that spasmodic story. "But that autobiography you were working at. Could I have a look at it?"

Mavin seemed delighted. About five-sixths was finished, save for a final review, and from a drawer of his filing cabinet he produced the roughly bound chapters.

"It was going to end where he left India," Mavin explained. "He had the tentative idea of doing a second volume later."

"Well, if you leave it here we won't keep you any longer," Wharton said. "You'll be handy if we want you?"

"In my room," Mavin told him. "There's the bell if you want me. But may I get you both some tea?"

Wharton began some hypocritical blether about not troubling anybody and I said bluntly that tea would be very nice. As soon as Mavin had gone I gave George a high-sign and went over to the telephone. It was still well short of six o'clock and I hoped I should be able to catch a man who'd been my own literary agent. While I was waiting for the number, Mavin looked in to say that tea was just coming, and then seeing me at the telephone he oozed off again and I heard him going up the stairs.

Just as the elderly maid brought in the tray, my inquiries were over. I hung up for a few minutes and by the time we'd polished off what was on the tray, I was rung up with the answers. Mavin, as an author, amounted to nothing, I reported to George.

"The fact that he didn't make money out of books doesn't prove he was on the rocks," was George's comment. "I'd say that he had private means."

"Then income tax has hit him hard," I said. "The proof is that he took this footling job."

"Why rush ahead?" George told me impatiently and illogically. I merely wanted reasons why Mavin should nip out of the house and crack Sir William on the skull and then nip back again. Mavin had said that he couldn't see very well in the dark, but he had walked close to me through the darkness on the way to the house and even when George's torch wasn't in action he did well enough, never once stumbling against me or setting a foot wrong.

"There you go," said George when I told him that. "We don't even know that Sir William got off that train." He gave me a glare and one of his best snorts. "Come on. Let's have a look at what was in his pockets."

There were the usual oddments and a quantity of loose change, but in his wallet were two fivers and some smaller notes.

"It definitely wasn't a snatch affair then," Wharton said. "Whoever did him in was after that attaché-case or else they'd have cleaned out his pockets."

There were various papers in the wallet too. One was a newspaper-cutting. I turned it over to see what paper it was from and there was the name and date in ink.

Daily Clarion. Dec. 4th.

The cutting itself was from the gossip column.

At the Universities Club I ran into my old friend Sir William Pelle, now extremely busy, he tells me, at the gifts branch of the Indian Famine Relief Fund. Sir William, who is also managing to snatch time for the completion of an autobiography that should be of absorbing interest to all Anglo-Indians, is very satisfied with the result of the appeal so far, though more gifts of jewellery would be welcomed. Bill ('Skittles') Pelle, Sir William's only son, whom many will remember as the holder of the mile record at Oxford, is connected with the Administrative Staff. But he still finds time for sport in those rare leaves which fall to the lot of our over-worked administrators, and only recently sent home a fine tiger skin. Sir William tells me that the bullet that settled the account of that particular tiger was clean through the centre of the forehead.

I was smiling rather wryly as I handed that cutting over to George.

"Someone else he's been blethering to," he said, and referred to the late Sir William. He clicked his tongue annoyedly. "If everybody in that Club of his didn't know about that attaché-case, then my name's Robinson. And what was amusing you about it?" he said, and referring this time to the cutting.

"The world in general," I said. "The sorrows of overworked administrators and how busy poor Sir William must have been."

Wharton gave another grunt and then was asking if there was anything else. All I could find was a half-sheet of notepaper on which was written something that struck me as a family motto. The handwriting turned out to be Sir William's and the whole thing was like this:

Par moy ton aide

(B.M. or K?)

And cts.

The last note about *cts.* was not in ink like the rest but in pencil, and seemed to have been added later. It was so badly written that Wharton said it wasn't *cts.* He said it was *etc.* and

I didn't argue the point, though why anyone should write down what was equivalent to "And etcetera," was beyond me.

Wharton said he had nothing else in mind and we'd better have that secretary down and then be getting back to town. We agreed on a question or two and the bell was pushed.

"Ah! come in, Mr. Mavin," Wharton said in his best avuncular manner. "We're just off but we thought we'd like a word or two first."

That was the cue for me. I handed him the *Par moy ton aide* paper, just to put him at ease, and asked if it conveyed anything to him.

"Sir William asked me about it," he said. "Several days ago it would be."

"Then it couldn't be his family motto."

"Oh, no," he said, and smiled primly. "That was *Fide non armis.*"

"By loyalty and not by weapons," I translated freely for George's benefit. "And he asked you about it, did he?"

"Yes," he said, "but I've never seen this paper before. He merely wrote the words down for me. He seemed very bucked at remembering them."

There was something definitely puckish and certainly very human about Mavin as he made that small revelation. I was actually beginning to like him.

"And what did you tell him?"

"Oh, just that it was Middle French. Then he asked how I translated it and I said, 'I will be your help.' He said that wasn't literal enough. His own idea was, 'Through me your help'."

That seemed to be that, and Wharton chipped in. Over his face came that Atlas look, the one where he carries the world, troubles and all, on stooping shoulders. Sir William's death was a bad business, he said, and a mighty serious one. Murder always was, but in this case there were wheels within wheels, though he was careful not to add what wheels they were. Then came the old formulae about the law holding everyone in suspicion till satisfied of innocence, and how that was no slur on character but something actually to be welcomed by the innocents themselves.

"Now take your own case," Wharton said, now heavily paternal. "You're young compared with me and you haven't come up against the rough edges. You don't know perhaps all that gossip can do. Gossip about yourself, for instance."

Over Mavin's face came a very distinct flush, and he wriggled uneasily on his chair.

"Did you know about Sir William bringing the jewellery down last night?" went on Wharton.

"Well, yes. He told me so himself."

"And about *The Case of the Purloined Letter*?" I asked amiably.

"Yes," he said, rather surprised.

"Well, there you are," cut in Wharton, and peered over the spectacle tops. "I take it you're not a wealthy man Mr. Mavin?"

"I'm not," Mavin said. There was something else he wanted to say and it was only after he'd moistened his lips that he got it out. "As a matter of fact, strictly between ourselves, I was only too glad to take this job."

"Paid well, was it?"

"Not too well," Mavin said. "A hundred and fifty a year and, of course, I lived here."

"There you are!" said Wharton, and waved a triumphant hand at me. "Just what we were saying. There's you knowing all about that jewellery. Not too well off for money—which I'm not if it comes to that. What alibi have you got for last night? None at all!"

Mavin was blinking away like mad and a growing horror was spreading over his face.

"What will the scandal be?" went on Wharton mercilessly. "You may not know, but I'll tell you. That jewellery mayn't be recovered and people will talk. Now do you see?"

"But really, it's too absurd," broke out Mavin, and then was all flustered again. "I don't mean what you were saying. I mean that I should have done . . . I mean . . ."

"Exactly!" said Wharton. "But that won't stop the talk and the harm to your career." He frowned portentously and his voice lowered. "And another thing—strictly between ourselves. Miss Chaddon!"

Mavin's face went a tomato red.

"You're not engaged to her by any chance?"

"No . . . I mean, not at all," stammered Mavin, and though Wharton's approach was funny in a way, I was somehow finding those little tricks of his somewhat misapplied.

"But you're very good friends."

"Well, yes."

"You dance together and all that sort of thing."

"Well, yes . . . sometimes."

"Exactly!" said Wharton, and gave me a look. "Just what we were saying. There's your scandal for you. You want to marry this particular lady. But you can't. You haven't the money. But you know how you can get hold of thirty thousand pounds. You see it?"

"But it's preposterous!" The worm turned so violently that the words were almost shouted.

"I know it is," Wharton told him placatingly. "All the same it may do you an incredible amount of harm. Miss Chaddon knew about the jewellery. You knew that, didn't you?"

"Well, yes," said Mavin and gulped.

"Used to have little talks with her on the 'phone."

"Yes, but . . . but not very often."

"Well, there you are," said Wharton with another look at me. "Even her name will come into all that scandal and you don't need me to tell you how. In fact, there's only one thing you can do. Two things. Make up your mind to give us every possible help, and the other is to write out a confidential statement which I'll collect in the morning. Everything you can think of in connection with last night. Everything connected with Miss Chaddon and yourself. Nothing's too unimportant."

He got to his feet. Mavin rose too, moistening his lips and doubtless wondering just what that extensive assignment meant.

"One little thing," Wharton said, and his tone was definitely magisterial. "You're to give me your word that you'll not communicate with Miss Chaddon till further instructions. The precaution is for the good of both of you. I can give you my word on that."

He picked up those roughly bound chapters of the auto-biography, frowned as he looked at a page or two, and then turned to me.

"Perhaps you'd better have a look through this. Just a quick look. Perhaps Mr. Mavin will wrap it up."

That was about all. The manuscript was duly wrapped up and Mavin was told he was to stay on at Kalpoor till instructed otherwise, and he needn't worry about his salary.

"If necessary I'll pay it myself," said Wharton with a final jocular touch to leave him at ease. "We'll be down again in the morning but you needn't worry about that."

When the door closed behind us the night looked as black as as coal. The driver switched on the lights.

"Come behind us as you did before," Wharton told him, "I shall be walking."

"We'll test the time properly," he told me. "Just a normal pace."

It took us exactly five minutes, and Wharton expressed himself as satisfied. Sir William knew the way better than we did, but our long legs might unconsciously have moved us more quickly.

"And now I'll tell you something that mayn't have occurred to you," he told me as soon as the car moved off. "At what time did the four-fifty from town get in?"

"Twenty past five," I said.

"Right," he said. "Then—and always provided he got off alive at Pangley Station—Sir William was well on the way for home at twenty-five past. Crack him on the skull and snatch the bag. That's done so quickly that it doesn't count. And what then?"

"From whose point of view?" I said. "That of the cracker-on?"

"That's it."

"Well, he nips into his car if he has one. If not, then he gets a train back to town."

"There *was* a train back to town, and a fast one," he said, and I knew then that that was what he had been leading up to. "And at five-thirty-five. Gets into town at six-five."

He waited a moment for applause that didn't come; grunted, and changed the subject.

"What did you think of that Mavin?"

"I thought you handled him well," I said. "But I'd bet a good deal he had nothing to do with the murder."

"I wouldn't be so sure," he said. "Because a man's been to Oxford or Cambridge, that doesn't make him God Almighty. What about that night club gang just before the war?"

I couldn't help smiling at that. Mavin and night clubs seemed rather funny, and I said so.

"Well, he and that Miss Chaddon have been to night clubs," he told me. "Does he look like one who can hold his liquor? Not he. He chattered and she chattered, and there you are."

"I wish you wouldn't keep all these things to yourself and then spring them on me," I told him irritably. "But you asked me for an opinion and I gave it, for what it's worth. Mavin would wince if he had to wring a chicken's neck."

"He didn't have to. All he had to do was crack the old man on the skull in the dark."

I said nothing.

"And what about his manner back there? Scared stiff, that's what he was."

"And no wonder," I said, "with that grilling you gave him!"

He chuckled at that and then was asking me for a cigarette. I was feeling tired and a bit hungry. George had wolfed most of what had been on the tray.

"Nothing else to-night?" I asked.

"Not for you, unless something's turned up," he said, and with a hint of reproach. And then I remembered something. Old Bertram Dane and his visit to Kenray's shop.

"He's a lad," said Wharton, and chuckled hugely. "Still carries that umbrella, does he?"

Then he said he could tell me some tales about Dane.

I said such as what.

"Well, there was that little business of Toby Nelder's," George began, "but that would be before your time. Toby was then the big tea man. Little fellow and piles of money. Had a fine place near St. Albans. Keep this well under your hat, by the way.

"But about Dane. He and Toby were pals, in a way. Both collectors, only Toby's was stamps. Now Toby—his real name was Tobias, and a hell of a name too—he had a grandmother who was incredibly old. Lived in Eaton Square, or somewhere there, and she had a ring that Dane wanted. This all came out *in camera*, by the way. Dane offered Toby a *quid pro quo* if he'd get it from the old girl, but Toby couldn't. Then Dane called on the old lady and the ring was missing. I believe there was the very hell of a row between him and Toby and it looked like ending in a case. We were actually called in and then everything was hushed up. Dane swore that if it was gone, then Toby had taken it. You never heard such a couple of liars. And then the ring turned up. Sent back to the old lady anonymously through the post."

"Dane had it?"

"Of course he had," George said with a snort. "Then got the wind up and sent it back. Talk about collectors being honest people! They're the biggest thieves and liars unhung. It's a disease. The only genuine kleptomania I know."

Before he could get going on further reminiscences we were crossing Westminster Bridge. I was run up to Trafalgar Square and George said he'd ring me if anything had happened.

Service meals were still obtainable at the flats and I stood myself a dinner and a tankard in my room. Just as I lighted my first pipe, George rang. His first news was that he was now in sole charge of the case and Carrow was handing over at once. To me it sounded good news too that we had no worries about Pelle and his personal affairs. The Powers-that-Be, as George called them, were making themselves responsible for the interment and all that. The bare news of death was being released.

"That stuff on his overcoat," he was going on. "It was sugar all right. Ordinary granulated sugar."

I'd rather forgotten about that, but George was going on.

"And they rushed through the time of death. About half-past five last night, if someone we know was telling the truth."

It was Doris Chaddon and the cakes that he meant. I cut hastily in.

"I take it we shan't be at Pangley after midday, shall we? What I mean is, I might overhaul that young lady myself."

Silence apparently gave consent, for he was giving the time of the morning's rendezvous—eight-thirty at Westminster Bridge.

"Nothing else?"

"Don't know that there was," he said, and then remembered something. "Oh, yes. About that skull of his. So thin that they'd like it as a medical curio in a bottle of spirit."

I started to chuckle, then changed it artistically to a cough.

"Right-ho, then George," I said. "Eight-thirty in the morning," and hung up.

Then I had my chuckle to myself. That mention of keeping Pelle's skull in a bottle had reminded me in some queer way of something my wife had once said about George himself, and in some outburst of affection—that if anything ever happened to him, she'd like to have him stuffed..

Chapter VI
THE ACE OF TRUMPS?

THERE HAS ALWAYS seemed to be a considerable amount of sense and reason behind the standard jokes of music-hall comedians. If you consider the statement a digression, you may later change your mind.

Take what I call the Anglo-Indian jokes, for instance.

I remember annoying considerably a bore of my acquaintance, whose sole topic was India, by bringing forward that argument about comedians making cracks, however stale, against the Poona type of Army man, and I claimed that there was in this case no smoke without fire. The worst comedian doesn't persist in jokes that won't tickle the risibility of his audience. It may be for the same reason, I added to his still greater annoyance, that the old-school-tie gags are always popular.

Or take mothers-in-law, who are the comedians' stand-by. The popularity of that particular joke seems to me to be a general resentment against interference. Mothers-in-law are only too apt to regard their own offspring's spouses, whatever their ages, as in need of perpetual advice, reminders and supervision; Peter Pans in real life, in fact, and never allowed to grow up.

And that's the kind of thing that often annoys me about George Wharton. Fifteen years ago I was a kind of apprentice, and learning my trade, and in his eyes I have remained much the same ever since. I don't mind his profiting by any of my chance inventiveness, for I'm in the game because it fascinates me, and it's a job worth doing. Kudos doesn't interest me and I'm actually scared of publicity, but that's no reason why George should regard me as someone to tag at his heels. Rarely am I allowed to see the pattern of the case. I know that he has a pattern or plan for attack, even if it is such a simple one as the gradual elimination of this and that suspect, but my sole knowledge of it comes generally from an apt reading of his mind. That's why our cases are so higgledy-piggledy at the outset. He works in the dark because it's his way, and I work in the dark, and surreptitiously, because it's the only way I can do work that seems to me progressive and worth while.

Take that morning at Pangley. If ever I wasted a morning, it was that. George had a couple of men with him and we made a methodical search of the grass verges and hedges all the way from the first fork to Pelle's garden gate. There wasn't a lot of traffic except military, but a voice from a lorry full of troops asked Wharton if he was looking for fag-ends, and I found the question funnier than George did. Only after an hour of searching did I venture to ask him just what we were looking for.

"If he was hit on the skull he had to fall somewhere?" he told me. "And wasn't there mud on his knees, and the front of his overcoat?"

I couldn't say anything to that last retort for presumably I should have noticed Pelle's knees when I saw him in the truck, but I did remind George that only the previous evening I had had my head bitten off for suggesting that Pelle had been on the four-fifty.

"Well, we know he was on it," George said, and then told me why.

Mavin had been in a state of panic when we left him the previous night, and he felt it was up to him to lend a hand in the case. What he did was to call on a man who lived in the first of the semi-detached villas on the side road from the station, and there he struck oil. The man had been delayed at the barrier, and his friend, who occupied the other villa, had waited for him. Then they had walked briskly home and, just short of the first gate, had almost overtaken Sir William. Though they had only identified his steps they knew him well enough, having seen him out for walks on Saturdays and Sundays, and, of course, he was one of the big men of their little district. The second man confirmed everything, and each said he had seen or heard nobody else on that road. Wharton was arranging to see the two men.

But there you see the kind of thing that Wharton kept to himself. There was no point in getting annoyed with him about it. As a matter of fact I was busy with thoughts of my own, and I was feeling uncommonly pleased. I told you I had the beginnings of a theory. George's information made that theory even more promising.

"About that sugar on the overcoat," I said. "Do you think he might have been knocked down by a tradesman's van? A van, say, that had been delivering sugar. The driver dumped him inside and then dumped the body in a railway truck to divert suspicion from himself?"

Rather crude that, but I was only wanting to be sure of the first part—if a car might have caused that injury to the skull. And then what should emerge but the fact that George had spent a great deal of the previous night in consultation with various people over that very same problem.

"Never a chance," he said. "How could a man's body be in such a position that a car should hit the base of his skull? If he'd been stooping down and doing up his bootlace then a car might have hit the *top* of his skull."

"Then why was the body taken away," I said.

"Well, you weren't so far out," he told me. "What we think is that he was knocked down and the attaché-case taken. Then along came a car and saw him. The driver thought he might be implicated somehow so he put the body in the car—tradesman's car probably—and moved it off."

That seemed as footling a theory as I'd ever heard. I gave him a look but it seemed he wasn't pulling my leg. When I asked what he was doing about it he said he had a man or two making inquiries about local vans and their overnight movements.

"Where's the nearest point where a van driver could have had access to the truck?" I asked him.

"Why, here, of course!" he told me. "The railway runs right alongside the road by the station, doesn't it?"

"Of course," I said, and tried to sound apologetic, but all the same it didn't sound right to me. A tradesman's van that had been carrying sugar by all means, but transporting a body which that van hadn't knocked down and then depositing it in a local truck, most certainly not.

We were getting near the house and all at once Mavin joined us. His eyes looked a bit puffy as if he had had a trying night. Wharton hailed him with all the friendliness in the world.

"Would you mind if I used your telephone?" I asked him, and told George it was something personal.

Sutton, the gardener, a sturdy-looking man of about fifty, was sweeping up the twigs that the last gale had blown across the lawn. He touched his hat to me and we had a minute or two's chat. It was a bad business about Sir William, he said. And he had his own theory, that a tramp or casual soldier had done the murder.

"What made you think of murder?" I asked him quickly.

Then it transpired that Mavin had been with him the previous afternoon when word came about the body. And since Sutton had seen us searching grass verges and hedge bottoms he had put two and two together and decided that Sir William had been killed on his way home from the station.

"That's what people don't think of," he told me. "Some won't hear a word against a soldier, but I look at it this way, sir. Everyone is called up, aren't they? Well, they call up the honest men and the crooks, and them that enter the Army as crooks, then they stay crooks. And burglars. And murderers."

"There's a lot in that," I said. "But you didn't hear a sound yourself that night?"

"Never a sound, sir," he told me. "I had my tea just after five and then I was too busy."

He told me how and why he was busy. He was a corporal in a local platoon of the Home Guards, and a new edict had gone forth from their Powers-that-Be that every N.C.O. now had to pass an examination, or rather a series of examinations in order to retain his stripes. Sutton had had the wind up and that was why he was devoting that evening to concentrated study of various notes. As for his opinion of the edict, it was definitely blasphemous. It was all a racket, he said. Those higher up trying to make out the Home Guard was still essential, so as to cling to cushy jobs and uniforms and comic ranks.

A word of sympathy from me and I went on to the house. Inside, three minutes I was speaking to Doris Chaddon.

"Oh, it's you," she said, and then, before I could speak again, "Isn't it dreadful about Sir William! Is it true what they say about him having been murdered?"

"Sh!" I went warningly. "Mustn't talk about things like that over the 'phone. But what about that lunch? You're free?"

There was doubt, coyness and then a touch of the flirtatious. Then she suggested the Hanover, in Arundel Street. That sounded all right to me. I didn't know it and so was hardly likely to be seen by an awkward friend.

"One sharp then, at Swan and Edgar's Corner," I said, and just to give her something to think over: "I may be able to save you a whole lot of bother."

Then I rang off. By the time I had rejoined Wharton and his merry men, the maid from the house was chasing me with a message, that Wharton was wanted on the 'phone. It turned out to be the Big Bugs, though from what habitat George didn't say. But he had to be in town that afternoon, a fact that suited my book particularly well. By half-past eleven the search had been completed to his satisfaction and an hour later I was dollying myself up in the flat. Only a darker suit and a black tie. I hoped that would make me look rather grim.

Doris wasn't dressed to kill but she did look the sort with whom in my younger days I'd have been proud to be seen. But something was on her mind and as soon as we were seated she was firing her question.

"What did you mean by saying you were going to spare me a lot of bother?"

"Oh, that," I said airily. "Just a figure of speech. Sort of ground bait."

"Oh," she said, but relievedly. "But why are you wearing a black tie?"

"Well, someone's dead, isn't he?"

"You mean Sir William?"

"Sh!" I went, and, "What is this? A lunch or a memorial service?"

We chatted away after that, if always on the fringe of things and, on her part, calculatingly, as if she was working out just to what that lunch was likely to lead.

"You *are* married, aren't you?" she asked me suddenly.

"Well, yes," I said, and hoped the tone conveyed the over-worked if always tragic fact that my wife didn't understand me.

"And do you dance?"

"Well, yes," I said, and that time truthfully. My dancing is that of an apprentice fakir doing his first try-out on red-hot coals. "Which reminds me. You know Roger Mavin, don't you?"

"Poor Roger," she said. "Rather a good dancer, though."

She'd first met him, she said, at Marion Blaketon's. I frowned.

"Would that be Sir Herbert's daughter?"

It wasn't, and for the good reason that as far as I knew there wasn't a Sir Herbert Blaketon.

"Oh, no," she said. "She's an awfully good sort. Doing no end of work too. Has a topping flat just off Lancaster Gate."

"That costs her a packet," I said, but the economics of it didn't seem to interest her. And the waiter was presenting me with the bill and telling me we could certainly have coffee in the lounge. I suggested she might want to powder her nose and after that we'd meet for coffee.

I went straight to the lounge and by the time she'd reappeared, had decided on direct action. And as it was to have an important bearing on that theory of mine, here is the theory for what it is worth.

Pelle had originally intended to go to Pangley by his usual train and his whole morning and afternoon had been planned accordingly. Then he had received a telephone call as a result of which he had changed the time of his train. Why the call should have at first annoyed him was easy to see, for an acceptance of something inherent in the call would mean his taking a later train. Then he realized that what he was being asked to do was ample compensation for the loss of the early train, and his annoyance went.

What it was that the caller asked him to do didn't so much matter. What it did apparently ask was that he should go somewhere, and probably to meet the caller. But to trace that caller was impossible, since the call was a local one. And yet it seemed to me most urgent that the caller should be traced, and this is why. *Might* not the object of the caller have been to make him miss the first train and travel by the second? The first train should get him home before the black-out, and an attack and the snatching of the bag would be impossible. By the second train he would get off at Pangley in the dark.

Vital considerations, I think, and having vital implications. That caller must have known about the jewellery and the attaché-case. But—and there was my point of attack —that call was not made till the very last moment, and the caller had to be sure that Sir William would be in the office to receive it. How could he be sure of that? Well, by ringing up earlier and asking if he was in or when he would be in. If he had been out when that exploratory call came, then Doris Chaddon would have taken it, and she could provide information about the caller. But I personally didn't think the exploratory call had been explicit, so to speak, for if so, Doris would have told me that when Sir William was out someone had rung him up, and she'd reported the fact to him when he came in. She hadn't given me that idea at all, and what I had concluded therefore was that someone known both to herself and Sir William had rung her on some private business, but had prefaced it with the casual remark that Sir William wasn't in.

"Oh, no," Doris would have said. "He won't be in for another ten minutes at the earliest." And then the gossip could have proceeded in peace, with the caller knowing just when to ring Sir William later.

How it would all work out I didn't know, but as soon as we were settled comfortably to our coffee I began putting on a Wharton act.

"About what you asked me this morning, and somebody being murdered," I asked. "I'm afraid you're right."

"No!" she said, wide-eyed, and then was looking guiltily round to see if she'd been overheard.

"And that attaché-case is gone."

"But how awful!" she said. "Whatever's going to be done about it?"

"I don't know," I said. "But I do know this. The police will probably give you a pretty thin time."

"Me?" Her eyes were popping again.

"That's right," I said. "I managed to get a private tip. That's what I meant when I rang you this morning. What I'm trying to do is head them off."

"I don't care what they do," she said with a pout, and drew herself up.

I disillusioned her in double time. The police were of the opinion that she was the only one who knew about the attaché-case, and therefore she must have given the information directly or indirectly to the murderer.

"It's ridiculous," she said. "And what about Roger Mavin? He knew all about it."

"And you haven't spoken to a soul?"

"Not a soul," she said. "Only Roger, of course. We were sort of privileged, and even then we only said what a risk he was taking."

"Well, I'll do what I can," I said, and suddenly decided to take a short cut. "But there's one other thing. Didn't you have a telephone call yourself that afternoon?"

"I?" She frowned. "Yes, I did."

"Nothing important?"

"Not really. If you must know, it was Marion Blaketon, asking me to a private supper and dance at her place on Saturday."

"Sir William wasn't there at the time?"

"He wasn't," she said decisively. "I told her he was round at the bank."

"I don't quite get all this," I said. "Why should you tell her that?"

"It's funny, really," she said. "They hate each other like poison."

"They know each other?"

She gave me the first suspicious look.

"I thought you said you knew everything."

"And so I do," I said. "Or rather, the police do. But I didn't know that this Miss Blaketon and Sir William knew each other."

"*Mrs.* Blaketon," she told me. "She was Lady Pelle's younger sister. She's a widow and she's really uncommonly nice."

"Now I'm getting the hang of it," I said. "But why the bad blood?"

She made a moue.

"Well, look at Sir William. A perfect old frump."

"And she isn't."

She laughed.

"I'll say she isn't!"

"And Sir William disapproved."

"You bet he did," she said, "though it wasn't any business of his. Besides, Marion's an awful good sort. She really runs that Prisoners' Institute Business. They do no end of good."

"I think I've heard of that somewhere," I said. "Isn't it called the Prisoners' Reformation Society."

"Of course!" she said. "I'm perfectly dreadful at remembering names."

"Then it all adds up to this," I said. "Mrs. Blaketon rang you, and she could talk more naturally if Sir William wasn't there. You said he wasn't, and that's that." I clicked my tongue. "If you ask my opinion, the police have found a mare's nest and I shall make it my business to tell them so."

"That's awfully good of you," she said, and was glancing at her wrist-watch. "I must simply fly. I've been away from the office for over two hours!"

The supplementary bill had been paid and I walked with her to Leicester Square.

"I wouldn't worry Mrs. Blaketon with any of this," I said. "It's all too footling. I suppose you've known her a pretty long while, by the way."

"I haven't really," she said. "Only about a month or so. But we've seen an awful lot of each other since. I simply love her place. And she's such an awful good sort!"

"Good," I said. "I must try and meet her myself some time."

You might not credit it but I was feeling as if I'd been playing chess for an hour and a half, and concentrated stuff at that, so at the Square corner I had a cold wash in the lavatory and then rang George from the kiosk above. He wasn't in, but they said he was due at any moment.

I strolled quietly to the Yard and by the time I got to his room, he was there. Before he could ask, like a mother of some errant offspring, what I'd been up to, I cut in first.

"George," I said. "I think I'm on to something big."

"Oh?" he said, and with that note of hostility that is always his opening gambit.

I took off my overcoat with some deliberation and drew in a chair.

"You follow this carefully," I said, and gave him the arguments that had led to my questioning of Doris Chaddon. When he heard the outcome, his eyes fairly bulged.

"Sounds good to me," he said. "Looks as if we've got something there," and I hope you noticed the 'we'. "That Blaketon woman's in it up to the neck, or my name's Robinson."

"It might have been a coincidence," I said, "but that word 'prisoners' sounded a good omen."

"What prisoners?"

"I forgot to tell you," I said, "but this Marion Blaketon is running a Prisoners' Reformation Society."

"What!" He fairly hollered the word, and then was pushing a bell and grabbing the inside 'phone. An Inspector Somebody whom he wanted seemed to be away, but he was making do with a Sergeant Somebody-Else. The 'phone was replaced and he leaned back.

"Prider's a good man," he said. "He knows all about this Reformation Society. They've been a bit quiet recently."

He wouldn't tell me any more till Sergeant Prider came in. Under his arm was a file of papers through which Wharton had a quick glance.

"Make yourself comfortable," Wharton told him, and peered at him over his spectacle tops. "Things have been quiet with our old friend Mrs. Blaketon."

"They have that, sir," Prider told him, and grinned. Then he cast a look at me as if he would have liked to add, "Has this gentleman come with some new evidence?"

"This is Mr. Travers," Wharton said, catching the look.

"I've heard about you, sir, but haven't met you," Prider told me, and we solemnly shook hands.

"We've quite a nice little *dossier* about Mrs. Blaketon," Wharton was saying. "Daughter of Sir Leyland Frame. Born in 1894. Married in 1923 a South African, a Colonel Blaketon, who turned out to be a crook. Nothing known of him since but supposed to have died while prospecting in West Africa. She's thought to have lived with Nevermind-Who, the diamond magnate, till 1936, and then she turned up over here, and with funds. Then she started the Prisoners' Reformation Society—"

"You'll pardon me, sir, but she didn't actually start it," Prider said. "She took it over when it was in a moribund condition"—damned good that!—"and made a go of it."

"She made more than a go of it," Wharton said grimly as he closed the *dossier*. "What I should say is that we thought so, even if we couldn't prove it. Tell Mr. Travers about that trap you set."

It was plain that Wharton himself had only a rough knowledge of the facts, for he listened with as much interest as I did. Those facts were that the police had reason for suspecting that the Prisoners' Reformation Society—which meant Marion Blaketon—had other activities than those which appeared on its pamphlets of appeal and its records of service. Ostensibly it was out to aid men released from penal servitude and to help them to go straight.

"That's all very well, sir," Prider said, "but just consider this. A man's had a stretch for robbery in a big way and he hasn't disclosed the whereabouts of the swag. This Society gets hold of him when he comes out and gains his confidence. You see now, sir?"

"I think I do," I said. "The Blaketon woman could put him in touch with a fence or even do business direct."

"That's it, sir. And that's what we had reason to suspect was actually done in one case. So, to cut a long story short, sir, we tried laying a trap. We fixed it so that her typist left her and then worked things with her agency so we could plant a woman of our own. You know her, sir," he said to Wharton. "Bertha Howard."

"A first-class woman too," said Wharton.

"Yes," said Prider and sighed. "Only she just didn't happen to be good enough, or else the other one was a bit too fly. She was there for a fortnight and hadn't discovered a thing, and then she was sacked. Bertha told us she was sure Mrs. Blaketon had rumbled her, and she couldn't spot why."

"Bad luck," I said. "And the Blaketon woman's given no cause for suspicion since?"

"Plenty of suspicion," Prider said wryly. "But nothing you could get down to. What we did in that abortive attempt, as you might say, was to make her more careful. At least, that's my idea." He looked hopefully at Wharton. "Something new turned up, sir?"

"Well, yes and no," said Wharton. "Just a gleam of something and that's as far as we can go."

"Nothing for me, sir?" He was looking like a dog begging to be taken for a walk.

"Not at the moment," Wharton told him, and gave him a pat on the back. "But you'll get the hooks on her before long, or my name's Robinson. And if anything does turn up, you needn't worry about not being told."

The door closed on Prider and George was telling me that there were wheels within wheels.

"Funny how things go round in circles," he said. "You've only got to wait and the conveyor belt comes past." His sigh had in it a tremendous regret. "I never handled that business Prider was telling us about. My idea was that it was bungled. Still, that's over and done with. Undoubtedly she was warier than ever, and there's the lesson for us. We can't afford to bungle anything. I'll let you see what we know about her and then we can work out our line of approach."

George had obviously skimmed extracts from the *dossier* when he read it to me, and I said I'd like more inside dope on Marion Blaketon. What we gathered was this. Her family had never approved of Colonel Blaketon, as he had called himself, and the wedding had been an elopement, with the bride cut off without a shilling. Hence the hostility between her and Pelle whatever the reasons she had told the gullible Doris and, indeed, the whole of the Blaketon circle. As to the funds with which she had arrived in London in 1936, they weren't guessed to be sufficient to support her way of living, and beyond £200 a year from the Society she had no ascertainable income.

"Look at this," George said, and handed me what I might call one of the Society's prospectuses. It had a list of patrons and patronesses as long as my arm.

"Every one of 'em that I know is a crank," George said. "Then there're the subscribers we never hear about. Even if their subscriptions were acknowledged, that isn't to say they appeared on the balance sheet except as part of a general lump sum."

"Sounds a good racket," I said.

"One of the best," He shrugged his shoulders. "I believe an attempt was made to catch her by means of a subscription, but either that was bungled too, or they had no luck. More might have been done but then the war came and we were up to our eyes. Not that we've lost sight of things. It's only that there've been bigger fish to fry and fewer hands to do the frying."

"And on the opposite side of the account," I said. "What's the record of achievement, as Prider might say?"

George handed me a booklet. A quick look through showed me a score of cases, labelled A. and B. and so on, who had been set on the straight and narrow path after careers of crime. It read very impressively.

"You bet it does," George said. "I believe that damned Society was actually congratulated in the House not so long ago."

Ten minutes later we had made our plans of attack. One excellent aspect was that she had never come into contact with George, and so suspicion shouldn't be aroused. The office of the Society was in Southampton Row.

"We don't want a trip there for nothing," George said, and rang for a call to be put through. "Hang up as soon as you get a Mrs. Blaketon," he said, and gave me a wink.

In a couple of minutes the buzzer went. George picked up the 'phone and grunted.

"It's all right," he told me. "She's there."

Chapter VII
MARION BLAKETON

As our car turned into the Strand I suddenly thought of something. Mightn't Mrs. Blaketon be alarmed at the very mention of Wharton's name.

"She's never heard of me," he assured me. "I've had nothing to do with her, or her Society."

From his tone I gathered again that if he had been in charge, things might have gone differently.

"It seems rather a pity that that kind of racket should be carried on with impunity," I said.

"It's a slow job uncovering a thing like that," he said. "Remember that philanthropic parson business and how it took us years to put him out of action? And there's even less to go on with this Blaketon woman. And she has pals in high quarters. Remember that list of patrons or whatever they call themselves?"

We turned out of Holborn and across into Southampton Row. At Russell Square the car was parked and we walked the few yards back. The office was on the first floor and facing us at the head of the stairs was a door marked 'ENQUIRIES'. George gave me a look, then knocked.

A moment or two and it was opened by a girl of about seventeen.

"Mrs. Blaketon in?" asked George.

"I'll see," she said. "What did you want to see her for?"

She was evidently a new hand.

"Give her this card," George said, "and tell her it's urgent."

She let us into a tiny waiting-room. George's eyebrows lifted at the sight of the wall prints—Dartmoor, Pentonville, Portland and Holloway.

"Regular home from home," he whispered to me, and then was cocking an ear. A voice from the next room said, "You oughtn't to have . . ." and then suddenly it was only a murmur. Then came a silence and a couple of minutes must have gone by before the door opened.

"Will you come in?"

That was Marion Blaketon. Her voice was the mannish kind, but there was no doubt about her having what Wharton called class. A striking-looking woman too, though a bit on the horsy side, but what struck me most at that first sight of her was her perfect self-possession.

"Always glad to see the police," she was telling Wharton heartily, and I had another quick look at her as I followed them into her office. Her clothes were good, I noticed that, and how wiry-looking she was. Five foot eight probably and just about looking her fifty years.

"Won't you sit down?" she said to Wharton, and was giving me a look of pleasant inquiry.

Wharton introduced me as a colleague and we took two of the hard-seated chairs. She was in a swivel chair at the roll-top desk.

"As I was saying," she resumed, "we're always glad to see the police. In our small way we do our best to cooperate. Prevention's always better than cure, don't you think?"

Before George could give an opinion she was off again. That woman, as my old nurse used to say, could jaw the hind legs off a donkey. A good half minute of the Society's aims and George simply had to come to the top to get breath.

"Pardon me, Mrs. Blaketon, but I don't think you know just what we're here for."

"How foolish of me!" She laughed, if the laugh was more of a neigh. "And what *are* you here for?"

There was a door beyond and through it came the tapping of a typewriter. That, I thought, would be the door-opener at work.

"On rather distressing business," Wharton told her. "To do with the death of your brother-in-law."

"Oh, that," she said, but apparently puzzled. She was frowning as she nibbled the end of the pencil.

"You knew, of course, that he was dead?"

"I saw the notice in the paper," she said, as matter-of-fact as they make 'em.

Things weren't going as anticipated and Wharton was already finding himself in the wrong gear.

"You don't consider it a distressing occasion?" asked Wharton with an unusual malice.

"Heavens no!" she said. "Why should I?"

Wharton shrugged his shoulders.

"It isn't as if we were friends. A ridiculous term but the best I can think of."

"But you weren't what I might call actively hostile?"

"One doesn't quarrel with a fool," she told him amusedly. "The man *was* a fool. And my sister was a fool to have married him."

"If it isn't too personal, then why did she marry him?" asked Wharton, just a bit nettled.

"My dear man, she didn't. He married her." She gave a shrug of the shoulders that in its amplitude was almost foreign. "Just to get in with our precious family. Pure opportunism." Another shrug of the shoulders and her head went sideways with a look that was Wharton's own. "But surely you haven't come here to ask me about Piggie Pelle? That," she said charmingly, "was always his nickname. So expressive, if you knew him. Indian pigs, of course; the kind that one sticks."

"And what if I told you that his death wasn't all it appeared on the surface?"

She raised her eyebrows.

"Strictly between ourselves," went on Wharton, and hesitated a fraction too long.

"Don't tell me he was murdered!"

The case had slipped so far out of Wharton's fingers that he had had to put on those ancient spectacles of his as a kind of sheet-anchor. Now he peered at her over their tops.

"What made you think of that?"

"But why shouldn't I? You were mysterious. You implied he didn't die naturally. Well, what else was I to think?"

"You thought right," George said bluntly. "It isn't public and it mayn't be made so, but murdered he was. And that's a serious business."

"I quite agree," she said. "What I don't see is how it concerns me."

"It concerns you in this way," George said, and his attempt at impressiveness was none too successful. "We have reason to believe that you were the last person to see him alive!"

"I?" The surprise seemed genuine enough to me. Then her eyes narrowed. "I haven't seen him or spoken to him for at least a year, and then the interview was none of my seeking." That must have slipped out, for she was qualifying it at once. "Not that that has anything to do with it."

"Well, our information is that he was seen entering this building at about four o'clock on Monday afternoon," Wharton told her. "An hour and a half later, he was killed."

"Entering here!" The frown went. "My dear sirs, it's absurd. You surely can't be serious."

"Only too serious," Wharton told her, and gave me a look. "Smith's statement was explicit, wasn't it?"

"It seemed so to me," I said unblushingly.

"If you *are* being serious," she said, and now she was including me for the first time, "then you have only to question my secretary. She was here till after five o'clock on Monday. No one could have come here without her knowing."

"Oh, no," Wharton said. "Your word's good enough for us."

"Pardon me," she said, and a nasty look was on her face as she got to her feet. "Now we've gone so far I insist on it."

A couple of minutes later her Miss Mortimer had duly confirmed. Wharton could only say he was extraordinarily sorry she'd been troubled.

"Misunderstandings will happen!" Marion Blaketon told him with what sounded to me like sweet malice. "But was that all you wished to see me about?"

"Yes," said Wharton, and got to his feet.

"Don't hurry," she said. "Do let me give you a cup of tea. We always have one about this time."

"Very good of you," Wharton said, "but we're rather pressed for time."

"Then perhaps you'd like to take these with you," she said, and was offering both of us a small wad of pamphlets. "We're always glad to add to our list of subscribers."

Wharton took his wad as if it was a slab of horse-dung.

"Thank you so much," was what I said, trying to give George a hint about tactfulness. "One does hear your Society so well spoken of."

"How perfectly sweet of you!"

We were then at the outer door. George mumbled something about being sorry but she and I parted with the most delightful interchange of smiles, and the door closed behind us.

Half-way down the stairs George was still speechless as I grasped his arm.

"Left my gloves," I whispered. "Just slipping back for them."

They had been left by design and well concealed by the leg of the chair. There had been no click of that outer door and it opened when I turned the knob. Then I tiptoed across the waiting-room, paused to gain confidence and applied my ear to the crack.

"Yes, Superintendent Wharton and another man—a Mr. Tracey or something like that," Marion Blaketon's voice was saying. "A tall thin man with heavy glasses. . . . Oh, just a stooge probably. . . . I see. . . . And you're sure you wouldn't like to tell me any more?"

And that's where I made a mistake, though the fault was not really my own, but that of my subconscious self. There was I, polishing my glasses, and as I knew that, I knew too that my foot had somehow kicked against the door. In a moment the glasses were on again and I was looking into that office. My smile must have been worse than fatuous.

"Sorry," I said, "but I left my gloves behind. There they are. . . . So sorry to have troubled you."

She had the receiver close against her chest. I had been scared somehow of meeting her eyes but I heard that receiver slammed down.

"Isn't it usual to knock at a door?" she was asking me. "Or don't the police ever knock?"

"I'm sorry," I said, "but I did knock."

The look had been definitely venomous and now she was trying to pass things off.

"Sorry I bit your head off."

"But you didn't," I said.

"All right," she said. "We'll leave it like that. Just one of life's little jokes."

She had followed me to the door and before I could utter a final word of parting, it closed behind me, and I heard the click of the catch. At the foot of the stairs Wharton was waiting impatiently. Two doors on was a tea-shop and I suggested a cup might do us good.

"What was the idea of that glove business?" he asked me as soon as I ordered the tea, and when I'd told him he was saying he'd give a fiver to know to whom she'd been 'phoning.

"What a woman!" he said, and let out a breath. "No wonder poor old Prider didn't get far."

"You believed what she said about seeing Pelle?"

"Can't do anything else," he said. "Even if she's nobbled that secretary, as she calls her, we can't do a thing."

"And that secretary will swear to what she told us, that they both left that office together at about a quarter-past five."

"All right. All right," George told me testily. "You needn't rub it in."

Then he felt that wad of pamphlets he had rammed into his overcoat pocket and with a kind of subdued roar he wrenched it out with his fist, glared at it and smacked it down on the floor behind him. That seemed to ease his mind for when he next spoke his tone was quite mild.

"Yes," he said. "A pity about that alibi. All bone and gristle, that woman. A smack from her and Pelle's skull would have cracked like an egg-shell."

The pot of tea came and he told me generously I could have the sugar. Saccharins were good enough for him.

"She's in it in some way," he told me, still harping on Marion Blaketon. "In it up to the neck, or my name's Robinson. Who could she have been 'phoning to?"

"Art thou come hither to destroy me?" I quoted at him.

George is pretty apt at Biblical allusion, but he chose not to understand.

"You mean you don't know?"

"How should I know?" I said.

"A pity." He gazed at his cup, then took a drink. "Wonder if it would be worth while getting in touch with that secretary."

"A bit dangerous," I said. "But why not have someone on the other one's tail?"

"Yes," he said, and gulped down the rest of the cup and got to his feet as if no moment could be too soon.

"A hell of a tea interval that, George," I said reproachfully, as I joined him on the pavement. "And where do we go now?"

He was going back to the Yard, he said. Something might have come in, and he had an idea or two himself. Then at five o'clock he was seeing Kenray by appointment, and he'd like me to meet him there.

"What to do?" I said.

"Having a final look at that alibi of his."

"But won't he rather resent that?" I said.

"Not if we handle it the right way," he told me, and the plural pronoun was a sign that things weren't going to be too easy.

George had me set down at the flat, but long before that I had been in a state of alarm. It was Grace Allbeck who was worrying me, and what she would think when she saw me arrive with Wharton. Why I should be squeamish about Grace Allbeck I didn't know, at least, so I told myself. And then I had to tell myself that I did know.

No sooner was I in my room than I was heroically picking up the receiver and dialling the number of the shop. A man's voice that I recognized as Kenray's spoke to me. I asked if I might speak to the particular lady who was generally in the shop.

"You mean Mrs. Allbeck?"

I said that was probably right. Then I gave my name and mentioned my visit.

"I remember, Mr. Travers," he said. "My sister mentioned it to me. She was very interested."

It was easy after that. Life was all coincidence, I said, and told him about seeing him later with Wharton, and how I'd hate to have Mrs. Allbeck think that visit with the piece of jewellery some sort of subterfuge.

"I'm sure she'd never think anything of the sort," he assured me. "But I'll give her your message."

"I couldn't tell her personally?"

"I'm sorry, but she's lying down with a severe headache," he said. "She's had them very badly this last year."

I said lamely that I was sorry, and then when I had hung up I wondered if I ought to have made any reference to the tragic death of her son. Then again I knew I had been fortunate in saying nothing. After all I was supposed not to have seen or spoken to Kenray in my life, and it hadn't been Grace Allbeck herself but Tom Fulcher who'd told me about Hugh.

After all that I had a clean up and then lighted my pipe and settled down for a half-hour to something that I'd been looking forward to—a quick study of Pelle's unfinished autobiography.

Somehow I couldn't get going with that book. The opening struck me as pompous and uncommonly dull, and I just couldn't get interested. And yet I had to read it.

That was a vital change of view. When Wharton first handed me that manuscript and I took it over, I'm sure neither of us regarded its study as other than a kind of routine. It could scarcely throw light on the killing of Pelle. He had not been killed by an Indian fanatic, for example, and in revenge for some injustice, shall we say, rankling from the days when Pelle had been an administration official.

Pelle had been killed for one reason only—that attaché-case of jewellery. Of that neither Wharton nor I had the slightest doubt, and how then could a reading of the manuscript throw light on the crime? All it might conceivably have thrown light on was Mavin—his editing, for instance, and literary ability— though how that might have connected him with the actual crime was something with which we had never come to grips.

Now, as I laid that manuscript aside and leaned back in my chair, I knew that things had vastly changed. That manuscript might throw a damning light on the killer *provided* that Marion Blaketon had been that killer or had engineered the crime. It was true that she had what looked like a perfect alibi, but alibis even more perfect had been broken before.

With long legs well out and eyes closed I tried to add fact to fact. In about *three weeks*—and the emphasis seemed essential—Marion Blaketon had made the acquaintance of and ingratiated herself with Doris Chaddon and Mavin. That clipping from the *Clarion* had announced—though doubtless the fact had long been public property—that Pelle was in charge of the jewellery, and the Blaketon woman had in the course of three weeks learned all there was to know. As for the fatal afternoon, that she had planned to make Pelle travel by that later train seemed an unquestioned fact. And then suddenly I thought of something—a question that should have been put to Marion Blaketon, but which Wharton and I had forgotten.

I grabbed the receiver and dialled before I should change my mind.

"That you, Mrs. Blaketon?"

"Yes," she said.

"This is Travers. The man who left his gloves behind."

"Oh, yes." The tone was distinctly unfriendly.

"I wonder if you'd be good enough to tell me something. Sir William had a telephone call at about a quarter-past three that certain afternoon. It wasn't you ringing him up, was it?"

"My dear man, what *is* this?" she was asking me, and the tone was more unfriendly still. "If I ran this office as you run yours I'd be thrown out on my neck."

"Sorry," I said, "but I'm afraid I don't follow you."

"You don't? Well, your Superintendent Wharton rang me to ask the same question a few moments ago."

"Oh," I said. "Just a little overlapping, I'm afraid. But would you mind telling me what you told him?"

"Oh, not at all," she told me sweetly. "I told him I definitely hadn't 'phoned and if I was pestered any more I'd complain to the right quarter. And the same applies to yourself."

Then the line went dead. I went sheepishly back to my chair and with the none too reassuring knowledge that Wharton had been thinking along the same lines. But in a minute or two I had my arguments in line again. That she denied having rung Pelle was nothing after all. That she was a fluent and calculating liar I had no doubt, even if I was of the opinion that she had not been such a fool as to ask him to come to her office. On the other hand it would have been perfectly easy to use a false voice and lure him elsewhere. And how? Well, by saying the speaker was bedridden, for instance, and asking him to call and collect a valuable piece of jewellery for the Famine Appeal. Sir William, I remembered, had at first been annoyed at the thought of losing his train, but when he had heard the whole message he had quietened wonderfully down.

Now as far as Marion Blaketon was concerned, the killing of Pelle might have meant two birds with one stone. If everything the police suspected was correct, then she was in need of money, and she was the one person likely to know a good and safe fence. As for the other reason, that was where the manuscript came in.

She must have learned from Mavin, and the *Clarion* cutting, that Sir William was writing his autobiography, and at once she must have been in a state of considerable alarm. *What if she herself was mentioned in it?* Just the kind of thing she might expect that obstinate, blundering fool to do, and with what consequences? Disastrous ones, as I saw it. If he mentioned the family scandal that would speedily winkle Marion Blaketon out of that lucrative job with the Society. For she hadn't changed her name, and, even if she had changed it it would have made no difference. While the original scandal had been hushed up and nobody suspected it outside the Yard, the probability was that she owed her position in whatever circles she frequented to the fact that she was Sir Leyland Frame's daughter.

So far the arguments had gone well, but all at once there began to be complications. If she questioned Mavin he might have told her that there was nothing in the manuscript about a scandal. Or he might have put her off with prevarications, since he himself was very much between two stools. He daren't antagonize Sir William; indeed, I didn't see how he dared let Sir William know that he was even acquainted with that gentleman's sister-in-law. All very complicated, as I said, and as my brain began to go in circles I suddenly caught sight of the clock. In five minutes I was due at Kenray's shop, and at once I was grabbing my hat and overcoat and making for the lift.

Chapter VIII
ONCE MORE KENRAY

THE SHOP WAS SHUT but the outer side door wasn't locked, so I made my way up the stairs. A lighted lamp stood on a wall bracket and showed a door across the landing. I pushed the bell and who should open the door but Grace Allbeck. She looked pale and somewhat drawn, but she smiled at me in a way far more friendly than I deserved. I felt a queer kind of warmth, like meeting again a friend whom one has hoped somehow to see.

"Unpardonable of me disturbing you like this," I said. "And is your headache better?"

"Quite better," she said. "I have some special tablets and the headaches always go after a little sleep."

"But they always leave you shaken?"

I said that because I could see that she was still nervy. Her fingers were moving restlessly and that poise which had so struck me was no longer there.

"Yes," she said. "It makes one feel as if . . . as if . . ."

"I know," I said. "I used to suffer from them myself. As if you'd been sandbagged."

It was quite a charming and cosy little sitting-room we were in and through an opened door I caught sight of the little kitchen and some white tiles and a little electric stove.

"Your brother gave you my message?" I asked.

"Yes," she said. "It was very good of you."

"Yes, the world's a small place," I said. "But about that piece of jewellery. I'm going to sell it now if only to prove my bona fides."

She told me laughingly not to do anything so foolish, but I said I would bring it in the next time I happened to be that way. I was taking a chance on Bernice but it seemed to me worth while. And I didn't mean the money. I liked Grace Allbeck and somehow I wanted Bernice to know her. Good opinions seemed to me in that moment to be worth more than a piece of jewellery.

"Is Superintendent Wharton here?" I asked her, for in some strange way I'd forgotten what I was there for.

"He's downstairs with my brother," she said. "Would you like to come this way?" Then she was remarking what charming manners Wharton had.

She switched on a light and there were stairs that led down. I could find my way, she said, and indeed I heard Wharton's voice before I reached the bottom. The lights of the shop were bright behind the black-out and there was George trying to look as if he knew something about the Sheffield candelabra that Kenray was showing him.

"Here *is* Mr. Travers," said George at the sight of me. "I don't think you've met Mr. Kenray."

Kenray and I shook hands and at close quarters he was just the same quiet, unemotional and likeable man I'd seen from the fanlight.

"Travers is a busy man," George said, "so perhaps we'd better do our little bit of business and be on our way."

He put on his glasses and consulted his notebook, and all to gain time and create an impression.

"About this jewellery business," he began. "How long is it since you were first called in as consultant?"

"About a couple of months ago," Kenray said.

"As long ago as that!" Wharton seemed surprised. Kenray had nothing to add.

"And did you ever actually see any of the jewellery?"

"Well, yes . . . once," said Kenray. His words were even more deliberate than usual, as if he was careful of committing himself. "I thought it necessary to call personally at his office and he showed me a couple of things that had come in that very morning. He was taking them later to his bank."

"Valuable, were they?"

"A pair of single stone drop ear-rings, and a ring," said Kenray reminiscently. "Quite nice stuff. Might have been worth five or six hundred."

"That Miss Chaddon was there?"

"Oh, yes," said Kenray, and very non-committally.

"What did you think of her?" Wharton asked. "Strictly between ourselves."

Kenray's shoulders moved slightly.

"As typists go these days she seemed fairly efficient."

Wharton grunted. I justified my presence by cutting in with a question.

"Just how long have you known about that attaché-case, Mr. Kenray?"

"You mean about his taking the jewellery down in it?"

"Yes," I said.

"Well," he said, and frowned in thought. "I suppose I first had an idea about three weeks ago."

"As long as that," said Wharton again. "Do you mind telling me about it again?"

"I thought it about time the proceeds were realized," Kenray said. "If any extras came in, I thought they might go into an ordinary sale. When I rang Sir William about it, he didn't agree. Then I asked if I might do my valuation of what had been sent and he wanted me to wait a week or two and do everything together. I said I'd come round if he rang me and then he said the valuation would be at his house. But I think I told you about that."

"There you are!" said Wharton to me. "Sir William talking over the telephone and that secretary of his taking it all in. She tells her pals. Mavin knows and he tells his pals. He might just as well have put an advertisement in the papers." He heaved a sigh, and then his remark was a subtle question. "Still, there you are. We can't expect everyone to be as discreet as that sister of yours. She knew all about it, but I'll bet a new hat that she never said a word to a soul."

"She knew just as much as I've already told you, and no more," Kenray reminded him quietly. "But she's just as much in this business as I am, Mr. Wharton. If I didn't trust her, then I couldn't trust myself."

"Exactly," said Wharton heartily. "Anyone can tell she's a fine business woman. And a most charming lady too, if you'll allow me to say so."

He took out his notebook again, had another look at it, and gave a grunt as he replaced it.

"Well, now I've got to do something that I hate doing, and I hope you won't take offence. It isn't my doing exactly. I give you my word for that."

There followed the old, old formula about alibis and how the innocent ought to welcome inquiry, and the variation of a frank admission that Kenray had reason to resent such inquiry.

"You see how it is," Wharton said. "As Travers here knows; some Big Pot or other will be bound to ask where you were that evening, If I say I don't know—well, that won't do me any good, or you either."

But Kenray was already moving towards the foot of the stairs.

"Grace! . . . Will you come down for a minute?"

We heard her coming. Wharton began expostulations, but Kenray waved them aside. It was he who explained to her what Wharton wanted.

"Where you were?" she said, and looked rather puzzled. "But that's simple. You were here!"

"Tell them all about it, my dear," Kenray said gently.

"But there's nothing to tell. You came in very tired. Let me see now. It was getting on for five o'clock and I thought you looked a bit grey, so I brought you a cup of tea. You said you'd have it in the office so I turned the stove on."

"That's right," Kenray said. "You said it wasn't more work I wanted but a quiet nap, and you were right. I did have a nap. As a matter of fact I had a good sound sleep. What time was it when you woke me, Grace?"

"Just gone six," she said, and smiled. "But I peeped in once before that and you were sleeping so comfortably I didn't disturb you."

Kenray smiled too.

"Well, there we are. After that—"

"We don't need any after," Wharton cut in. "It isn't me you've satisfied. I didn't need any satisfying. The thing is I'll have an answer if any busybody asks questions." His voice took on a syrupy quality. "Might I have a look at that office of yours?"

"Why not?" asked Kenray, unperturbed as ever, and the three of us went along the passage.

It was a comfortable little office with the usual furnishings. Silver and bric-a-brac stood on the desk top and among the books and files of the shelves.

"A bit untidy," Kenray said, "but I like it like that. Every dealer does." His voice lowered as he looked about. "My sister always wants to have it tidied up. This is her doing, by the way," and he pointed to the antimacassar kind of cover on the back of the easy chair. "That's the chair I had my nap in."

He might have gone on to add that there was the electric stove, and there the side-table on which his tea had stood, but again Wharton was expressing himself as more than satisfied. And he said that any Big Pot who poked his nose into the matter of Kenray's alibi would get a rap over the knuckles, however big he was.

He waited till we were back in the shop and with Grace Allbeck again, before he put his next question.

"Haven't you a man here? You told me, I think, that you had one."

"Yes," Kenray said. "Fulcher's his name. Tom Fulcher. Been with us for years."

"A good fellow, is he?"

"There isn't a better," Kenray said. "I believe he'd cut off his arm for either one of us."

"Well, I'd better have a word with him," Wharton said regretfully. "It's all red tape but it's got to be got over. Is he handy?"

"He's in his room," Grace Allbeck said.

Kenray was moving towards the stairs. The last thing I wanted was for Tom to see me, so I stayed put.

"Perfectly lovely those candelabra," I said.

"Aren't they fine!" she said. "We don't often touch that class of thing, but I simply couldn't resist them. They're going to America."

"But you're not taking them?"

She smiled. "No. I'm a stay-at-home Jill. Mr. Kenray will probably be going in about a week's time. He's expecting the permit almost at once."

"Aren't they liable to get scratched in transit?" I asked, fingering the lovely smoothness of the stems.

"They're most carefully wrapped," she said.

"In cotton wool?"

"Gracious, no!" she told me. "That'd be unobtainable these days."

From a cupboard she produced some ordinary newspaper. That of *The Times*, though better paper, wasn't so good as that of the *Clarion*, she said, and proceeded to illustrate. Certainly the flimsier paper folded much more softly, though it wasn't really a fold but a twist. Then the twisted paper was wrapped wound the delicate scroll work and it was as if it was covered by a cushion.

"Like everything else, so simple," I said. "But let me show you what a fine detective I am. I'll bet you read *The Times* and your man Tom reads the *Clarion*."

"But I could have guessed that," she said, and then Wharton was heard calling from the head of the stairs. In a way I was sorry to go. I liked talking to Grace Allbeck and we had just arrived on the fringes of something near to intimacy.

"Duty calls," I said, and waved her to the stairs.

She laughed back at me and said she didn't believe I was a detective at all. I begged her not to give me away to Wharton, and by then we were nearing the landing.

"Thought you were in a hurry," Wharton told me accusingly. Then he was saying good-bye to Grace Allbeck.

"I didn't tell you, Mr. Kenray," he said as his hand went out again, "but you'll probably have a communication in the morning from the Powers-that-Be. They'll ask you to get a valuation of the missing jewellery from the actual donors. I've got a spare list you can have if it's any help to you."

"Sorry, but it just can't be done," Kenray said. "That job would take days."

Wharton gave a nudge and a wink.

"Yes, but the India Office pays."

Kenray shook his head.

"That may be, but I expect to be in New York in ten days' time."

"Well, it's their headache," Wharton said resignedly. "Afraid Travers and I have been a bit of a headache too."

"Mr. Travers is a very charming sort of headache," Grace Allbeck told him, and on that blushful note I said my own good-byes. Another minute and we were out on the pavement.

There was a little restaurant just round the corner and Wharton thought we might do our talking there instead of going to the Yard. It was still short of half-past five but neither of us had had a real tea.

"Well, I'm bound to admit I was wrong about Kenray," he said. "He's got a regular Rock of Gibraltar of an alibi."

"Personally I'm pleased he's out of it," I said. "I'm not saying, 'I told you so,' but honestly, George, he never was the type for murder and theft." Then I had to add something else. "But what's worrying you about Kenray?"

"I'm not worried," he said, and then went off at what looked like a tangent. "That's a funny thing about our game. You learn everything you can about a person and watch him under a microscope, and when you've finished you don't know what's a clue and what isn't."

I nodded, and feelingly.

"For instance," George went on. "Kenray's going to the States in ten days' time. A nice chance to take that jewellery, if he has it." He held up a pontifical hand to check my comment. "I know he's liable to be searched by Customs, but then again he mightn't be. And that's not all. I saw that man of theirs. Nice old boy he was, just as you described him. And where was he on the particular evening? Not there. He was with his sister at Woolwich. She wasn't well and he'd been given half a day off. Which reminds me."

He made an entry in his notebook, and doubtless to have Tom Fulcher's alibi checked.

"I know they're trivialities," he said as he put the notebook away. "The main thing is that Kenray's out."

"Very definitely so," I said. "The only problem now is, where do we go from here?"

"Wait a minute," he said. "There was something I was wanting to ask you. I know. Just why did you ask Kenray how long he'd known about that attaché-case? It struck me as if you'd had some sort of brainwave."

"Let me ask you a question first," I said. "Something had been done about the actual sale of that jewellery, hadn't there? Wasn't it tentatively arranged for this day week?"

"That's right," he said. "It didn't need advertising except in next Monday's papers and to the trade. Kenray probably wanted the sale over before he left for the States. Maybe he would have made some purchases."

"Exactly," I said. "And so that Blaketon woman's time was getting short."

"What do you mean?"

I told him. For three weeks she'd been working on Doris Chaddon and Mavin, and that was why I'd put that question to Kenray. Two birds with one stone, I said, and told him about the autobiography.

"We've got something there," George said, and set down his cup of tea just as it was at his lips. "We'll try and break that alibi of hers first." Then up went his hand. "But wait, though. She wouldn't do the job herself. I'll lay a fiver she had a dozen crooks up her sleeve. She'd pass one the wink to collar that case."

"Then where does the killing come in?" I said.

"He never was intended to be killed," he told me. "He had an abnormally thin skull, hadn't he? The killing just happened."

"Then that autobiography business is all wasted," I said. "There was only one bird—the jewellery."

"Now, now, now," he told me. "No need to rush things. Even if it wasn't intended to do more than knock him out, there might be something in it after all. Why shouldn't it have been a kind of warning. You know the sort of thing. She rings the old boy when he's recovered and says, 'Sorry to hear you've been hurt. It just shows you, doesn't it,' or words to that effect. Telling him in so many words what's coming to him if he doesn't keep his mouth shut." That seemed to me about the most preposterous thing in theories I'd ever heard, but before I could say a word, George was off again.

"Wait a minute, though. How do we know she was interested in that autobiography?"

"We don't," I said. "Mavin's the one who can give us the answer to that." Then I remembered something. "Did he give you that confession you asked him to write?"

"Nothing in it much about Mrs. B.," he said. "Only that he went to one or two shows at her place."

"What sort of shows?"

"Parties, if you like. Dancing to a gramophone, and a little friendly roulette. Nothing we could pull her in for." Then he was suddenly pulling out his notebook and he was nodding to himself as he stowed it away again.

"Look here. No time like the present. There's a train from Charing Cross at ten to six, that's in six minutes' time. You can just make it."

He was bustling me off and out, and so much in a hurry that he didn't bother about his change. As his hand took my arm his voice was a wheedle.

"This is just the sort of job you can do a hundred times better than me. You go and have a chat with Mavin."

"But suppose he isn't in?"

"He is in," he told me. "I had to ring him this afternoon about something and he told me he was going to be in. You nip off now and catch that train and I'll get hold of him and tell him you're coming. I expect he'll find you a bit of dinner."

The clutch on my arm had gone, and when I looked round in the dark, he had gone too.

* * * * *

I made that train with half a minute to spare, and no more. Perhaps it was a good thing that I was so rushed, for if not I might have attached myself to Kenray.

You know that kind of subdued light in a blacked-out railway terminus, and how when compartment doors are opened a sort of neon lighting from the blue shades just shows up the occupants and gives their faces a greenish pallor. Just as I was passing a door it opened and I saw Kenray, but the door closed quickly again. He hadn't seen me for his eyes were on an evening paper, and I took a compartment a door or two on where another open door revealed a seat.

The train was packed by the time we left London Bridge, but a man had got out and left me his evening paper, so I read that till we got to Hurstham. My compartment half emptied then and I took a look out to see Kenray's back. But I didn't see him at all, and I knew that he must have nipped out of his compartment quickly and was well along the platform before mine had emptied. By the time we had moved on, most of the Hurstham travellers had disappeared down the stairs, and I settled to my paper again. In any case it had been no more than the idlest curiosity on my part and I thought no more about Kenray. That was, till I got out at Pangley.

Most of my fellow passengers got out there and I made my way along the platform in the midst of the swirl. With my vantage of height I could see right ahead of me to the dimness of the far stairs, but what I was suddenly startled to see, and only a few yards ahead of me, was the back of Kenray.

You know how in a startling moment you can think of the most footling things. I thought that Kenray must have overshot his station, and then I knew he hadn't. Then I told myself he might have, and that he was going down the stairs to change back to the up platform. But when we reached the foot of the stairs he turned right, and by the time I'd handed in my ticket he was out of sight.

There seemed the very devil of a crowd in front of me, but I quickened my steps and just as we came to the first fork I caught sight of him again. But he didn't take the left-hand to the town. He took the right-hand and at once I lost him in the dark. And then it suddenly struck me that he must have some appointment or other at Kalpoor. Something he had to see Mavin about and in connection with that jewellery.

It was on the tip of my tongue to holler. The words shaped themselves in my mind.

"Hallo, there, Kenray? What on earth are you doing here?"

But I didn't holler. I don't know why to this day, unless it was that I suddenly wondered why he had said nothing to Wharton and me about having an appointment at Pangley. At that moment too, I was walking on the grass verge and I remember I halted for a moment and heard his steps ahead on the hard road. Then I moved on, and still on the verge, and it was like that that we passed the double villa and came to the second fork.

I halted and listened again. He *was* going to Kalpoor, for again he went right, and once more I followed noiselessly on the verge. Then I halted again and that time I didn't hear his steps. So he was walking on the verge too, I thought, and then all at once I saw the flicker of a torch. It flashed across the verge ahead of me by a good thirty yards, and disappeared and then flashed again. I listened for a sound of him and then I heard the most peculiar noise like the snapping of twigs. I remember I thought that he must have stepped on a fallen rotten branch, so I moved on again. And now I knew that he must really be going to Kalpoor, so I quickened my own steps. Before I was at the white gate I should have caught up with him, and yet I hadn't. Strange, I thought, and halted just before the gate in case he was ahead of me. But there was never a sound on the gravelled drive.

I was now more used to the darkness and I stepped back to the verge and listened again. Never a sound of him and never a flash from that torch of his. Then I went through the gate and stood for a good couple of minutes just inside, and listened again. Against the velvety dark of the sky I saw the darker shape that would be Sutton's cottage, but of the movement of a torch there was never a sign, and of Kenray never a sound. And then I had another idea. Maybe Kenray was going farther along, and at the spot where he had disappeared there was a stile and a field-path which he knew for a short cut. And yet, whom should he be going to see in that open country that lay beyond Kalpoor? And a strange thing that he should come, and designedly, so near to the house while his business lay elsewhere.

And then I shrugged my shoulders. The whole thing was beyond me. And yet it was queer, I kept saying as I moved towards the house. One might almost go so far as to say it was secretive, but just as I thought that I almost came a purler on the lawn edge, and I switched my thoughts back to the drive. Mavin must have been listening for me, for when I reached the door he was there.

Chapter IX
CONCERNING A MANUSCRIPT

I HAD INTENDED to think out, on my way from Pangley station, the questions I ought to put to Mavin, but that queer business of Kenray had given me no chance. All the same, I didn't see why I should have to spend more than half an hour in the house, but when I gave Mavin a hint to that effect he was quite upset. He had had dinner advanced, he said, and it would be on the table in a matter of minutes.

I had a clean-up in the downstair cloakroom and as we left it Mavin said there was a rather fine tiger-skin I might like to see, and switched on the drawing-room light. I said it looked a fine one to me and added that I'd seen a reference to it in a gossip paragraph in one of the newspapers. He'd seen that paragraph too, he said. Sir William had shown it to him.

"What was that son of his like?" I asked.

He hesitated.

"Strictly between ourselves," I added quickly.

"Well, he was fairly popular," he said, and it seemed to me that 'fairly' was the operative word. Then he remembered something and was finding for me a page of *Society News* with a picture of Bill ('Skittles') Pelle, with the usual 'friend', at Newmarket races.

"When was this taken?" I asked.

"Last summer," he said. "He was home on special leave."

"Ah, well," I said, thinking of our overworked administrators, and just then the front door bell rang. I moved on to the study and left Mavin to deal with it himself. And the voice that I heard at the door was Kenray's.

I guessed that the two would come to the study and something told me to make a quick exit. Luckily the door led to the dining-room and from that was another to the hall. I circled round and by the time I was in the cloak-room again, Mavin and Kenray had disappeared. Then I moved quietly across the hall rugs and listened at the study door. The voices were only a murmur so I nipped back to the cloak-room again.

A minute or two went by and then a maid came to the hall and sounded the gong. I was in a bit of a fluster and wondering if Kenray would have been persuaded to stay for the meal. But he hadn't. Another couple of minutes and he and Mavin appeared in the hall. Kenray was saying he wouldn't have to trouble Mavin again and Mavin was saying it had been no trouble at all. Then there was a farewell handshake and Kenray saying he had a torch and could see his way quite well. But what had interested me more was the sight of Kenray's shoes as viewed through the crack of my door. To me they looked as if he'd been ploughing through mud and had afterwards tried to clean them with handfuls of grass.

It's funny, as I said, how things will come to you. All at once I was laughing to myself at the mystery I'd made out of nothing. Kenray had had business with Mavin, and probably about the jewellery. Just short of the house he'd had a pain in his belly and had nipped through the hedge to relieve himself. It was true the operation had taken him ten good minutes, but there was everything plain as a pikestaff.

"I wondered where you'd gone," said Mavin as I suddenly appeared.

"You didn't mention to Kenray that I was here?"

"Should I have done?" he asked guilelessly, and I made some lame reply. Then as we went through to our meal he was telling me that Kenray had the idea that Sir William had made some private notes about the jewellery, and he had called personally for them to save time, if, of course, Mavin knew where they were. Mavin knew nothing about any notes, and that's all there had been to it. Then I was wondering to myself why Kenray should suddenly be wanting notes about the jewellery when he had told Wharton and myself a couple of hours previously that he had no intention of carrying on with the job. Then finally I could shrug my shoulders at the whole thing. Kenray, like anyone else, was at liberty to change his mind, and maybe he had yielded to persuasion after Wharton and I had left him.

I'm not going to drag you through all that meal and conversation. What matters is the information I gathered, and here it is in the summarized form in which I wrote a brief report for Wharton.

Marion Blaketon had apparently used Doris Chaddon for making contact with Mavin, and at their very first meeting she had told him—roguishly, I gathered—that she was in Sir William's opinion a bold, bad lot, and that he'd be furious if he knew that Mavin had attended one of her parties. Mavin had taken the hint and Sir William had remained in ignorance of the fact that his sister-in-law and Mavin were acquainted. I gathered too that Mrs. Blaketon had taken the same line with Doris Chaddon.

And Marion Blaketon had very definitely questioned Mavin about the autobiography, if in the same arch way. "I'll wager Sir William has had some pretty nasty things to say about me," and so on. Mavin assured her that there was no reference to her whatever, unless it was to "an unfortunate family matter," which had been referred to in the vaguest of terms. Then she had confided in the strictest secrecy that she had married the man of her choice, so to speak, against the express wishes of her family, and that was the molehill out of which she thought Sir William might have made a mountain.

But something that was much more startling to me emerged from that conversation. About a week previous, Mavin had been on the far lawn one afternoon with Sutton when he saw Mrs. Blaketon pass the house. He had thought of calling to her and asking her to tea, and then remembered with almost a cold sweat that if the servants or Sutton happened to mention the visitor to Sir William, there might be the devil to pay.

Two days later—the last occasion in fact on which Mavin had seen Mrs. Blaketon—he asked if it were she who had gone by. She didn't deny it. She had friends at Bewford, two miles farther on, she said, and as it was a fine afternoon and the office had seemed oppressive for once, she had decided to pay a country call. She loved walking, she said, and in her younger days a twenty-mile tramp had been nothing.

"Did you believe that?" I asked Mavin quizzically.

"Well," he said, "I did, perhaps. I did think she was taking advantage of having friends there to have a look at this house. I'm not talking scandal, of course," he added diffidently. "I meant that she might be interested to see just where he was living."

I agreed, though with reservations of my own. To me it seemed glaringly patent that she had been making a reconnaissance of the road from the station. Melodramatic it might sound, but if she had passed the tip to some thug or other that a certain man with a valuable attach£-case might be going that way some dark night, then she would have added further details and suggestions.

One or two other oddments emerged from that evening's talk, and all to fit snugly into the mosaic of that case. Mavin was quite frank about himself, for instance. The war had hit him very hard. His private income of the best part of six hundred a year net had been principally in foreign securities, and the war reduced that income to under a hundred. That was why he had been glad enough of that badly paid job at Kalpoor. And he owned frankly that Wharton had been right to regard him as a suspect.

I asked him what Sir William had been intending to do with the jewellery that night at Kalpoor.

"There's a safe," he said. "It's up in his bedroom if you'd care to see it. That's where he was proposing to keep it and he was taking it back to the bank next day."

I went up to have a look. It wasn't a bad little safe, though a modern cracksman would have made short work of it, and I told Mavin so. Then something else emerged that seemed to me to show an amazing remissness on Mavin's part.

"That's funny," he said, "but I thought I heard a strange noise that night. I couldn't sleep very well, you see, wondering about Sir William. I came downstairs and had a look round, but I couldn't see anything." He smiled sheepishly. "To tell you how muddled I was, I switched on the light in the drawing-room and had it on for quite a few minutes till I remembered it wasn't blacked out."

"Let's get this clear," I said. "You thought there might have been a burglar."

"Well, yes. I did."

"And was there any trace of one?"

"I really don't know," he said. "Yesterday I did notice that someone might have been trying to force the catch of the french window in the drawing-room."

"My hat!" I said. "I wish to heaven you'd mentioned this before. Let's go in with your torch and have a look."

To my mind there wasn't any doubt about an attempt at a forced entry. Mavin was most apologetic. Burglaries and burglars' methods weren't in his line, he said, and he'd been worried to death about things in general. Also it hadn't struck him that an abortive attempt could be of interest.

"As soon as I'm gone," I said, "and that will be in a very few minutes, ring up your local police and have them send a man round at once. For all we know that window may be covered with prints."

I said he was to ring the Yard and have the result passed on to Wharton as soon as the local men had finished. After that I prepared to go, and it was while we were in the hall that I thought of something else.

"One very tiny thing has been worrying me," I said. "It just shows a tidy sort of brain that simply can't stand loose ends. About that *par moy ton aide* business. You remember Sir William asked you what you made of it. Now that's rather puzzled me. Surely his own French was first class? His people had lived in Paris for years."

"His French *was* first class," he said. "It was the medieval flavour of that particular phrase that might have puzzled him; at least, that's what I think. After all, heaps of well-educated Frenchmen would be very much at sea with even late middle French, just as Englishmen would be with anything between Chaucer and Spenser."

That seemed to me an admirable and satisfying answer and I gave it no more thought. What I did think mostly about on my walk back to the station was that attempt at burglary, for there I did seem to see the Blaketon hand. And there again it was complicated and confusing. She doubtless had a burglar up her sleeve, but why have him run the risks of burglary by night when all he had to do was collar the jewellery on Sir William's walk from the station to Kalpoor. That was utterly beyond me and I decided to pass it on to Wharton.

After that I switched my thoughts to Pelle. The more one learned about him, the less likeable he seemed to be. Nobody, as far as I could think back, had volunteered much in his favour, and as for that son of his, Mavin, who had known him from their school days, had implied that there wasn't a lot to be said for him either. In the *Society News* picture he had looked to me a well-fed, beefy sort whose weight might reasonably have been employed against the Burmese Japs. Not that he had anything to do with the case in hand, but thinking of him made me suddenly think of something else, and it was as if a dozen ideas had coalesced into one.

What about that crook husband of Marion Blaketon? Was he dead or still flourishing somewhere under an assumed name? In less than no time I was weaving quite a thrilling story round Colonel Blaketon. Suppose he had turned up in England and run his wife to earth. A demand for funds, perhaps, and a hint of blackmail, and she getting rid of him by giving a free hand in the matter of Pelle. Or had she double-crossed him? Had one man collar the jewellery, or done that job herself, and let Blaketon make, later on that night, the abortive attempt at burglary. A fascinating series of ideas, I thought, and yet something told me that it might be as well not to put any of them up to Wharton.

But they kept me busy till I reached Charing Cross. It was then only ten past nine and I rang Wharton from the station to see if he was in, and five minutes later I was in his room. But there wasn't time to tell my story. What I was just in time for was to hear a piece of new evidence that muddled up the case still more.

Wharton had had a report which had made him decide to send for the particular constable concerned, and he had arrived at the same time as myself. Sandley was his name: a youngish fellow who looked pretty smart.

"You tell us all about it," Wharton told him when he had him comfortably seated. "Not witness-box stuff, but just your own words."

"Well then, it was about twenty past four last Monday afternoon, sir," Sandley began. "I was on the south corner of Faversham Square, waiting for my sergeant, when a gentleman came up to me all excited. Officer,' he says, 'will you tell me where Number 54 is, I've been looking and I can't find it.' 'Number 54, sir,' I says, and I had to do a bit of a grin inside, sir, because there isn't a fifty-four, and that's what I told him. 'Are you sure?' he says. I told him I knew every house and number in that Square and the last one was forty-eight. Then he didn't half let out. Reckoned someone had made an appointment with him for four o'clock at this Number 54, and how he'd wasted his time looking for it and how he had a train to catch."

"'Sure you didn't take the number down wrong, sir?' I asked him. 'Maybe it was forty-five and not fifty-four.' 'God dammit, officer,' he says, 'do you think I'm deaf? I tell you it was fifty-four.' and then he whips out a piece of paper and shows me it all written down. 'Sorry then, sir, but I can't help you,' I says, and then I wondered if someone had been pulling his leg. He gave me a regular glare at that, sir. Looked as if he was going to burst, and then off he went."

"And why did you connect him with Sir William Pelle?"

Sandley took out a wallet and handed Wharton a newspaper-cutting. It was a photograph of Pelle from the *Daily Record*.

"I recognized him by that, sir. And there was a bit of talk at the station about something fishy about his death, so I thought I'd better send in a report."

"And very sensible too," Wharton said. "But what did he look like?"

"A smallish gentleman," Sandley said. "Looked a regular little fighting cock, sir, if you know what I mean. Talked like a machine-gun, sir, all explosive like."

"And his clothes?"

Sandley described them and there wasn't a shadow of doubt in Wharton's mind or my own. Sandley had a warning to keep that report to himself, and then went out with his tail wagging at Wharton's word or two of praise and pat on the back.

"And now what?" Wharton asked me with something of a glare.

"Lord knows!" I said. "Pelle's the only one who could have given us details about that telephone call, and he'll never tell us now. All the same, we *are* a bit further. We've verified the call and know what it was about."

He grunted.

"No wonder that Blaketon woman could swear blind he'd never set foot in her office that afternoon. You can bet your life it was she who sent him on that fool's errand. And where's that get us? Nowhere. Back where we started from."

Then he was asking what I'd found out at Pangley, and I told him everything, except about Kenray. His eyes fairly popped when he heard of that attempted burglary but by the time I'd finished he'd changed his mind.

"You can say what you like," he said, "but my idea is that Mavin faked those marks himself. He'd do it on the Monday before Pelle got home. In the morning the jewellery would have been missing. And why? Because he'd have rifled the safe. He'd every chance to get a key."

"But the safe was in Pelle's bedroom."

"Why not?" he told me with a glare. "They always had coffee after dinner, didn't they? What was to stop Mavin slipping something into his cup? Or into his night-cap, for that matter. I'll wager the old boy always had a whisky the last thing."

The buzzer happened to go just then and George picked up the receiver with something of resignation. A moment or two and his look altered.

"Oh, yes, Mr. Mavin? . . . I see. Nothing at all. . . . Yes, a pity. . . . Just a minute. Something I want to know. Was Sir William accustomed to having a night-cap before he went to bed? . . . He was? . . . Oh, just getting a few personal details. Nothing more than that. Good-bye, and thank you very much."

"There you are," he told me. "He did have a night-cap. And there wasn't a print of any kind on the french window."

"All hypothesis," I said, "and one-sided at that. No self-respecting burglar would have left a print. And the fact remains that Mavin didn't dope the coffee or the night-cap, and for the simple reason that Pelle never came home."

"That's no reason why we shouldn't try to find out if Mavin bought any sleeping tablets in preparation," he said, and made a note in his book. "The trouble with you," he went on, "is that you have your likes and dislikes."

"I can only give you an opinion," I told him. "That opinion is that Mavin had nothing to do with that crime, no I admit I can't prove it, but as an opinion it's a very strong one."

"All right, then. Say he's out. And Kenray's out. All that leaves us is the Blaketon woman."

He grabbed a piece of paper.

"What've you got against her? Facts, mind, not theories."

"If you mean what would convince a jury, then I don't think it would be hard to prove that she began making a dead set at both Doris Chaddon and Roger Mavin three weeks ago."

"Yes?"

"We could prove she questioned him about the autobiography," I said. "What we couldn't prove, unless we can get the Chaddon girl to talk, is that she questioned her about the jewellery."

George wrote down something about the autobiography.

"And there the facts seem to end," I said, "and we come to suggestion. We could suggest to the jury that her visit to Pangley was for the purpose of reconnoitring the ground. To do that we'd have to prove she hadn't any friends at that Bewford place where she told Mavin she was going."

Wharton made a note of that last.

"The only other thing is also suggestion," I said. "We can prove she rang Doris Chaddon and suggest it was to find out when Sir William would be back in the office. From that we might go on to suggest it was she who lured him to Faversham Square and made him miss his train. I admit she'd have had to do some skilful disguising of her voice."

"Well, we'll put down a barrage on that Blaketon woman," George said. "Do some Montgomery stuff. Go at her from all angles, particularly that alibi."

That seemed to be all so I rose to go.

"Tell me, George," I suddenly said. "I take it even Montgomery has a plan of campaign."

George chuckled. I didn't say anything. If George thinks me funny, who am I to dispel the delusion.

"Your plan of campaign is eliminating suspects. Is that it?"

"Didn't I say so?" he told me. "Kenray's out and your pal Mavin's out."

"There's one person we haven't considered," I said, and switched to a question. "What's happened about that sugar inquiry?"

"Never a thing," he said. "Not a tradesman's van in all Pangley or the district was that way that night." What his men were now employed on was tracing ration lorries.

"That's a good idea," I said. "There might have been sugar spilled on the floor of a ration truck. But there's another suspect, George. The one who put the body into that truck. It'll be interesting to know just why he put it there and carried it off. And why and how it found itself in that goods wagon."

It was after ten o'clock when I got to my flat, but somehow I wasn't feeling too tired. I'm a night bird for one thing, and for another I was rather pleased at George's suggestion that I'd better take things easy in the morning. He'd ring me, he said, if anything important turned up.

I got into a dressing-gown, poured myself a drink and then settled down to a reading of that autobiography. There were two hundred and forty pages of manuscript, double spacing, and I told myself that I'd read the lot or succumb in the attempt. It turned out that I was reckoning without the author.

I'm not going to bore you with even the briefest resume of that book, but since certain facts and conclusions were to have a vital bearing on the case, I will confine myself to them, and no more. Generally speaking then—and that fact is comparatively unimportant—the book had a stodginess, a dullness and a pomposity that seemed to me incredible. Unless Pelle's son was prepared to finance its publication, I couldn't see a publisher even beginning to take an interest. There was also an utter absence of humour. A few good stories sprinkled here and there would have carried a reader along through the aridities, but the whole book had no more than two and they were spoiled in the telling. Not that Mavin was to blame for the quality of the book. He, I imagine, had learned only too well the lesson that Gil Blas failed to learn in time—that it doesn't pay to offer criticism, however constructive, to a self-satisfied and pig-headed employer.

The descriptions of Indian landscape were monotonously done, and with too great an intrusion of the speaker. Accounts of this and that commission were interminable and I don't mind owning that I was soon skipping most of them. Of little human touches there were few. One—and much overwritten—was his meeting with Laura Frame, whom he subsequently married, and another—coloured by the passing years—was the birth of his son. And so to facts.

My brain works best at night, and it was after midnight when I began collating various facts that seemed to me to stand out. The first was that there was never a mention of the name of Marion Frame. There was a too glowing tribute to the character and work of Sir Leyland, and mentions of various receptions, balls and conferences, but that his other daughter should not be mentioned seemed to me very deliberate. And yet there was one reference—the one that Mavin had mentioned. Laura Pelle caught a feverish cold and pneumonia supervened, and she died with tragic suddenness.

> Hers was a gallant spirit but she never had been over-strong. I had long been urging her to spend the summers in England, but she had always refused. Her place, she said, was by my side. *An unfortunate family affair over which she worried a good deal, helped also to hasten the end.*

Those were the exact words, and the sole reference to Marion Blaketon, and in reading it no one could say that a labouring man, though a fool, could not err therein. Few people would identify Marion Blaketon with that family affair, and since Mavin had told her that wording, why should she worry about the publication of the book? And worry sufficiently to have taken action so drastic.

As to the oases of interest in the book generally, I did read with something of pleasure the accounts of the young Pelle's holidays in Paris, and I envied him the opportunities he had missed. His father had been an art dealer of international reputation, and all the great figures of what I might call the late Victorian and early Edwardian schools of France had frequented that shop in the Rue de Rivoli. I admit that a long chapter was devoted to Paris but those giants of the age were catalogued rather than described.

After he went to India he returned to Paris on leave, and that was in 1911. There again was a chance to give a first-class insight into the mentality of France before the last war, but there the opportunity was not so much missed as utterly ignored. One chapter ended . . .

> and in June of that year I was once more in Paris.

> As for the next chapter, that began

> when I returned to Mysore in the late winter of that year . . .

You see what I mean? Perhaps the failure to mention Paris at all was artistic, I thought. An attempt, that had badly missed fire, to show the reader how India was to such an extent in the blood of a young administrator as to exclude everything else.

When I put that manuscript away for good, it was about one in the morning. And in case you should think that what I have told you about that manuscript is unnecessary digression or mere padding, let me hasten to add that you are a considerable way out. When I got into bed that early morning, I was making the same mistake. Except as purely negatively—and in the express case of Marion Blaketon— I was regarding the long night hours as completely wasted. Days and days afterwards, and at a very strange moment, I was to find myself much mistaken.

Chapter X
CONFIRMATION OF A THEORY

HAVE YOU EVER gone to bed with, say, an unsolved crossword clue on your mind and then woke next morning with the answer pat on your tongue? Doubtless you have, and doubtless you know far more about the reasons, subconscious or otherwise, than I happen to do. But I woke the following morning, not with the knowledge that I needn't get up, but with something on my mind that I'd completely forgotten.

This was it—a fragment of conversation and no more.

"Chaddon will probably get a packet when he dies. He or his daughter."

My conscious brain went into action. A morning at the club. Whom was I with? Then I remembered, and how we'd been talking about Bertram Dane. Colley had said that when Dane died, old Chaddon would come into a packet, or else his daughter would.

I scowled in thought and then had the connection. Dane was Chaddon's uncle. Chaddon was the only nephew, and since Doris was Chaddon's only child, she was Dane's only great-niece. Doris Chaddon and Dane, my mind went on. She in the case from the beginning and I'd seen him making that queer exit from Kenray's shop on the morning after Pelle's death.

There are moments in a case when a new suspect is a gift from heaven, but this wasn't one. What Dane could have had to do with the killing of Pelle was utterly beyond me, and even beyond surmise, and if I hadn't been indulging in wishful thinking I'd have thought the same about the theft of the jewellery. That theft, even if it involved a comparatively harmless bludgeoning of Pelle, wasn't beyond the scope and inclination of Bertram Dane, provided there was something in that attaché-case that was coveted for his collection of rings. And Doris Chaddon would have been his source of information. With an eye on the old man's money, she'd have blabbed for all she was worth.

But there again was something that I had no intention whatever of putting up to Wharton, and, as I told myself within a matter of seconds, no intention of proceeding with myself. Except perhaps for satisfying one small curiosity. Now I was on friendly terms with Grace Allbeck, mightn't I induce her to tell me just why old Dane had shaken his fist at her that morning on the pavement. Grace Allbeck struck me as the last person at whom one would want to shake a fist, and Dane's hadn't struck me as playful but distinctly minatory.

By that time I found myself out of bed. It was about half-past eight, so I dressed and then rang down for breakfast to be brought up. Then I remembered letters, and found two for me on the mat. One was from my wife and I read it over my meal. There was a postscript:

Yours just come. Think I should sell the brooch thing.

Out of that came a quick warmth of anticipation. Some time that morning, if Wharton didn't want me, I'd take that piece of jewellery to Grace Allbeck. Then I had an afterthought, not so pleasant. Doris Chaddon might think it strange that I had not looked her up again after that lunch. Maybe I might drop in on her too, and there mightn't be any harm in bringing the conversation round to old Bertram Dane and trying to ferret out what the relations were between great-uncle and great-niece.

After breakfast I went through my paper leisurely for once, but when I'd finished I thought it still a bit early to call on Grace Allbeck, and that was why I began thinking about the case again. Then among the notes in my pocket, what should I find but a copy of that memorandum that Pelle had had in his wallet. Somehow I had had no time to have a real good look at it, but now began an attempt to discover just what it meant.

Par moy ton aide

Late-middle French, perhaps, as Mavin has said, and "I will be your help." A perfectly good translation.

B.M. or K?

That conveyed nothing, unless it was the title of reference books that Pelle had intended to consult.

And cts.

Cts. was surely an abbreviation, and, if I remembered rightly, was short for carats. The thought brought a little thrill. Then suddenly I found myself fumbling at my glasses, and then I was making for a dictionary. And there it was. *Ct.—Cent. Carat.* Carat seemed the more likely of the two. What Pelle had written down was virtually, "How many carats?" And obviously in connection with the stone or stones in one of those gifts that had reached his office. And then, before I hardly knew it, everything was clear as daylight.

B.M. would be British Museum, and it was the authorities there whom he was proposing to consult. *K* was Kenray, and he was undecided which was the better authority. Then what of that French motto?

That came easily too, or at least I thought the solution I found must be correct. That piece of jewellery was a ring, and a posy ring at that. The French was a motto incised inside the gold of the stone mounting. Common enough those posy rings. Names of betrothed parties were their simplest form, and when I looked up the encyclopaedia I found half a score, and some in the most native of English. "My Deere, Love me and Mine", "Harte to Harte, Both I Binde", and "My Love True Love", were the quaintest. But the French motto seemed to me to be early seventeenth century at the latest, and that particular ring would therefore be more rare.

And that made me open my eyes. Who would be more interested in a rare ring than Bertram Dane? The thought brought me to my feet and set me fumbling at my glasses again. Ideas came, and went, and circled, and then suddenly it seemed to me that I had heard of that French motto before. And in some context that had to do with a ring. That set me frowning and thinking again, and the more I concentrated the less I could remember. And then just as suddenly I was smiling to myself. Grace Allbeck might know. Indeed, if she didn't know, who would.

I glanced at my watch and it was about half-past ten. Time to move on, I thought, and I could leave word at the exchange downstairs if a message from Wharton should come for me. And then just as I was having a look at the set of my hat in the glass, the telephone went.

It was Wharton, and the tone His urgent one.

"It's you," he said relievedly at my hallo. "I thought you might be out. I'm ringing from Pangley, by the way."

"Anything happened?" I asked quickly.

"You'd never guess," he said. "It's that missing jewellery. It was sent by post addressed to Sir William, here at his house. Arrived this morning. Aldgate postmark, if that means anything to you."

That last had been something of a hopeful question.

"I'm flummoxed, George," I said. "Absolutely flummoxed."

"Well, there we are," he said. "Mavin opened the parcel and quite right too. He let me know and I got hold of Kenray. He's now checking everything against the lists."

"You don't want me down there?"

"Don't think so," he said. "Look me up this afternoon at the Yard."

"Oh, George," I said quickly. "One small thing, but don't ask me questions about it. I'll explain later. But when Kenray's checking that jewellery, make sure if there's a ring with probably a goodish-sized diamond. It'll have a French motto engraved inside. I'll ring you about it later."

"What's the idea?"

"Tell you all about it later." I said. "Don't forget. A ring with a French motto inside the band."

I'd had some facers in my time but that news about the jewellery seemed about the worst. Why in heaven's name had it been returned? Had the thief got the wind up badly after learning through the papers that Pelle was dead?

That seemed a likely solution. Pelle had been knocked unconscious and then the thief had made off. By rights Pelle should have recovered in a few minutes and the affair would have been robbery with violence. Serious as that was, it was petty larceny compared with murder.

But whoever it was, the return of that jewellery seemed to me to let out Marion Blaketon. Somehow I couldn't imagine her having several thousand pounds in her possession and then returning it to the owner. Indeed, if the situation before had seemed to me complicated, to say the least of it, it now seemed illogical to the point of chaos, and if I shrugged my shoulders with something like despair it was because three days of inquiry had landed us behind the point from which we had started.

And then I had a brainwave. It was more than that; it was something that made me heave a sigh of more than relief. Suppose, I told myself, that that ring was missing. Mightn't that prove that Dane had been after it, and after nothing else? Once the ring was his, then the rest had been sent back.

I admit straightaway that I was jumping to conclusions, but at that particular moment I was ready to jump at anything. And it did seem a reasonable theory, and one that could almost be put up to Wharton. And I realized something else. If Kenray was examining the collection of jewellery, then there would be no need for me to question Grace Allbeck. Kenray would be the absolute last word. Even if that ring wasn't there, he could deduce its value, and if it had any special history, then he would certainly know it.

With that I made my way out, and a dull muggy sort of morning it was. As I opened the door of Kenray's shop I saw that the light was on. Grace Allbeck heard my entry and came in at once from the office. It was quite a moment or two before she smiled a welcome at me, and I was wondering if in some way I could have offended her.

"I've come on business," I told her, and laid my little parcel on the counter. "Here it is, and I want you to send the cheque direct to my wife."

She took down the address.

"You're looking more yourself this morning," I said. "The headache quite gone."

"Quite gone," she said.

"Good," I said, and it didn't seem too easy to make conversation. And then I thought of something.

"Tell me," I said. "You remember when I brought that piece of jewellery in and how you asked if I'd mind telling you how it had come into my possession? Was that some sort of formula?"

"In a way, yes," she said and her eyes seemed to be questioning me about something quite different.

"Then pardon my being importunate," I went on, "but let's imagine a concrete case. I come in here down at heel and I offer to sell you something which you strongly suspect has been stolen. What do you do?"

She looked relieved and I don't know why. Then she was smiling to herself and looking as if trying to remember.

"I did have a case like that once," she said. "The customer wasn't really suspicious, as to circumstances, I mean, but her manner was. I took her name and address and then said I wasn't able to purchase. She was most indignant and flounced out of the shop."

"And what did you do then?"

"Nothing," she said. "There was only my word against hers, and she looked the sort to make trouble."

"Very interesting," I said. "And very tactful on your part, if I may say so."

"Please don't repeat it," she was telling me anxiously.

"I'd never dream of repeating it," I assured her, and in the same moment I was realizing that there was one more question I simply had to ask her. And why I had to ask it I can't quite say. She had mentioned a woman, and I was thinking of Marion Blaketon and how she'd maybe got hold of stuff that she'd try to sell.

"I know I'm unblushingly curious," I said, "but tell me just one more thing, and in the very strictest confidence. Have you ever heard of a Mrs. Blaketon? Marion Blaketon?"

What I saw on her face was fairly staggering. She looked away and then she was smiling feebly, or trying to force a smile and shaking her head.

"I don't think I have. But why?"

"No particular reason," I said, and then she was changing the subject with a haste that couldn't be concealed.

"But about the receipt. Shall I ask your wife to send it or would you rather give me one now?"

"I think I'd rather you let her send it," I said. "She'll love to handle things herself."

Somehow I wanted to get quickly out of that shop and pass on what I knew to Wharton. But there was that other business to do.

"What I really came for," I said, "was something semi-official. I've just learned from Superintendent Wharton that the missing jewellery's been recovered. Or did you know?"

"Mr. Kenray did say something," she said. "I'm afraid I was rather busy and didn't gather more than you've just told me."

"I'm glad things have turned out as they have," I said. "I mean I'm glad that your brother is doing the job he was asked to do, and that everything will be cleared up before he leaves for the States."

"It's possible there may be an alteration," she said, and she was giving me that queer, direct look. "I may be going myself."

"But how lovely for you!" I said. "The change should do you all the good in the world. Get rid of those headaches for one thing."

"But nothing's settled yet," she told me, and began moving towards the door. "I suppose you haven't been to the Jugoslav Exhibition?"

"I ought to have gone," I said, "but somehow I haven't had time." Then I gave what I hoped was my most bewitching smile, though to her it was probably fatuous. "What about your going with me some afternoon? We could have lunch first?"

I could honestly say that that was the first moment that morning when she seemed really friendly. Somehow she was suddenly quite a different woman.

"I'd love to," she said. "I've been once but it's something one ought to see several times. I don't mean that I'm accepting your kind invitation," she added hurriedly. "Everything's so rushed at the moment."

"But you'll keep it in mind."

"Yes," she said gravely. "I'll keep it in mind."

Our eyes met in a good-bye smile and I was out on the pavement again. It was dull as ever overhead and everything about me was dull too. I had looked forward to that call on Grace Allbeck but everything seemed to have gone wrong, and with a chastened sort of irony I was wondering if I was the kind of person whom one could stomach only in small and rare doses. Even that dramatic discovery about Marion Blaketon wasn't as cheering or even as important as it had first seemed. Maybe I had called rather too soon on the heels of the previous night, and with that I shrugged my shoulders resignedly and put an end to introspection. Grace Allbeck, I told myself, was a highly attractive woman, but that was no reason why I should make myself a pest.

Doris Chaddon opened the office door, gave a little gasp and then admitted me.

"Oh, it's you!" she said.

"What's wrong with me this morning?" I demanded humorously. "This is the second time I've had a cold reception."

"You called here before?"

"Forget it," I said. "And what about a cup of tea?"

"I was just making one," she said. "It won't be a minute."

She left the door open as she went through.

"Heard about the jewellery?" I called.

"What jewellery?"

"My dear girl," I remonstrated. "Your jewellery. Sir William's jewellery. It's been recovered. Arrived by post at Kalpoor this morning."

"No-o-o!" she said, and appeared at the door. "Do they know who sent it?"

"Santa Claus," I said flippantly.

"Don't be ridiculous," she told me. "But do they know?"

"Not the foggiest notion," I said. "It was sent back anonymously."

She disappeared again at that, but only for a second or two. In came the tray and she was asking how I liked my tea. I said I liked it that way, sitting there with her.

"Can't you ever be serious," she told me, but not at all displeased. "Like a biscuit with it?"

We munched biscuits and sipped the hot tea and talked for two minutes about the weather.

"By the way," I said. "Isn't my old friend Bertram Dane some relation of yours?"

I saw her stiffen. It was at least ten seconds before she answered, and I knew that because I had suddenly remembered that I hadn't mentioned him to Grace Allbeck.

"He's my great-uncle," she said off-handedly.

"Often see him?"

"Oh, sometimes."

"How often's sometimes?"

"Oh, just sometimes."

"I only asked," I said, "because I was wondering if he still had that wardens' post under him."

"Isn't it too priceless?" she said. "Rather handy though."

"I suppose he hasn't his collection still in his house?"

"He had it moved as soon as the blitz started," she said. "Poor dear! I believe he goes and moons over it sometimes. It's in a strong-room somewhere."

"I suppose you haven't by any chance seen him quite recently?"

"On Sunday week," she said, and then stopped short. "Why did you want to know?"

"Only that I hadn't seen him about myself," I said. "Give him my compliments when you see him next. I doubt if he'll remember me though. It was my father he knew best."

She poured me another cup of tea.

"You can be rather nice, you know, sometimes," she said.

"Hallo!" I said in mock consternation. "What's coming now?"

"Oh, nothing," she said, and gave me a coming-on look. At that moment I was sure that if I'd put out a knee, she'd have sat on it. "Only I've got rather to like it here. I'd hate going back, and I just wondered. You must know heaps of nice jobs."

"Do I not!" I said, and was probably looking like a rather inebriated Don Juan. "But wait a minute, though. Aren't you in a reserved occupation?"

"We can always get round that," she said. "Besides, Daddy knows heaps of people."

I gathered relievedly that it was not myself but her father to whom she was referring, but things were getting rather too intimate all the same.

"You leave it to me," I told her. "It may take a little time but I'll have a scout round."

I got to my feet to make a more artistic switch to the conversation.

"But going back to that jewellery. You used to see it as it came in?"

"Why?" she said, and was on her guard at once.

"Something curious has happened," I said. "I didn't quite get the hang of it but there's a ring or something with a French inscription inside. Nobody seems to know quite what it is."

"I saw it," she said, and looked quite relieved. "Sir William was awfully puzzled. Uncle Bertram—"

Then she stopped short. I didn't look at her. It was best to pretend I hadn't heard.

"I don't see what the fuss is all about," I said. "It'll fetch what it's worth at the sale. Those things always do."

Then I said I'd really have to be going. I thanked her for the tea and said if she kept on being good she should make tea for me in heaven. She asked what I meant by good, and I said, "Just good," and we left it at that. Down the stairs I went and she waved a good-bye from the top. A kiss was blown to accompany it and I blew one back. I suppose I must have walked a good few yards before I came to my better self. A hell of a game I was playing, I thought, and consoled myself with the knowledge that it was worth it. She *had* seen that ring and she *had* told old Dane about it. And that knowledge seemed so vital that I made for the kiosks in Piccadilly Station, for I simply had to ring up Wharton. I made a queue of one outside the likeliest box and in about a minute was ringing Kalpoor. George was at the other end.

"This is Travers, George," I said. "Anything about that ring yet?"

"It isn't here," he said. "According to the list there's only one article missing and that's a ring, sent by an anonymous donor. What's the idea?"

"I can't tell you. I mean, over the 'phone. But what about Mavin? He couldn't have taken it?"

"Why should he?"

He gave a grunt, then said Mavin was at the funeral. And if he weren't, what was the point of questioning if there was nothing to go on.

"Look here," he said. "You'd better see me about it straightaway. We'll be back in about an hour. Half-past one suit you?"

I said it would and added that I might also be able to tell him an interesting discovery about the Blaketon woman. And when I'd hung up, was I feeling pretty pleased with myself! Everything had turned out superbly, and if Dane wasn't our man, then in Wharton's words my name was Robinson. I looked at my watch and there didn't seem time for a regular meal, even if I could get a table, so I went to a cafeteria and had a cup of coffee and an incredibly indigestible bun, and while I was tackling it I was thinking about old Bertram Dane. Eighty he would be, if a day, and as hale and vigorous as a man of sixty. A menacing-looking figure too, with his untidy beard and vastly bushy eyebrows and a hooked beak over his slit of a mouth. A law unto himself, like most eccentrics, for the essence of eccentricity is to damn the conventions. Unscrupulous and predatory, that was old Dane, and I remembered Wharton's story of how he'd obtained a certain ring and then, when the pace of the law had got a bit too hot, had returned it anonymously, just as that jewellery had been returned.

But when I began thinking what I should say to Wharton I realized there was something that ought to be done at once, and I left that cafeteria before I should change my mind. It was something I didn't like doing, and it seemed to me that my best policy was to make the visit official. By the time I was at the shop I thought I saw the best approach.

"I'm so sorry," I said to Grace Allbeck, "but I've got to bother you again."

"Why call it a bother," she asked me, and her tone was much more friendly.

"Official business is always a nuisance," I said. "I hate doing it but I must ask you to give me your word that you'll regard what I say as highly confidential. In the same way I'll assure you that whatever information you can give me will be in the strictest confidence too."

It seemed to me she was looking a bit alarmed.

"I wouldn't worry you," I went solemnly on, "but in a few minutes I have to see Superintendent Wharton and your brother about that jewellery. It appears that a ring is missing."

"A ring missing?"

"Yes," I said, "and here's where the pledge of secrecy has to operate. You give me your word?"

She nodded, but so disconcertingly direct was her look that I turned my eyes away.

"Good," I said. "Then the fact is there's reason to suspect Bertram Dane as having been concerned in it."

"Bertram Dane," she said, and almost to herself. Her eyes met mine again. "Won't you tell me the reasons? Why should you suspect him, I mean?"

"At the moment things haven't reached a sufficiently advanced stage," I said. "We do know he knew of the existence of the ring, and it was probably one he would give a good deal for. We also know his little propensities, as you do."

I ventured on a smile at that last remark. She smiled rather wryly too.

"What sort of a customer was he?" I said.

"As a customer—good. We've sold him quite a lot of things in our time."

"And yet you didn't like him."

"Well, perhaps not," she said. "There was always the feeling that he might be likely to let you down. I can't explain the feeling, but . . . well, I didn't feel happy with him."

"Well, let me put something to you," I said. "It's pure guesswork, but if I'm right I shall be very pleased. I saw Dane leaving here last Tuesday morning and his attitude struck me as peculiar, even for him. He looked, in fact, as if he were shaking his fist at this shop. I almost said, at you."

"He probably was," she said, and smiled.

"Well, my guess is this," I said. "I think he'd asked you for an opinion on that missing ring. He'd know you knew nothing about it."

"Heavens, no!" she said, and laughed. "What he came here with was some extraordinary story about someone having written him, I think it was about a piece of jewellery and asking quite a big sum for it because we'd offered the same sum. I told him, of course, that even if this customer of his was telling the truth, we couldn't divulge names. Then he accused me of sharp practice, and that's when I virtually showed him out of the shop. I believe he even added that the whole thing was a conspiracy and we were in it to extort money from him." She smiled. "That's probably when you saw him shaking his fist."

"Well, that satisfies me," I said, "even if it doesn't let him out of that other business."

I held out my hand.

"There's nothing else you want to ask?" she said.

"Not a thing," I said. "Unless it is when you and I are going to that Exhibition."

As I strolled slowly towards the Yard I was far from perturbed about the badness of that guess of mine. After all I should have been considerably alarmed if it had turned out to be other than the stalking horse for which I had intended it. For if Dane knew all about the jewellery, then the knowledge might have included the fact that Kenray was in charge of the selection and valuation, and therefore to have brought that ring to Kenray's shop would have been stark madness. What I had wanted from Grace Allbeck was anything that might throw light on Dane's mind and actions on that morning after Pelle's murder. That I had gathered little or nothing was of small consequence compared with the fact that I had been told nothing of negative importance. Dane, I could tell myself, was just as strong a suspect as when I entered the shop, whereas Grace Allbeck might have revealed, however inadvertently, something that knocked that theory endways. In fact, I was feeling that the theory had had its first test, and had survived it more than well.

When I entered Wharton's room he was there, and Kenray with him.

"Been waiting for you," George said with just a touch of accusation.

I told him sweetly that I was five minutes ahead of time, but he was helping me off with my overcoat and generally bustling me round.

"Now then," he said, as soon as I'd taken a chair. "What's all this about that ring?"

Chapter XI
BEARDING THE LION

I TOOK OUT that copy of Pelle's memorandum and George and Kenray gathered round. Each agreed with my deductions, and then I hesitated before going on. George read my thoughts for once.

"You needn't worry about Mr. Kenray," he told me. "You just tell us everything you know."

That being so I spilled all the beans.

"We're on to something," George said, and pursed his lips. "That Chaddon girl told him every damned thing. He wanted that ring and he didn't want anything else. That's why he sent the rest back. What do you think, Kenray?"

"You gentlemen know more than I do," Kenray told him with a little shrug of the shoulders.

"Do you think him capable of snatching that attaché-case?" persisted Wharton.

"I've known collectors do some queer things," said Kenray, and the answer evidently satisfied Wharton.

"And what about the ring itself?" he said. "Assuming Travers's deductions are correct. Would it be valuable?"

Kenray spread his palms—the most expansive gesture I'd ever seen him make.

"You're asking something impossible," he said. "Was it a single stone ring, or what? Was the stone genuine or perfect or flawed? As Sir William apparently wondered, what was the weight of the stone or stones? If the stones weren't valuable, the gold would be only breaking-up price—if it *was* gold."

Wharton smiled sheepishly and said he hadn't thought of all that.

"What about historical value?" I said. "Suppose, for instance, one could trace original ownership from the incised motto. If it belonged to Catherine de Medici, for example, or the great Duc de Guise or Marguerite de Valois."

"I don't think it would make all that difference," Kenray said, "at least, not for what I might call the general market. To a collector, possibly yes, but only if the history were thoroughly established."

"You've never run across that particular motto?" asked Wharton.

"I don't know that I have."

"Would your sister be able to help?" I asked.

Kenray shook his head.

"Rings aren't her particular line. I've always rather specialized in them."

"That's a good enough answer for me," Wharton said, and got to his feet. There were profuse thanks to Kenray and apologies beforehand for a future meeting, and then George and I were alone.

"What was that news about the Blaketon woman," he was wanting to know.

I told him what I thought I'd discovered from Grace Allbeck, and at once he was pursing his lips and frowning away to himself.

"I think you're right," he said, and made a note in his book. "Should I have a confidential word with Mrs. Allbeck or shouldn't I?"

"You can't, George," I said. "She didn't give it to me as a fact, and it was in strict secrecy. Also if you did get the facts from Mrs. Allbeck it would only be on the condition that she was never called upon to witness. Blabbing about any sort of customer would do a business like hers incalculable harm. But about the jewellery," I went on, "where is it now?"

"In the possession of the Powers-that-Be," he told me gloomily. Then I was learning that there had been nothing to be gleaned from the actual parcel in which it had been sent to Kalpoor.

"This is the very devil of a business," he said, and scowled at me over the tops of his spectacles. "Everything looks so simple. But is it? How can we go to old Dane and ask him where he was at half-past five last Monday night? At least, till we've a damned sight more to go on."

"Why not?" I said. "Who's he that he shouldn't be questioned?"

"Who's he?" He glared. "The biggest liar in Europe, for one thing. He'd swear blind he never left his house. Make out that someone was impersonating him."

Perhaps he saw I thought that a bit far-fetched for he went on to qualify it.

"What we've got to do is find someone who actually saw him leave his house. And who saw him come back."

"He has some domestic staff?"

"A man at least," he said. "But it's going to be a ticklish job. That old ruffian would just as soon throw you out of the house as look at you."

"Does that imply that you want *me* to inquire into his alibi?" I asked blandly.

"Not necessarily," he said, and shot me a look. "Alibis," he went on bitterly, "where do they get you? Fulcher has one—not that he was ever a real suspect. And that Blaketon woman."

"You've had a go at hers already?"

"What do you think I'm here for?" he asked me. "We had a go at her the same night, through that typist."

"Well, I've got an idea," I said. "Somewhere or other I've heard about that motto that was on that ring. If it should turn out to be highly desirable from Dane's point of view, that strengthens the case against him. And another thing," I went on, "I don't prophesy for a moment that that ring is a famous one—"

"How could it be?" he cut in. "Kenray would have known it if it was."

"Not necessarily," I told him obstinately. "But what I was going to say was that if I can get information about that ring, then there might be a very full advertisement put in the Personal Columns, asking the donor to come forward in confidence. He or she might fill in the gaps. Besides," I went on hastily again, "the Powers-that-Be will want some sort of information like that. The loss of that ring from the funds will have to be made good, and they can't make it good till they know its probable value."

I admit I had been getting a bit muddled, but all the same it made a good deal of sense. George said that inquiries on those lines wouldn't do any harm, though it seemed to me that he was sparring for time. The idea of tackling old Dane was far from attractive.

I asked for a call to be put through to Luddly at the Victoria and Albert, and in a couple of minutes I had him on the line.

"There we are then, George," I said. "If anybody knows this chap, Luddly does. Inside half an hour I ought to be giving you a call."

My rendezvous with Luddly was at a little tea-shop near South Kensington Station, and at my own request, and by the time he'd arrived I'd finished the toast and tea that made the balance of my various lunches. He had a pot of tea too, for the good of the house.

First I told him that what I was going to ask was desperately hush-hush and I reinforced that with a showing of my credentials. But when I did begin to describe that ring, as far as deductions allowed, I saw him at once sit up and take notice.

"A single stone ring?" he asked, and I knew he was trying to make his tone casual.

I said it probably was, and probably a diamond of considerable weight. Yet I knew that it wasn't that that had interested him. It was that *Par moy ton aide* that had literally made him start.

"Somewhere I've heard about a ring and a motto like that," I said. "I don't say it's on the tip of my tongue, but it's there if you know what I mean."

"A pity you couldn't give me more information," he said. "It might have fitted in with something I was wondering."

"What was that?"

"Oh, something preposterous," he told me off-handedly. "There probably isn't a ha'porth of truth in it."

"Tell me in any case," I said.

"Honestly it isn't worth while," he insisted. "I mean, even the very yarn itself has never been definitely confirmed. The best history books wouldn't print it."

"What an annoying bloke you are!" I told him with humorous exasperation. "*What* yarn?"

"You're a pertinacious bloke yourself," he said. "Still, if you're prepared to believe it, that's your headache. The yarn is that ancient one about Queen Elizabeth and the ring she was supposed to have given Essex."

I hoped I hadn't betrayed the fact that he had as good as told me where I'd read about that motto.

"You know the yarn," he said. "Fairy-tale is probably a better name for it. She was supposed to have given him a ring and if he was in trouble he was to send it back. Later on he tried to raise a rebellion in London and she clapped him in the Tower, and he *was* in trouble: plenty of it, right up to the neck. So he tried to smuggle that ring out to her to remind her of her promise. Gave it to a friend—I think it was the Countess of Nottingham. But this particular lady hated Elizabeth like hell and never sent the ring. In fact it was supposed to have disappeared."

"But isn't the story backed up by a certain amount of truth?" I said. "Isn't it a fact that although Essex was guilty as hell, Elizabeth wouldn't sign the death warrant for the devil of a time? And because she was expecting him to send her that ring?"

"That's about the only backing it's got," he said. "And even that can be explained in other ways."

"And what about the motto? Is that a fake too?"

"As far as I remember," he said, "that motto was first mentioned by an Erasmus Harte, a late seventeenth-century divine, in a queer book called *Vicissitudes of Favourites*. What he doesn't mention is where he had the story from."

"I see," I said. "And how then do you explain the existence of the actual ring?"

"What you mean is the existence of *a* ring," he said. "But there were fakers in those days and just as opportunist as there are now. That ring might have been made after the publication of Harte's book."

"And a valuable diamond used for the purpose?" I asked rather incredulously.

"You've got the wrong end of the stick," he said. "A ring was in existence already, and all the faker had to do was to cut the motto."

"I suppose that is so," I had to admit. "But fake or not, would that ring be of value to a collector?"

"Most decidedly," he said.

"Let me see," I said. "Doesn't old Bertram Dane collect rings?"

"Does he not," he told me enthusiastically.

"And would he know the legend, if that's what you call it, about that ring?"

"I should say he certainly did."

I gave a Whartonian grunt and then called the waitress over and paid the bill.

"Tell me," Luddly said, and his voice was a seductive whisper. "Has old Dane been up to any tricks again?"

After that we exchanged scandals. I told him the yarn Wharton had told me and he told me one about a ring missing from a museum in the Midlands. He also told me a lot about the collection. The papal rings alone were worth a fortune, he said, and added that he wouldn't mind lifting one or two of them himself.

It was half-past three when I managed to ring Wharton. Hard as it was to explain things over the telephone, I gave him a brief history of that ring, and told him the new approach it provided for a first attack on Dane.

"You go and see him," he said. "You're the very one to handle him."

"Suppose he isn't in."

"Of course he'll be in," he told me. "Haven't got the wind up, have you? Anyone would think you were going lion taming."

When I'd hung up I thought of quite a few retorts I might have made, not that they'd have penetrated that hide of his. And then for the next half-hour I was busy preparing my questions for Dane and by the time I was outside St. John's Wood Station I felt myself equal to twisting the tail of any lion. As I made my way towards Manfred Road I had only one problem, and then that was dismissed with a shrug of the shoulders. George hadn't told me what to say or what not to say. I had, in fact, been given *carte blanche* and I was proposing therefore to take whatever action that circumstances might direct.

I found the house easily enough—a large, yellow-bricked house standing in spacious grounds, and the site alone, I knew, was worth a packet. But all the property had gone down in the twenty years or so since I had last seen it. Gardens, lawns and shrubberies were hopelessly neglected and the house itself was clamouring for paint and pointing. But with an exception. The lower story looked neat, and as I neared the front a warden in uniform appeared at the door. He was calling to another warden who was digging on a piece of open ground between two shrubberies.

I left the weedy drive and followed a path round the side of the house. It was a cold day and an east wind cut at me across the bare lawn, but I was sheltered again as I came to the back. There the door was wide open and stairs led upwards. As I mounted them I felt a curious excitement. It was like going to an interview with a ghost, but a ghost who was likely to be very much alive.

At the head of the stairs was a passage and a neat arrow to the left had a notice beneath it about a tradesmen's entrance. I went to the right, my feet making no sound on the strip of carpet, and then the passage ended at another door. Voices were coming through it, and they ceased at my knock.

The door was opened by an elderly man in shirt sleeves and wearing a green baize apron.

"Is Mr. Dane in?"

"I'll see, sir," he said, and took the card I handed him.

"Who is it?" bellowed a voice, and I stepped unannounced through the open door. Glaring at me was Dane himself.

He was evidently just about to take a walk, for he was wearing an Inverness cape and an old deerstalker, so that, but for his dishevelled whiskers, he would have looked like Sherlock Holmes in senility. I had heard about those garments, which were his suburban wear. In town he always wore a topper and a frock-coat that age had mellowed with a sheen of green.

He fairly snatched the card. His eyes must have been good for he read the name at once.

"Travers," he said, "Never heard of him."

"May I show you my credentials, Mr. Dane," I said.

"Credentials? What credentials?"

I gave them to him, and then he was waving impatiently to his man to get out.

"Scotland Yard," he said to himself, and then gave me a look from under those buttresses of eyebrows. "What is it you want?"

"Just a little information," I said, very humbly. "We think you can help us."

"Us? Who's us?"

"Scotland Yard," I said. "It has to do with a very valuable ring."

"Ring? What ring?"

But the old man's look had become wary—infinitely wary. I tried a bit of Whartonian wheedling.

"If you would be so good as to give me a minute or two of your valuable time, sir, I shouldn't have to trouble you again."

His eyes bored into mine for a moment or two, and then he was going across the hall and opening a door. Then he drew back and waved me through with a curt hand.

When I was a small boy it was the custom to embellish railway carriages with photographs and one that I particularly remember was an interior at Sandringham. The room I entered was its very spit. Every inch of space on the walls was crowded with pictures, photographs and china plates, and I noticed among other things two pieces of majolica that made my mouth water. As for seating space, there seemed to be none, so packed was the room with side-tables, chairs, two grandfather clocks and a piano, and to move an elbow would have meant a cascade of yet more photographs or cups and plates that stood everywhere on stands.

"Take a seat there," the old man said, and I backed carefully to the plush armchair. "You'll have a cigar?"

"Thank you, sir, but I won't," I said. "I don't want to take up more of your time than I can help."

His tone had been conciliatory, to say the least of it, indeed compared with his earlier barks and ejaculations it was friendliness itself. I seized the favourable opportunity to begin with Sir William Pelle.

"Who's he?"

I told him and went gabbling on for fear he should cut in again. A valuable ring was missing and as he was the most famous collector, the police wondered if he had been approached by the thief, and if he hadn't, would he notify the police at once if the thief did make any approach, and at the same time try to detain him.

He gave a grunt or two and was snatching in a fumbling sort of way at his whiskers.

"How do you know the ring was likely to be offered to me?" he asked me shrewdly.

I threw discretion to the winds and described the ring. I even said it was probably the ring that Elizabeth gave to Essex.

"Rubbish, sir, rubbish!" he told me. "Damme, sir, you don't believe all you read?"

"That's for my superiors to say, sir," I answered. "I'm merely obeying instructions."

"Yes, yes, yes," he said impatiently, and hoisted himself out of his chair.

"You will be willing to help us?" I asked.

"The situation's not likely to arise," he told me. "I'm not the man, sir, to entertain offers from any Tom, Dick or Harry."

He growled a something under his breath and was making his way through the door to the hall. I followed and for the life of me I could think of nothing else to say.

"Good day to you, sir," he said to me, and gave a funny little bow, though he didn't hold out his hand.

"Good day and thank you, Mr. Dane," I said, but already he was turning back from the door.

When I came round to the front of the house I kept well beneath the wall and then nipped through the front door. There I was in the usual kind of wardens' post, if a more spacious one than most. Somewhere a man was humming to himself and there was a smell of cooking. As I peered along the passage a warden came out.

"Anything I can do for you, sir?"

I told him I wasn't there on business but for reasons of pure sentiment. He was interested when I told him how the place used to be a police canteen and recreation room, and he told me the billiard-table was still there.

"Pretty snug quarters you've got here," I said. "Does Mr. Dane bother you much?"

"Not him, sir," he said. "Grumbles sometimes if there's too much noise. Sends that man of his down, and then we have to use the soft pedal for a bit. There *is* the old boy now."

Dane, his loose cape flying, was making for the front gate, the inevitable umbrella beneath his arm.

"Queer old gentleman," he said. "You don't often see his kind nowadays. And lousy with money, so they reckon."

"How old would you put him?"

"Him? Oh, about eighty-five. And he walks a darn sight better than I do. Had a bit of trench foot in France in the last war."

We swapped war reminiscences for a minute or two and then I said that Dane was certainly a peculiar character. Last Monday I should have seen him at half-past four but when I rang up to confirm, he was out.

"Did you see him go out?" I asked.

"Last Monday?" He frowned, and began mumbling names of people on duty. Then he opened a door.

"Fred, was it on Monday afternoon we saw old What's-his-Name going out without his umbrella?"

I didn't hear what was said but my warden came back with a beam on his face.

"It was Monday, sir, and about half-past four. My mate he said to me, 'Lummy, Dick, look at that!' and there was the old boy without his umbrella. First time any of us ever saw him go out like that."

"And you didn't see him come back?"

He shook his head and I didn't press the point. But as I made my way back to the station I was feeling none too happy. That he had left his house at four-thirty ought to have been good news, and yet it wasn't, and this is why. Four-thirty would never have given him time to catch the four-fifty at Charing Cross. *In other words, old Dane had a perfect alibi for the essential time on that Monday evening.* By no combination of circumstances, so it seemed to me, could he have been the one who snatched that attaché-case.

But when I got back to the Yard I found myself confronted with quite different views. By throwing a cloak of modesty over my interviews with Dane I had created the impression that I had scored a tremendous success, and George was out to prove otherwise.

"Why shouldn't he have taken a taxi?" he said. "That would have got him to Charing Cross in time?"

"I doubt it," I said. "In any case it's up to you. Have all taxi-drivers questioned."

"A hell of a game, that," he said. "Far better go to the fountain-head and ask at Charing Cross if he did or didn't take that train.'"

"Of course," I said, and wondered why I hadn't thought of that myself. And then, in case George had ideas of sending me to make that particular inquiry, I said if he didn't mind I'd be getting back to the flat. George said he might ring me there later and added that I hadn't done a bad day's work, and that told me that up his sleeve he had a card or two of which he hoped I knew nothing. Indeed he probably had a couple of packs.

<h1 style="text-align:center">Chapter XII
WHEELS WITHIN WHEELS</h1>

GEORGE PAID ME an unexpected visit soon after breakfast. There were times when he was always dropping in, but of late his visits had been so rare that I wondered if he had something on his mind and wanted a change of scene to stimulate his ideas. And he was looking a bit subdued and not because it is hard to be hearty in the early morning. George, if he has a mind, can be hearty at any time.

He had had breakfast hours ago, he said, but he didn't give the expected glare when he said it. And it was in a tone that was almost casual that he told me that Bertram Dane had not only taken the four-fifty from Charing Cross that Monday night but had also got off at Pangley.

"Then you've as good as got him," I said. "But how did he get to the station?"

"There's a cab rank not fifty yards from his door," he told me. "Just round the corner into Holliwell Street. We've even got the very taxi that took him to Charing Cross. And the man there who punched his ticket. And the one who saw him through the barrier at Pangley."

"When did he come back?"

"By the six-forty," George said. "That gave him an hour and a quarter in Pangley."

"Rather long, wasn't it?" I said.

"Yes," he said. "That's one of the things that've been making me think. You'd have thought he'd have shot back to town like a pea out of a pod."

"Yes," I said thoughtfully; and then thought of something. "I suppose you couldn't tell him you'd been making inquiries at Pangley, and having learned by chance that he was there, and on that train, you were wondering if he saw anything abnormal? Mightn't that make him go into details as to why he was at Pangley at all?"

"Not it," George said curtly. "He had a perfect right to be at Pangley. Hundreds of people were on that train. Coincidence has to operate sometimes, hasn't it?"

I rather stared.

"That might be one of his lines of argument," George went on. "And why should he tell us what his business was? We've got to have a damned sight more on him before we ask questions. Dane's a wealthy man."

"What difference does that make in the eyes of the law?"

"Every difference," he told me, and his tone had nothing cynical. "He can afford to use the best legal advice, can't he? If I make one little slip, what am I in for? Unlawful inquiry and an action for damages."

"What's come over you, George?" I said. "I've known you take bigger risks in far less important cases."

"All right," he said. "You go along and question him yourself. I'll give you a free hand. And I'll bet a fiver that you get thrown out on your ear, and that you hear more about it in under a week's time."

For a moment I had an idea that that was the original scheme behind George's visit of that morning—to get me to tackle old Dane, and then he was uttering a disclaimer. "Not that I'd let you make such a fool of yourself."

"Then what are you going to do?" I said.

"Something we probably shan't be able to do," he said. "Try to prove that he was in the neighbourhood of Pelle's house at the right time. Try to connect him with sending back the jewellery. Prove collusion with the Blaketon woman."

"I hadn't thought of that last bit," I said. "He went on the four-fifty because she'd made Pelle lose the earlier train."

"There you are then," George said. "Didn't I tell you there were wheels within wheels? We've got to conduct two parallel inquiries—him and her—and find the points of contact. Those two birds have got to be killed with one stone. When we've got one to talk, then we'll have the other."

"And Marion Blaketon's the most vulnerable?"

"Maybe," George said guardedly. "All the same, I've had men on her tail and she hasn't made a suspicious move since we saw her."

"What about that Bewford visit?" I said. "When she went past Kalpoor for the purpose of spying out the land."

"Two curious things there," he said. "She did go to Bewford but she had tea in a tea-shop. That's all her movements we've managed to trace."

"You mean that if she'd really been calling on friends, she'd have been having tea with them?"

"That's it," he said. "There is, of course, the fact that she might have found these friends out. And then again, she ought to have telephoned to make sure. Or they mightn't have a telephone."

"Wheels within wheels," I said, and could appreciate some of George's problems. "But what's the other curious thing you were talking about?"

"There are ten thousand people in Bewford," George remarked casually, and then cocked an eye at me.

"You mean it might be impossible to trace her movements?"

"Yes and no," he said. "But there's a railway station there, isn't there? She could have taken a different line from Charing Cross. Therefore she did go by Pangley to spy out the land, as you called it."

He had pulled out his pipe and was regarding it contemplatively. I passed him my pouch, but he shook his head.

"Time to be getting along," he said. "Meeting Prider outside Covent Garden Station in twenty minutes."

"Something on?"

"Yes," he said, "and I thought you might like to come along. We're seeing a bloke called Harry the Snoot."

"Who's he?" I said. "Someone from Damon Runyon?"

He looked as if he was going to ask me where that was. Then he changed his mind and got to his feet, and we were turning into Long Acre before he began spilling the beans.

I think the idea was Prider's, even if George was tentatively claiming credit; or should I say that he was manoeuvring himself into such a vantage position that if things went right he could pronounce the benediction. And the idea was this.

Prider—George did give him credit for that—had been puzzling out the methods by which Marion Blaketon might have profited by that Society of which she seemed to be virtually in sole charge. Of the dozen ways of which he thought, two made a special appeal.

> *a.* She could tip off some 'reformed' yegg about the jewellery and habits of friends or patronesses, and so facilitate both easy and profitable entries. If this were skilfully done there would be no risk of a squeal, and she would be sure of her share of the swag.

> *b.* In the case of a jewel thief who had served a term without disclosing the whereabouts of the swag, she could put him in touch with a fence as soon as he got outside. If there were sufficient intermediaries there would be little risk, and again she would draw her percentage. Maybe her share in either case, as Wharton admitted, had occasionally been an item or two of jewellery. When she wished to raise the wind she had later disposed of these, or tried to, as in the case of her visit to Grace Allbeck's shop.

With regard to the first—and Wharton was careful to disclaim full agreement—Prider thought that Marion Blaketon had been behind that abortive attempt at an entry which had been upset by Mavin. I saw the reason for Wharton's disagreement. Why should Marion Blaketon arrange for Pelle to take a particular train and gain no profit from it? It didn't matter to her what train Pelle took provided the jewellery was in the house that night.

But the second was the promising opening, though the problem there had been to find a suitable man who had either just been or was about to be released. And as there wasn't one, Prider had suggested Harry the Snoot. Harry Sanders was his official name, and he had a snoot, according to Wharton, that made night work his only hope of survival. But Harry had been out for best part of a fortnight after doing twelve months for lifting a jewel-case from a parked car in Hanover Street. And the jewellery had been recovered.

I was getting a bit puzzled. Harry the Snoot, according to Wharton's account, was the very opposite of the right man. But before Wharton could tell me more, we were in sight of the Opera House and there was Prider waiting for us.

"Everything all right?" Wharton asked him.

"Everything okey-doke, sir," Prider told him, and I saw George wince. "In Morgan's coffee-house at half-past ten. I've fixed up a table."

That coffee-shop was almost empty when we went in and our table was at the far end. The seats were high-backed to give privacy, and except for the faint whoosh of the broom of the waiter who was sweeping the floor, there was very much of a hush.

"Come in here any time up to seven in the morning, and you wouldn't hear yourself speak." Prider told me, eyes on the door.

The waiter came up and George ordered three large coffees. I thought him a bit ambitious. The chipped cup I got and the stains on the saucer made me wonder if I'd have survived a small one. Then Prider was nudging Wharton. My back was to the door and it was not till Harry was on top of us that I had my first sight of him.

He looked a humorous sort of cove, quite well dressed and as mildly spoken as you'd find them. Precious little accent either, and with a self-possession that staggered me. As for that nose of his, it was something to fascinate. At all sorts of moments I found myself wrenching my eyes away from that monstrous beak. Frontways it wasn't so bad, but seen from the side it was something incredible.

Wharton was calling for another large coffee. Prider was holding out his hand.

"How are you, Harry? Make yourself at home."

"How's tricks with you?" asked Harry and sidled into my seat. Wharton's hand went across too. To me it was something out of Gilbert and Sullivan, with special reference to the *Pirates of Penzance*. Maybe Harry never should have been a burglar. Some one had blundered, and his indentures should have bound him apprentice to a bugler, and everyone knew it and dealt out a little sympathy on the sly.

"What about something to eat?" Prider asked him when the coffee came.

"Not for me," said Harry, and squinted at me.

"We've brought you a mouthpiece," Prider explained. "Mr. Travers, this is Harry Saunders."

"How are you," I said, and I felt somehow that I should have said, "How're you, Harry?" and out of the corner of my mouth.

"He'll look after your interests," went on Prider. "If anything slips up—which it won't—you'll be in good hands."

Wharton leaned forward.

"Glad you're coming in with us on this," he said. "About time you did yourself a bit of good."

"Draw it mild, Super," Harry told him with a grin. "Since when have you been a friend of the working man?"

Wharton nudged Prider in the ribs.

"Always one for his little jokes, eh?" He leaned forward again. "But you *will* do yourself a bit of good, take it from me. Besides, there's what we know about that Henrietta Street job. We're not holding that against you, are we?"

"Come off it, Super," Harry told him. "You can't pin that on me."

"Mr. Travers here might tell you different," Wharton said. "Still, we're not talking about that. You stick close to us and you're on a good thing. Prider's given you an outline?"

Harry said that a ruddy outline was about what it amounted to. Wharton handed him a sheet of printed paper.

"Did you get one of these when you came out?"

Harry had a look at it and said he didn't remember. I saw it was one of Marion Blaketon's tracts.

"Put it in your pocket," Wharton said genially. "It's going to be one of the best friends you ever had. You tell him, Prider."

"This is the lay," Prider said, and his voice lowered. "Everyone's supposed to have one of these handed him when he comes out. That one is yours. Crease it well and rub it in the dirt and make it look as if it's been in your pocket for days. See that name at the bottom? Marion Blaketon, Secretary. She's the one you're going to tell the tale to."

And so gradually to the tale itself. Harry would produce the tract and say the police weren't giving him a chance.

"Don't choose the language," Wharton said. "That dame's pretty hard-boiled."

Prider said he'd probably have to fill in a confidential form or else answer questions which she'd enter on a form. Everything he told her was to be true, with one exception, and that was what needed careful handling.

"You see, you're supposed to have got away with that Hanover Street stuff. She won't know any better. Nothing ever came out. So you sort of hint that you aren't too hard pressed for a job. You can go on living for a goodish while yet."

"And what if she asks me point-blank?"

"About that stuff?" cut in Wharton. "Then you try to look crafty and say that's nobody's business. Don't overdo it. Deny you ever took it, if you like, and then you can weaken a bit. You get the idea?"

It took him another quarter of an hour before he got it to Wharton's satisfaction, and then there had to be another quarter of an hour of rehearsals, with Wharton as Marion Blaketon.

"Keep your eyes off her," Wharton told him for the dozenth time. "Let her think you're shifty. You're telling the tale, and she's got to know it. The only thing you've got to get into her mind is that you've got that stuff salted away."

"You'd better wear those duds you've got on now," Prider said. "Look as if you've got a bit of money behind you."

"Then what the hell am I going to her for?" Harry wanted to know.

"Because you want to go straight," Wharton told him with an infinite impatience, "and the police won't let you. If necessary you say indignantly that they're tailing you because they think you can give them a lead where you've cached that stuff."

"Which I never had."

"Exactly! You tell the truth and you lie like hell in the same breath. All you've got to get into her mind is that you know where the stuff is."

The first arrivals were coming in for dinner before Wharton could sound anything like satisfied. I took out a card and gave it to Harry.

"If ever you want me, that's where you can get me," I said. "Better than calling my office. If I'm not in, you can leave a message."

"Mr. Travers is just our little present to you," Wharton told him roguishly. "You'll be in the clear about this business but life's a funny thing." The tone changed to the impressive. "Who got Fred Harris off on that Acton job. And Peeper Marks, when Prider here as good as had him in the pen."

Harry the Snoot was looking a bit bewildered as we got to our feet.

"Wharton's always kidding someone," I told him on the quiet. "What you've got to know is that if the Blaketon woman tries any double-crossing, that's where I come in."

Prider and Harry went first, George and I hung back and made our exit together, and turned right for Long Acre again-

"When's the balloon going up, George," I asked.

"Early this afternoon," he told me. "They're settling the details over a drink in the Golden Eagle."

I didn't ask him point-blank why he'd taken me to that coffee-shop, for though I wasn't sure about the part I'd been supposed to play, I did have ideas. Between Harry the Snoot and the law as represented by Wharton and Prider was a certain amount of respect and the same amount of trust. But Harry would have been at sea in trying to place one like me. Whether or not he had been influenced by Wharton's vague threats about a Hanover Street job, I didn't know, but I did sense that my silent presence had been intended as a kind of warning. The one thing a crook fears is what he doesn't understand, and I was something outside Harry's experience; something dimly threatening, like that mention of Hanover Street and Harry's future need of a first-class mouthpiece.

"I like your pal, Harry the Snoot, George," was what I did say.

"Harry's all right," he told me. "He's been going straight the last two or three years. Then he saw that jewel-case and it was too much for him."

"What's his job?"

"Works for his brother. Nice little chap, the brother: has a greengrocery business in Hamilton Street. Straight as they make 'em."

The sun had come out and on the lee side of Long Acre it was more like a day in April.

"When do you expect things to happen?" I asked George.

"No sense in hurrying," he told me. "All this has got to work itself out in its own way. One step at a time and no rushing."

"Then if there's nothing doing for me I think I'll take that manuscript back to Mavin," I said.

George seemed in quite a good mood so I added that I might as well drive down.

"I doubt if you'll pick any more up down there," was all he said. "Look me up when you get back, though. We ought to know then how Harry's got on with the Blaketon woman."

He wouldn't join me in a meal at the flat, so we parted company at St. Martin's. I treated myself to a service lunch and then I rang Mavin. I got him all right, but he said he wouldn't be in. He wanted the manuscript pretty badly and asked me to give it to Sutton.

It was about two o'clock when I picked up my small car at the Yard. The sun had gone in again, but that didn't worry me, for there wasn't a sign of rain. Afterwards I was to tell myself I'd been amazingly lucky. I hadn't either the wish or the need to take that manuscript back to Mavin, at least till the sun came out that midday. That was what gave me the sudden urge to get out to the country and revel in a wholly fictitious spring. And if I hadn't gone, then we'd never have found things out.

I took my time on that drive to Pangley for I'd rather thought of coming home by Bewford and joining the London road beyond Bromley. What I hoped to find at Bewford I didn't know. Maybe I only wanted to have a look at the place, and with the hope that it might stimulate ideas about Marion Blaketon. Not that there was any special need of stimulation.

For at last, as I could tell myself, the case had a perfectly clear pattern. Wharton had toyed, and from the first with very little purpose it seemed to me, with Francis Kenray. He had been discarded and suspicion had shifted to young Mavin, with Doris Chaddon as a very minor accomplice. Those two had gone and the attack had shifted to Marion Blaketon. That attack had looked promising and then had petered out, only to take the limelight again when Bertram Dane had become a suspect too. And now there seemed little doubt but that Dane was the man we wanted for the actual murder. One thing only was needed to clear the case up—direct evidence or such a chain of circumstantial evidence as no defending counsel could break down.

I think that knowledge that the case was almost over was the real cause of my dawdling, but at any rate it was nearer three o'clock than two when I got near Kalpoor. What made me draw up the car just short of the house was remembering the night when Kenray had slipped through the hedge. Now I thought I could see the very gap through which he had slipped, though that straggly hedge had gaps in plenty. Beyond the hedge was a kind of common, and there were gorse clumps here and there' with the gorse in bloom.

I didn't enter the drive but left my car parked on the verge by the front gate. There wasn't a sign of Sutton so I went through a privet arch to where I guessed the kitchen garden would be, and there he was, spreading wood ash for an onion bed. He scraped his boots on his spade and came to meet me. Mavin had told him about the parcel, he said, and he'd take it to his cottage for safety.

"And how're things with you, Sutton?" I said.

"Can't grumble, sir," he told me. "I don't get no younger—that's all."

"It's a curious thing, but that's how I feel myself," I said, and then was wondering if he was brooding over a failure in that Home Guard examination he'd told me about.

"Oh, no, sir," he told me with a knowing grin. "I got through all right. Heard the result only this morning."

"A pity there isn't a handy pub," I said, "and then we could celebrate."

He didn't make any comment on that, perhaps because he was too eager to tell me about his manoeuvring.

"What I had the wind up about," he said, "was that Sten gun. Never had no real chance to study it. The old Northover—that was my job, till they took 'em all away."

He opened the front gate for me and it seemed only right that I should hear the rest of the story, so I went on walking.

"There's a young chap," he went on, "who's stationed at Manwood. Service Corps he is really, but what they call mechanically minded. Nice fellow he is. A corporal. Got an eye on my daughter—the one that works in that big fishmonger's in the High Street. So he came along and put me through it."

Sometimes I amuse myself trying to trace back a train of thought from the point at which I stop to the point where it began. It's an easy enough feat when confined to one's self, though a certain client of Sherlock Holmes found it almost black magic when applied to himself. But I don't propose to make a logical analysis at how I arrived just where I did when Sutton mentioned his daughter. I did remember staying with my sister and her asking me to bring some fish from a certain market town on a Monday, and how I found the shop shut and how later she'd apologized for troubling me since fish-shops were always closed on Mondays, and she should have remembered it. Maybe that corporal had fixed the coaching of his future father-in-law for the Monday since the daughter would be there, and at that point I tried pulling Sutton's leg about it.

"Did he come to coach you, or see your daughter?"

"A little of both, I shouldn't be surprised, sir," he told me with a grin. "Not that he stayed very long. He had to be back pretty sharp."

"Let me see now," I said, and frowned in thought. "That would be on the Monday night when Sir William was missing."

"That's right, sir," he said, and then halted in his tracks.

"It's all right," I said. "I wasn't thinking that your corporal friend had anything to do with that. What I was wondering was if he heard or saw anything suspicious when he came out."

"That I can't say, sir," he said, and then added a shrewd rider. "Depends what you mean by suspicious."

"Exactly," I said. "All the same, I'd like to have a talk with him. In our game you never know what might turn up."

Trigg was the name, he said. Corporal Ernie Trigg, and stationed at Manwood Junction Supply Depot.

"It isn't all that important," I said airily. "Any time I'm that way will do."

I might have saved myself a heap of trouble if I hadn't been so Machiavellian, but I didn't want Sutton to see that I was more than politely interested. But no sooner did I leave him than I was pushing the car on. My map showed a side road that would bring me to Manwood and that was the road I took. And why?

The reason was this. By Sutton's cottage the grass verge was uncommonly wide. Alongside his very gate was a rut made by a lorry, and that lorry might have been the one in which Sutton's corporal came to the cottage that Monday night.

CHAPTER XIII
SATURDAY HOP

MANWOOD WAS little more than a hamlet and when I drew up by the church I had seen no sign of a Supply Depot. Then I hailed a couple of soldiers and they told me it was at the station, and I'd come to that if I kept straight on for somewhere round half a mile.

The station seemed a busy little place and it had quite a decent little marshalling yard, much of which was new. Forty or fifty lines of tracks perhaps, and row after row of army huts alongside, both for storage and personnel. I drew up the car by the nearest one and got out.

A passing sergeant told me where I could find the O.C. Depot and that happened to be in the second hut. A waiting runner challenged me and then told me to knock on a certain door, There I was told to fill in a form stating my business and after that came five minutes' wait. The O.C. was a R.A.S.C. Major and he had my chit in his hand when I was shown in. I produced my credentials.

"Damn those fellows of mine!" he said. "Always up to some ruddy mischief—or worse."

"Nothing like that this time," I said. "Something purely formal."

He looked relieved at that and asked me to sit down and passed me a packet of cigarettes.

"You do have a Corporal Trigg here?" I said.

"Oh, yes," he said, and I knew he had been making inquiries during my five minutes' wait. "At the moment he happens to be on seven days' leave."

That's when I cussed myself for not talking a bit more with Sutton.

"He's due back at midnight on Monday," he was going on. "You could see him on the Tuesday morning if that will do."

"Where's he on leave?"

"Wolverhampton," he said.

"It doesn't matter," I said. "I was only thinking I could have seen him direct and short-circuited you people. Not that it's anything important. The fact is that we think he's known a certain man we want to interview—a man with whom he was once billeted."

"That would be at Colchester?" he asked, consulting some record or other.

"That's it," I said. "We want this particular man badly and we think Trigg might help."

"I'll fix it," he said, and got ready to make notes. "See he doesn't leave camp on the Tuesday morning, till you get here."

"Fine," I said, and left it temporarily at that. An eye went cynically round the room. "No fewer Army Forms than in my time?"

"You were in the Service yourself?"

There followed a good ten minutes of yarning and it was with a sigh of reluctance that I rose to go. He wanted me to have tea in the Mess but I said I had to get home before the black-out.

"One thing you might do for me," I said. "You can save me a hell of a lot of trouble by sending Trigg to me instead of my coming down here to him."

He was only too willing and we looked up trains. I said the one that got to Charing Cross at nine-twenty would suit me fine. I'd be at the barrier and Trigg could be furnished with a description of me.

"You won't mistake Trigg," he said. "A nice-looking chap with black hair, and a grin on his face. About five foot nine."

"Good," I said. "I don't think I'd tell him, by the way, just what he's coming up for. Spin him some yarn about a new job. Once these fellows start to worry, they don't talk so freely."

We were almost sworn brothers when I left, and I had to travel pretty fast, for dusk was in the sky and I didn't want the black-out to descend on me till I was in familiar streets. But I was on the best of terms with myself for all that. Never had a Supply Depot been more conveniently situated for everything that I was now beginning to have in mind. And if the deductions were correct—and already they seemed pretty near fool-proof— then Wharton would be a mightily surprised man when Corporal Trigg and I walked into his office on the Tuesday morning. And so, for that matter, would Corporal Trigg.

It was best part of six o'clock when I got to the Yard. Wharton was out but I got hold of Prider.

"How did things go this afternoon?" I asked him.

"First class," he told me. "Harry turned up trumps."

"Tell me all about it," I said, and he was off the mark at once.

First of all Harry had given the typist the tract with his name written on it. After a bit of a wait he had been called in.

"I've got a copy of his statement here," Prider said. "You read it for yourself. It's a fair scream."

There definitely were some amusing touches and a piece or two of rhyming slang that I'd never run across. Harry had been asked for his complete record and Marion Blaketon had entered the details on a form. Everything was highly confidential, she had told him. Papers were not even left overnight in that office but were taken to her house and locked in a safe. When Harry told her that he might come round and see it some night, she thought it a priceless joke. After that a comfortable time was had by both until she began asking why he hadn't kept on going straight. Harry reckoned the game, as he called it, was in his blood. Then she was wanting to know why he had come there if that was the case, and Harry reckoned it was because he was bringing disgrace on a hard-working brother. And he worked the gag about being tailed by the police.

Naturally she wanted to know why he should be tailed, but Harry shrugged his shoulders. Then she started finding out in her own way. ("Regular human ferret, she was.") Hadn't that sentence of twelve months' hard been pretty stiff for snatching a case? Harry gave her a suspicious look at that, and then she became really confidential. Could it be that he still had the jewellery? Harry got a bit truculent. ("What happened to them sparklers, lady, is between me and myself, and I don't want no nosy business—see?")

Next came a little Salvation Army work. ("Nearly had me crying me perishin' eyes out.") How could he make a fresh start if he didn't clear up the past? Harry said he wasn't worrying about the past, but about the future. And he wasn't worrying too much about that. He wasn't without something behind him. If it weren't for that brother of his and them perishin' coppers he'd never have come there.

Marion Blaketon told him—and I could almost hear the heartiness of her tone—that she thought a way could be found. If he gave a definite promise to go straight, he might be found work that would take him out of the ken of the police. Harry asked what sort of work, and she hinted at something in his own line. Not greengrocery actually, but, say, gardening. Harry said that would suit him a treat, and then she had artistically hedged. Everything would have to be thought over. Perhaps he had better come back again on the Monday morning. Harry said he would be there.

At the parting ("Shook hands with me as if I was a regular toff") there was a bit of cryptic advice. Harry wasn't in the meanwhile to do anything rash. That was covered by the statement that the job would be well paid, if still available. It would be with one of the Society's warmest supporters, and might be worth as much as five pounds a week, all found.

That was the end of the statement. Here and there in the margin were pencilled lines and I asked Prider what they meant.

"Just things that struck the Gen."—he caught my eye at that slip into George's nickname, and ventured on a grin— "the Super and me. That one, sir. The crafty way she led him on about that jewellery. And this bit specially, where she tells him not to do anything rash."

"I don't get it," I said.

"Anything rash," he repeated. "Don't go getting a fit of repentance and sending that stuff back to the police. That's what she meant, sir. And Harry took it that way, and she knew he knew what she meant. And this other bit about getting five quid a week all found."

"I get that right enough," I said. "He'd only be capable of the roughest work and the pay's too much."

"An agricultural worker gets three pounds five a week," he told me. "That makes an under-gardener get three pounds ten at the most."

"Very suggestive," I said, and gave him the report back. "And all you've got to do now is wait till Monday."

"That's it, sir." Then he was giving me a queer look. "Not that we haven't a few ideas."

"Such as what?"

"Well, to tell you the truth, sir, I was to keep them under my hat."

"And not even tell me?"

My cynical grin might have told him that I was already in the know.

"As a matter of fact, sir, the Super mentioned you by name. He said there was no need to worry you about anything till we knew more ourselves."

"Very considerate of him," I said as I got to my feet·, and once more we exchanged grins. Maybe he was amused because he knew Wharton's little tricks. I was amused because it seemed that on the Tuesday morning the laugh would be on my side. George wasn't the only one who could palm a few aces or keep a spare pack or two up his sleeve.

When I got to the flats there was a message for me. A Mrs. Blaketon had rung me and asked if I would call her as soon as I came in. They had the number handy, but I preferred to put the call through from my own room. Five minutes later I was ringing Wharton at his house. I guessed he'd be there taking a breather.

"Something unusual has happened, George," I said. "Mrs. Blaketon wants me to go to a party at her flat to-night."

There was a pause and I could almost hear him thinking.

"What did you tell her?"

"I left it open," I said. "I told her I'd make it if I could."

He was doing some more thinking so I added that he probably remembered the party. Doris Chaddon was to be there and Mavin. Probably Mavin had spent the afternoon in town which was why I hadn't seen him. Then as he still didn't seem to remember I called to his mind how Mrs. Blaketon had rung Doris Chaddon that Monday afternoon especially to invite her—at least, that was what was claimed.

"I know," he said testily. "What she wants you there for is to prove she was telling the truth."

"Probably yes," I said, but I hadn't thought of that. "But what had I better do, George?"

"Go," he said, "and keep your eyes open." He cleared his throat rather noisily and I guessed afterwards that it was to gain time. "Oh, and if you happen to see a man there by the name of Leverton, you might let me know. To-morrow morning will do."

"Leverton?"

"Yes, Leverton. Montague Leverton. Oily sort of cove. You can't miss him."

"Right," I said, and: "Suppose you can't tell me any more?"

But he had hung up and I was wondering if that particular concealment had anything to do with that other one that he seemed to have confided to Prider. But there wasn't a lot of time left if I was to get to Lancaster Gate by eight o'clock. Indeed, by the time I'd bathed and changed and rung the local service for a car, I was a quarter of an hour late already.

But when I got inside the block of flats I opened my eyes. They were really in Hobart Street and, as a glance round showed me, about the last thing in ease and style. The hall alone was big enough to take a couple of tanks. A gentleman who looked like a shopwalker came across and bowed from the hips.

"Mrs. Blaketon, sir? Up the stairs and to your right. Number three, sir, first floor. Or, if you prefer it, sir, there's the lift."

I told him I thought I might just manage to stagger up the stairs, and proceeded to do so. A wide corridor with carpet that seemed to rise above my hocks led away to the right. From somewhere was the sound of dance music on a gramophone and there on a door was a 3.

A trim little maid took my hat and coat and showed me through the door, and there I was in the midst of the young hilarity. A dozen people were there. Two men were in uniform and two more in what I judged to be mufti, and there was a paunchy, elderly man. The women were all young or youngish, and the first who met my eyes was Doris Chaddon. She looked startled at first and then disentangled an arm to give me a wave. Then the music suddenly stopped. Mrs. Blaketon saw me and came beaming and booming across.

"So glad you could come."

Most of the women were dressed to kill, but all I could say about her was that she was damn' well dressed. Perfectly poised of course, and I might have been the oldest of friends.

"Turn that record over," she called to a young Air Force man, and to me: "You dance, of course?"

"Devil a bit," I said. "Dowagers even in my youth used to call me the Menace of Mayfair."

She grabbed some people who stood by and made some introductions, and all I know about their names is that none of them sounded in the least like Leverton. The fat gentle-man, who might have filled the bill, turned out to be a Czech refugee. Then the dance was on again. Quite a big room it was, with the carpet rolled back, and the floor seemed good.

"Now we're complete," Marion Blaketon told me. "Six of each, and so you'll simply have to dance."

"Maybe later," I said, and allowed her to draw me towards a couple of easy chairs in the far corner. Roger Mavin grinned sheepishly as we passed and I remember his partner had the longest finger-nails I'd seen for years.

"Tired?" she asked sympathetically as I flopped down.

"Just a bit," I said. "Had a busy day."

"Not arresting people!" she told me with mock horror.

"Not too many to-day," I said. "Hoping for better luck next week. Everyone gets very peevish when you fall behind in your quota."

"I believe you're making fun of me," she said, and roguish though the look was meant to be, it seemed to me to have a touch of the anxious. Then she was asking if I'd like to see the evening papers, but it was a quarter of an hour before she came back with them. Something made me wonder if she'd been doing some telephoning, and to the mysterious Leverton.

As I sat in my corner for that quarter of an hour, I couldn't help wondering what the devil I was doing—or was meant to do—in that particular galley. Maybe Wharton was right and I was there only to confirm that Marion Blaketon had had good reasons for ringing Doris Chaddon that Monday afternoon. But I wasn't actually bored. The first impressions of hilarity had gone and it was somewhat cynically that I could watch the dancers, vapid-eyed and monotonously moving with the same unchanging rigidity of tempo to music which now seemed a yammering cacophony of trumpet making itself heard in an ooze of slush. Then I knew my cynicism was rather cheap. Those young people had the right to their own form of amusement—or had they? Why should Doris Chaddon be in need of relaxation? What fibres, bodily or mental, needed to be braced against the stresses of war by Doris Chaddon, or that yellow-headed flapper who was dancing with Mavin?

"Well, enjoying it?" Marion Blaketon asked breezily when she rejoined me.

"Quite a mental change for me," I said guardedly.

That made small talk for a minute or two and then she was asking if I had no parlour tricks at all.

"Very few," I said. "I used to be rather good once at telling fortunes with cards."

"But how exciting!" she said, and clasped her hands in ecstasy. Then she frowned. "I don't believe you."

"Lady, lady," I said reprovingly.

"You honestly can tell fortunes?"

"Finger wet, finger dry," I said. "I know the way I do it, but I don't know how, if you follow me. Seventh son of a seventh son, or something."

"Do come and tell mine," she said, and was literally pulling me out of the chair, and as I followed her I knew I'd made rather a fool of myself. Once in my life, I'd done a case a good turn by an exhibition of that sort of mumbo-jumbo, but now I had the feeling that I ought to go warily.

We went into what looked like a dressing-room and I wondered if the tête-à-tête would end in an attack on my none too solid virtue. She was opening up a folding card table and finding cards.

"What do I do?" she said. "Just sit and watch?"

"That's it," I said, and drew in a couple of chairs.

I made play, but not too much, with shuffling the cards, then asked her to divide into three piles, and choose any one of them. Then I began paying the cards out. The third was the queen of clubs and I paused to frown.

"Something ominous?" she said.

Let me explain that I had to extemporize, and at speed. I know as much about fortune-telling as Hitler does about the Pentateuch.

"Not necessarily," I said. "Depends on what comes next."

Next came the ten of spades. I frowned heavily.

"A dark lady of middle age," I said. "Definitely an enemy. Someone to watch out for."

Before she could comment I was laying out more cards.

"You don't mind my being frank?" I asked, suddenly looking up.

"Do, please," she told me earnestly.

"Well, here's a tragedy," I said. "A great tragedy in your life. This card says it happened many years ago." I frowned even more heavily. "Something across the seas, or to do with the sea."

"But how wonderful!" she said, and her voice was awestruck. "That's my husband. He was drowned at sea, you know."

"I didn't know," I said, and that was only too true. Then I gave a little chuckle. "But it isn't all tragedy. Here's something more promising. Depends on the next card."

By the mercy of heaven the card—and the penultimate one of that heap—was the seven of hearts.

"But this is fine!" I said. "You're engaged on something and it's going to bring you extraordinary good luck. Let's see this last card of all."

That was the six of diamonds.

"Better and better," I said. "You're going to make a whole lot of money. There's a man in it. An elderly, or middle-aged man." Again I frowned. "Yet it doesn't look like a legacy."

One more frown and I swept the cards together.

"Perfectly marvellous!" she said, and then puzzledly: "But is that all?"

"Yes," I said slowly, and pulled off my glasses and blinked. "You're not going to laugh at me?"

"My dear man, why should I?"

"Well, it's this," I said lamely. "People never believe me, but after I do one of these shows, however quick, I feel absolutely limp. Just as if something's gone out of me."

"You poor man!" she said sympathetically, and then was springing to her feet. "Do let me get you a drink."

I had a whisky with very little soda and said we ought to be getting back. It was then about a quarter to ten, and in a matter of minutes the party was temporarily breaking up. The little maid came in and the carpet was rolled into place. A few minutes later we were having a hand-round supper, and there seemed to be plenty of drinks. I had some talk with the Czech, who spoke very good English. Then Marion Blaketon button-holed me again and asked if I liked a little flutter. In for a penny, in for a pound, I thought, and said a flutter was just up my alley.

It turned out to be rather innocuous but good fun all the same. Roulette apparatus was laid out on a central table and we were each given a bag of nothing but coppers in exchange for a ten-shilling note. You could bet how you liked but there was no borrowing from friends. Once your pence were gone you became an onlooker. I was down to my last shilling when the party came to an end. Midnight was closing time, it appeared, and a quarter of an hour later we had all gone. Marion Blaketon gave my hand a warm squeeze and said I must certainly come again, and I felt as if I'd been kicked by a shire horse.

I got a lift as far as Leicester Square with Doris Chaddon and the Air Force man. I gathered he was her particular property at the moment, for she was shy of showing any friendliness to me. But she did ask me when I was getting out if I had had any news about I knew what, and I said I was still hoping. What she meant, I gathered, was finding her another cushy job.

When I got back to the flat it was too late to ring Wharton and I was far too restless to sleep, so I got myself a drink and sat in my dressing-gown before the electric fire. And I still couldn't see just why I'd been asked to that party. Then I had the glimmerings of an idea. Two reasons perhaps. The one Wharton had suggested, and the other to make me a witness of how well conducted those parties of Marion Blaketon's were.

The drink was soothing and the room cosy and in a minute or two I dozed off. It was only about ten minutes later that I knew I had fallen asleep, and then as I began making resolutions about going to bed, I had a queer idea. Maybe that day had been just a bit too exciting. It had produced Harry the Snoot and the absent Corporal Trigg, and had ended in that party, and that was why the sub-conscious had been so active.

You will pardon me a moment if I do a little more explaining, and, believe me that brief explanation is going to be important. When I woke it was as if I'd had a dream, but a dream which I tried vainly to recapture. That's how vague it all was, and yet I felt the dream had been vivid. It was as if I had been flooded by the high tide of it, and now all that was left was wispy seaweed and the vague marks of receding waves. A pipe-dream was how I somehow thought of it, though nothing could have been less apt. Yet that expression remained as a kind of tag, and it's a tag that you might remember it by.

Then like someone going deeper and deeper into a tunnel I began looking for a hopeful pin-point of light. What had I been thinking about just before I dropped into that quick sleep? Then I seemed to remember. I'd been thinking of Mavin and how Wharton had suggested that he'd intended to dope Pelle's coffee and so facilitate the burglary. And odd and disjointed as that clue was, it made me sit up. I found myself moving on from there, and what had been a pipe-dream became the vestiges of a theory.

Then everything went again and all at once I was feeling very tired. But when I woke next morning, that pipe-dream or theory—call it what you will—was still like a queer brooding depression at the back of my mind.

Chapter XIV
NEARING THE CLIMAX

BY THE MONDAY MORNING that pipe-dream of mine—I still prefer to call it that—was more vague than ever, even if the uneasiness persisted, and the reason for that uneasiness lay largely in the fact of its curious persistence. Though I could tell myself that it was preposterous to worry over vague new theories when the case was well on the way to being solved, yet I couldn't clear that depression away. That was why I was so glad when ten o'clock came and it was time to make my way to the Yard.

A Chief Inspector Cumfit was with Wharton, and Prider was there too. Cumfit, I suspected, was the one who some years before had handled that previous tentative inquiry into the activities of Marion Blaketon's Society, and the guess proved true. And there seemed a kind of zero hour atmosphere in the room.

"Everything's very hushed," I told George when I'd been introduced to Cumfit. "Anything special on?"

"Harry's due at Marion Blaketon's place at half-past," he told me, and gave me a quick glance at the clock. "As soon as he gets clear he's going to ring us."

In a matter of seconds I was learning the ins and outs and just where the mysterious Leverton came in. Cumfit spun the yarn because he had handled things.

In 1940, which was when Cumfit had last concentrated on that particular case, there had been a couple of highly successful jewel robberies, and the methods were those of a certain O'Sullivan, *alias* a string of names as long as my arm. The police had spread the net but O'Sullivan slipped through the meshes. In fact he dropped right out and it wasn't till the autumn that the police ran across him, and then by pure luck. And even when they'd found him they had nothing definite to pin on him, and as the hunt was on for Fifth Columnists, Cumfit was loaned shortly afterwards to the Special Branch. Nevertheless, some curious things emerged, and were docketed for reference.

O'Sullivan was actually discovered working—or passing his time—as a gardener at the Woking place of Montague Leverton, a gentleman who was ostensibly 'something in the city.' Nothing was done about O'Sullivan to rouse his or Leverton's suspicions, and shortly afterwards he was seen back in town. He was a young, active chap in the late twenties and the last heard of him was that he was missing in the Middle East. He'd joined up, it appeared, under a wholly new name and had been spotted by an ex tec. from the Yard who was in the same battery.

But there was something more interesting to it all than that. Leverton was the owner of four pawnshops, and the manager of one turned out on inquiry to be a man with a record. Almost at once he disappeared and nothing further was done about him. Then another of those pawnshops, this time the one in Beresford Street, Camden Town, was under suspicion of receiving; at least a man subsequently apprehended and sentenced for a jewel robbery was seen using the back door.

"Now you see what it all adds up to," Cumfit told me.

I said I couldn't miss seeing, and I asked if there'd been anything since.

"Not since 1942," he said. "That was when we had ideas about that Camden Town place of Leverton's. And we couldn't hook it up with the Blaketon woman, though we had ideas."

"Well, it looks hooked up now," I said. "Too much of a coincidence that Harry the Snoot should be offered a job as a gardener if it isn't at Leverton's place." Then I wondered something. "Do you think she kept him hanging around all the week-end while she was making inquiries?"

"Leverton would do the inquiring," George told me, and then gave a chuckle and a sideways nod of the head. "But he won't get anything fishy out of Harry, or about him."

I think everybody was expecting Harry to be closeted with Marion Blaketon for some considerable time, and when the buzzer went at about ten to eleven, George merely reached languidly for the receiver. Then he sat up.

"Yes . . . yes. . . ." was all that came out of him. Then came a quick, "No, no, no. You go down there. . . . No, no. No! You get pulled in down there. On the station. . . . That's it. . . . She did, did she?" He chuckled, added a "Good luck, Harry," and rang off. A minute, perhaps, as I've written it, but he had been nearer five at that receiver end.

"There we are," he said, and peered at us whimsically over the tops of his spectacles. "Harry's been offered a gardening job at Woking. Due there for inspection at two o'clock."

Cumfit gave a little chuckle. Prider grunted.

"Everything's going to dovetail beautifully," Wharton said. "If the A.C. agrees." It was an Assistant Commissioner he meant, and a quick conference looked due.

"Who pulls in Harry?" Cumfit wanted to know.

"The local people," Wharton said. "They're supposed to spot him, and with the stuff on him. Prider will see to that." He gazed up reflectively. "By three o'clock the raid should be over, if it materializes, and I'll see the Blaketon woman at four."

He got to his feet and I picked up my hat.

"Where are you going to be from now on?" he asked me.

I said I'd be at the flat if he wanted to get hold of me.

"Like to take part in the raid if it comes off?" he said. "He'll make a good cover for you, Cumfit."

To you everything might not be too clear, but the way I read things was this. Harry the Snoot was to be roped in at Woking Station, and that would cause a few wonderings at Leverton's place. If the raid came off and whether it were lucky or not, the managers concerned were to be given a chance to get through to Leverton, and that would add to the perturbation. If stolen property were found, then Leverton himself would be pulled in, and he would doubtless try to get into touch with Marion Blaketon. And from what Cumfit told me as we went downstairs, there was more than a hope of a haul. The previous week had seen no less than three big jewel robberies, and some fence or other would be handling the stuff. As for Marion Blaketon, Wharton would see her when she'd hardly had time to recover from the shock. He wasn't stirring from the Yard. His role was a spider's in the middle of the web, and co-ordinating the news that came through.

I lunched at the flat and then sat nervously waiting. Then soon after two o'clock I had a call. The raids were timed for three, and I was to be in Charing Cross Road, opposite Manson's bookshop, at twenty to.

I'd expected a car crammed to the bonnet with men but it was an unobtrusive saloon that drew up at the kerb, where I was waiting. Cumfit was driving and I got in alongside him. When I asked about his men he said they'd gone on.

We went north along Tottenham Court Road and Cumfit began telling me where I fitted in. I was to enter the shop and I'd probably be attended to by an assistant whose attention I was to engage by arguments about the value of the cigarette-case which I was to pawn. That was all, except that there might be some fun downstairs. And there was only one word of warning. When I heard Cumfit himself in the shop I was to ignore him.

We made the bend by the Cobden statue and were in Camden Town. A quarter of a mile on was the shop and Cumfit drew the car in to the kerb and waited, watch in hand. Then he drew on again and my watch made it two minutes to three when we halted again.

"The shop's about twenty yards back," Cumfit told me, "Go in naturally. Look a bit embarrassed if you like, but no more. Everything'll be over before you can say knife."

A yard or two and the three brass balls were above my head. As I opened the door I could see an elderly man tidying a shelf at the far left and I gave a little cough. He looked round and merely peered at me. I fumbled a bit before I produced the cigarette-case.

"I don't know anything about this," I began. "I mean, about pawning things, but ..."

His hand went out and he gave the case a contemptuous look.

"Fifteen bob? It isn't—"

"The manager in?"

That was Cumfit's voice and he had come in so quietly that I hadn't heard him. The assistant gave him a quick look.

"Tell him it's Jim," Cumfit said. "He'll know."

"About the cigarette-case," I said, but the assistant was out of sight to the left. Then things happened so quickly that I don't know where to begin. Cumfit nipped through behind the counter and was on the assistant's heels. Half a dozen men were suddenly in the shop and two made their way through a door and before it slammed to I caught sight of a staircase. Cumfit was heard reassuring someone and the assistant was backing out, scared to the back teeth of him. He backed so close to me that I leaned forward and took that cigarette-case from his shaking hand.

"No panic, chum," one of Cumfit's men said. "Sit down there and take it steady."

Cumfit came through, nodded at me as he passed and went up the stairs. I knew that for I had followed him and already I could hear noises like scurrying rats above my head. There were noises under me too, and then I saw the stairs that led down. They had been masked by a curtain which the rush had drawn partly back. Light had been switched on below and I made my way down.

It was something of a rabbit warren down there and though I could hear noises I couldn't locate them. Then two of Cumfit's men appeared and with them was a furtive-looking little man, coat and hat on as if ready for the street. I drew back to the wall as they passed me and then went on. An open door, splintered at the lock, threw a beam of light across the dark passage. Cumfit was there in the far corner, gently blowing what looked like a neat pair of bellows, and he turned as I came in.

"Nice little lay-out," he said. "Have a look at this."

Everything, as he said, was fitted up to the nines; not gaudy but certainly neat. Crucibles and the tiny forge went back on a pivoting steel plate and fitted snugly into the wall. Even the bellows moved back to a hidden recess.

"What's it all for?" I said. "Melting down stuff?"

"That's it," he said. "And re-setting. Bring a pair of ear-rings in here and before you can wink an eye, you've got a brooch or a ring or a ruddy tiara."

And that's about all there is to tell. In the pocket of the man who'd been collared in that downstair room were the keys of a couple of safes, and according to Cumfit the staff inside looked like being just what the doctor ordered. When we got upstairs to the shop, the shutters were up and the lights on. The manager and the lad from downstairs had gone off in a police van and all that remained to do was to give the premises the thorough search.

"One thing I don't quite follow," I said. "Why was Harry the Snoot to have that fake pulling-in at Woking? Why not up here?"

"Ah!" he said, and chuckled. "That was the old General's own idea. A bit of split timing, if you follow me. Harry's arrested at Woking. The local police ring Leverton's house and say they've arrested a man they were looking for and how he's spinning a yarn about going to see Leverton about a job. Now if Leverton is at home, then he's called to the 'phone. If he isn't, then his butler or whoever it is tells us where he can be found. That's how we know his whereabouts." He gave himself a little congratulatory nod of the head. "I reckon that by this time he's been pulled in too." He went off to telephone Wharton and I watched the men systematically going through the shelves. The noise above told me that the same process was going on there too. I wondered what had happened at those other pawnshops and when Cumfit at last came back he told me. Two had clean bills as far as could be judged. The Pimlico one had had some bales of furs hidden in a cellar and Cumfit guessed they'd come from a recent Hounds-ditch job.

"I shouldn't be surprised if I'm here for an hour or two yet," he said, "so you might like to be getting back. If so I'll get you to take that bag of stuff we've collected from downstairs. They'll be able to check up on it at the Yard."

He took me out to where a police car was waiting with a man as escort. Just as I was moving off I remembered one last thing.

"What's going to happen to Harry?" I said.

"We'll park him somewhere nice and cosy," he said. "Harry'll be all right. He mayn't even have to give evidence."

I handed over the bag as Cumfit had directed me and then went up to Wharton's room. I had expected to find him cock-a-hoop but somehow he wasn't.

"Anything worrying you, George?" I said.

"Yes and no," he told me. "Leverton won't talk, but I expect-ed that."

"What's wrong then?"

"This," he said. "He swears blind that there was no appointment to see Sanders. Swears he never heard of him."

"But surely Harry's got some written evidence?"

"That's just what he hasn't got," he said, "and that's where we slipped up. Shows how damned cunning they are. When Harry saw the Blaketon woman this morning she made him write down Leverton's address. Everything was done by word of mouth."

"Then she may deny knowledge of Leverton."

"Exactly. She won't deny that he went there and that she said she'd do what she could about a job, but you bet your life she'll swear blind she never mentioned Leverton's name. And she'll call in that typist of hers to prove it. That'll mean Harry's word against theirs, and what chance does he stand in a witness-box with that record of his?"

"I wouldn't worry," I said. "Leverton will be bound to talk."

"And put another couple of years on his stretch?" He snorted. "Don't you believe it. His line will be that he's the innocent victim of crooked managers whom he trusted. Any admissions about the Blaketon woman would blow everything sky-high."

"I don't know, George," I said. "The mass of general evidence seems to me strong enough. But does this mean you're not seeing the Blaketon woman after all?"

"I'm just going," he said. "I'll have to hear what she has to say, and before a witness."

"If you were thinking of me, George," I told him hastily. "I don't think it would be good policy. One of her ideas in asking me to her place on Saturday night was to split our forces. Get me on her side, if you like. I know it's a dam-fool idea," I went on, "but if she thinks she's worked that particular trick, then we oughtn't to disillusion her. At some unguarded moment she might let something drop to me that she wouldn't to you."

George said there might be something in that, but what he didn't know was that the glib reasons I'd given him were far from my actual thoughts. In many ways I'm very much of a moral coward and somehow, after that Saturday night, I simply couldn't face Marion Blaketon in the company of George. What

I didn't know at the time was that I was never to be so cowardly to such good purpose. Maybe if I had gone with George, that case would have ended in mid-air.

It was at about six o'clock when he rang me at the flat. What he had anticipated had turned out dead accurate. Marion Blaketon had denied indignantly that she had given Harry any name at all. In fact, she asserted that she had distrusted him from the first and she produced a copy of a letter which she was about to send to the Society's President, to the effect that she had an idea that some insidious forces were trying to queer the Society's pitch!

"The letter was written after Leverton had given her the low-down this afternoon," I said.

"Of course it was," he told me with the usual snort. "But that typist swears it was written after Harry left the office this morning. A wicked little liar, that typist. Absolutely under the other one's thumb."

"What did you actually say to the Blaketon woman?" I asked.

"Oh, I kept my temper," George said. "Butter wouldn't have melted in my mouth. But I did leave her with something to think over. I told her Leverton was in pretty bad and we were dead sure he was going to talk. If he didn't, I said, it didn't matter. We had other sources of information, and some she'd never even dream of."

"And have you?" I asked blandly.

"Pure bluff," he said.

"And did it work?"

"I think so," he said, and he sounded really confident. "If she sleeps to-night, then my name's Robinson."

"You really think she's scared?"

"I'm damned sure of it. She's got a poker face, that woman, but she couldn't deceive the Old Gent."

"Good for you, George," I said. "And what about our friend B. D.? If she doesn't talk, won't it hang things up with regard to him?"

"Don't know yet," he said. "We're trying to trace his movements after he left the station at Pangley that night."

"That reminds me," I said. "Will you be in to-morrow morning? I rather think I'm on to something—not necessarily about B. D.—and I'll be dropping in at about half-past nine."

He hesitated before he asked me what I meant, and I got in a quick, "See you in the morning, then," and rang off.

After the evening meal I tried to read a paper, but somehow I couldn't concentrate, for that pipe-dream of mine began suddenly to intrude. As I said before, it was a queer feeling and just as if I was in a tunnel, with pin-points of light in some far, remote distance. And yet that was fantastic, for as far as the case was concerned I was not in a tunnel at all, but out at last in clear daylight. Dane had killed Pelle and he and Marion Blaketon had been in everything together. Everything was hastening to prove it, and whatever the immediate set-backs, it was only a matter of time before that thesis would be overwhelmingly proved. And yet there was I—setting all that aside and leaving the daylight of facts to wander and grope in a tunnel of my own ideas.

I think I must have smiled somewhat wryly to myself when I realized just how much of a fool I was. I do know that I picked up the paper again and began to read the war news which I'd missed at six o'clock. Then a glance at my watch showed me that in ten minutes the nine o'clock bulletin was due, so I went across to switch on in case I should forget. So unforgettable was that moment to be that I can see myself now, hand going out to the knob, and I know I was humming to myself at the time. Then the telephone bell went.

"Yes," I said. "Travers speaking."

"Get round to Kenray's shop quick." It was George's voice and I had never known it so urgent.

"What's happened?" I cut in.

"Mrs. Allbeck's hurt. Stabbed or something."

That was all. I stood with the receiver in my hand, and once again it seemed as if the world was all fantastic and awry. I was back in my tunnel and the far light was suddenly stronger, and then just as suddenly everything went, and I knew I was standing in that room at the end of a dead line.

It took me a matter of seconds to grab overcoat and hat, and I didn't wait for the lift. But the black-out steadied my progress. There was a faint drizzle in the air and the night, as they say in Tom Fulcher's county, was black as black hogs. From my flat to Kenray's shop is well under a quarter of a mile but it took me a quarter of an hour to get there. And when I did everywhere was dark.

I rapped at the side door and it opened. Nothing faced me but more dark.

"That you, Travers?"

"Yes," I said, and George's hand went out to guide me in. Then the door was closed behind me and he switched on the light again. At the head of the stairs a woman was looking from a door to the left, and then her head went in.

"Where is she?" I said.

"Mrs. Allbeck?" He shook his head. "They took her away in the ambulance just before I got here."

Two plain-clothes men appeared from the door on the right at the landing head. One said there was nothing to report and George told him to go on trying for prints.

"What happened, George?" I said.

"Don't know," he said. "All I do know is this. That landing up there serves two shops—Kenray's top rooms and those of the fancy shop next door on the left. No one was there except a woman fire-watcher. She happened to come out to the landing about half an hour before I got here—that'd be about twenty past eight or so—and saw something lying at the foot of these stairs. When she saw who it was and the knife, she thinks she fainted. Only for a minute or two though. What she'd done instinctively was to open that door and a warden happened to see the light. He rang the hospital and us."

"Badly hurt, was she?"

"Yes," he said, and shook his head gloomily. "I'm waiting for the preliminary report from the hospital. The knife got her in the lower ribs, clean through the lung I guess."

"Struck from behind?"

"Looks like it. Someone came down these stairs with her and stuck the knife into her and then switched off the light and bolted."

"Then she wasn't dressed for going out?"

He shook his head again.

"It was a caller all right. What I'm beginning to think is that he rang the outside bell and she came down to let him in, which looked as if she'd expected him. Maybe he knifed her as soon as the door was shut."

"Yes," I said slowly, and then thought of Kenray.

"He'll be here as soon as he can make it," George said. "But it's that man of his—Fulcher—we really want. He's probably at a local pub playing darts, Kenray said. He ought to be here at any minute now."

He had hardly finished speaking before there was a rap at the outside door. There was Fulcher and one of Wharton's men with him. Wharton nodded to the man to get upstairs.

"You've heard what's happened, Fulcher?" he asked quietly.

Fulcher was blinking in the sudden light, and his tongue nervously licking his lips. Then he gave a quick glance up the stairs as if he expected Grace Allbeck to be there. His eyes passed over the dark stain on the lowest step and the floor. Maybe he thought it was only shadow, if he saw it at all.

"Somebody attacked and stabbed Mrs. Allbeck," Wharton went on as if to lure him into talk. "Was she expecting a visitor, do you know?"

Tom stammered that he knew nothing. He had gone out at seven o'clock, which was his usual time. Grace Allbeck knew where he was, and she'd have telephoned the pub if she had wanted him.

"In other words, everything was normal," Wharton said.

"That's it, sir," said Tom. "Normal, that's what it was. I looked in as I always do and I said, 'Just off now, Miss Grace,' and she nodded, same as she allust do. If she'd have wanted me for anything, she'd have told me then."

"What was she doing when you saw her?"

"Readin' a book," Tom said. "She sorta looked up and then nodded."

"A bad business, Tom," I said.

"Can't see how it's true," he told me. "Don't know who in the world should want to go hurtin' *her*. Never did a livin' soul no harm in her life. It can't be true, sir."

"It's true enough," Wharton told him, and his hand fell on the old fellow's shoulder. "But you get up to your room. Mr. Kenray should be here soon. Maybe we'll want you again then."

Wharton and I went up with him. On a table by the chair in which Grace Allbeck had sat was an opened book, face down-wards. It looked a much read book and I glanced at the worn title on the cover: Henry Wilson's *Silverwork and Jewellery.*

"What about the shop, George?" I asked quickly. "It couldn't have been a burglary?"

"Nothing disturbed down there," he said. "Never a sign of entry. And the alarm's in order."

He drew in a chair at the table and began dialling and I guessed he was calling the hospital. They must have told him to wait, for he began talking to me with a hand covering the mouthpiece. The telephone showed everything was normal, he said, for it was switched to the extension when the shop was closed at night. Then he was pricking his ears.

"Sounds like Kenray," he said. "You keep him down there. I'll be with you as soon as I'm through."

Kenray looked a broken man. His shoulders were sagging and he found speech hard. And there was nothing he could tell. He had left town without returning to the shop, having spent the afternoon at a sale. His sister had never an enemy in the world, he said, and his eyes went towards the shop door.

"It wasn't burglary," I said. "Wharton's sure of that. But here is Wharton now. He's probably got the latest from the hospital."

Kenray's eyes asked the question.

"Not too good," Wharton said. "There's a fighting chance and that's all they'll say. At the moment there's a spontaneous arrest of haemorrhage. If only she gets a bit stronger and there's no secondary haemorrhage, then they might operate in the morning."

And the devil of an operation that would be, as I knew, though Wharton didn't say so. Ribs cut away, and a major operation generally.

"I must go there," Kenray said. "I've got to be there for myself."

"You stay here," Wharton told him gently. "Go upstairs and try and get some sleep."

"Sleep?" He brushed Wharton aside and turned to the door. Wharton's hand held him back.

"We'll go with you then. There's something I ought to do myself."

And that would be to examine the knife, I thought, while Wharton called up the stairs to a man of his that he'd be at the hospital if wanted. Then out we went and were making for Lower Regent Street. On the corner of Duncannon Street I halted.

"I don't think I'll come any farther with you, George," I said. "Perhaps you'll give me a ring later."

I couldn't see his face, but he said he would. Then I shook hands with Kenray and he and George crossed the street, and George, I knew, would be thinking that that was the second time that day that I'd left him in the lurch. But this time the reasons were far more personal. I've known men in the old days who simply couldn't listen at critical moments to a broadcast of the Boat Race or a Test Match. What they had to do was sneak away and then come back when they thought the crisis was over, and things once more going their desired way. But I wasn't suffering from nerves, even if my fears were something of the same kind. So incredible was that attack on Grace Allbeck that I was refusing to believe it, even if I knew it was true, and to have gone to the hospital with Wharton would have shattered that illusion and set me to thoughts that would have meant a sleepless night.

As soon as I was indoors I got into a dressing-gown and sat before the electric fire. I had taken my time over undressing and that was why Wharton's 'phone call seemed to come so soon.

"No more news," he said. "She's fairly comfortable and that's all."

"Could she make a statement?"

"They wouldn't hear of her being disturbed," he said. "In the morning there might be better luck."

"I owe you an apology," I said.

"For not being here?" he said. "You couldn't do any good here. You stay where you are. I'm just getting a statement off to the Press." His voice lowered a bit. "And I've got an idea."

He told me what it was before I could ask him. In that Press statement would be the claim that Mrs. Allbeck was still alive and that it was hoped she'd recover sufficiently to give an account of what had happened.

"Fine!" I said. "That will make somebody sit up and think. I suppose you aren't aiming at any special person?"

"Yes and no," he said.

"You think you know!"

He paused for a second or two before answering.

"*Think's* the right word," he said. "This time to-morrow I may be sure."

That was all, but the noteworthy thing was what he left unsaid. You don't know George as well as I do, but to me it was significant that he hadn't added, ". . . or else my name's Robinson."

Chapter XV
OUT OF THE BLUE

I slept badly that night though I woke fairly late. Indeed it was the sound of the post that woke me, and I hooked on my glasses and yawned my way to the door. There was only one letter, from Bernice, so I made my way back to bed and read it at ease.

But I was not at ease for long. Towards the middle of the letter she said she'd had a cheque from the people to whom I'd sold that piece of jewellery, and a brief note had accompanied it.

I think the name was Allbeck, but it was really a charming letter. She must be an awfully nice woman, so tell me about her when you write.

That was all but it was enough to bring me back to the events of the previous night. At once the letter was limp in my hands and I was back in that pipe-dream of mine, and all at once, as by a flash of inspiration, I knew who had killed Grace Allbeck. That was the word that went through my mind: *killed*, not *tried to kill*, and when I knew that I knew that I had rushed too far ahead. Maybe she was not dead, and yet that thought was not enough and I had an overwhelming urge to know.

At once I was putting on my dressing-gown and making for the telephone. In the old days I had been a governor of that hospital, and maybe, I thought, the matron would tell me what I wanted to know.

"This is Ludovic Travers," I said, and repeated the name carefully. "Could I possibly speak to Matron?"

The feminine voice asked me to wait, and I waited for about two minutes.

"I'm sorry," she said. "But Matron isn't available. Will you leave a message?"

I gave my telephone number and said I was inquiring about a Mrs. Allbeck who'd been brought in the previous night. Might I be rung any time up to half-past eight.

I put on the same clothes that I had worn when I went that afternoon to Manwood Junction, and so that Corporal Trigg could recognize me. Then I had breakfast and when my first pipe was alight it was still well short of half-past eight. The headlines in the paper looked promising but before I'd had time to read more than a paragraph, the telephone bell went. My heart began to race as I made my way across.

"Who?" I said.

"Wroce," he said. "You remember me, Travers?"

"Of course," I said. "How are you, Wroce?"

"Pretty fit—considering. You were asking about Mrs. Allbeck, weren't you?"

"Yes," I said, and waited.

"Friend of yours?"

"Yes," I said again.

"Sorry then," he said, "but there's some bad news for you. She died at five o'clock this morning. Secondary haemorrhage, and nothing could be done about it."

"Did she recover consciousness?"

"No, no, no," he said. "Quite a peaceful end. We'd put her under morphia."

"Thanks, Wroce," I said. "Very good of you. Look me up some time and we'll have a yarn."

He said he would, and that was that. I made my way slowly back to my chair, and there for a time I sat. Then I began looking through the pages for that account that Wharton had handed out, and at last I found it. War news had crowded it to a corner but it was all there; all that was vital, that is, in a single paragraph. A premeditated crime, Wharton had said, and probably with the idea of theft. The assailant had been disturbed by a fire-watcher and had bolted, but the police expected immediate developments. Inquiries at the hospital had said that while the conditions of the injured woman was grave, she might be able to make a statement in the morning.

Nine-fifteen found me at a platform barrier on Charing Cross Station. Five minutes later the train drew in and I was watching the approaching passengers. I spotted a corporal that fitted his C.O.'s description of Trigg, and at the same time he spotted me.

"Corporal Trigg," I said, and smiled.

"That's right, sir," he told me with a grin.

"This way then," I said, and made left. "Did you get a seat or did you have to stand?"

I kept blethering on like that for I didn't want him to question me about what his new job was and where I came in. He was a good talker too, and it was only as we neared the Yard that I mentioned what was in his mind.

"Like your present job?"

"It's not too bad, sir," he said. "A bit dead-and-alive."

"Round here," I said, making for the side entrance, and I saw his eyes opening at the sight of a couple of uniformed police.

"A fine building, sir," he whispered. "The War Office, isn't it?"

"More or less," I said, making for the side staircase. The man on duty gave us a questioning look and I flashed my card and up we went.

"This is it," I said, and rapped on Wharton's door. His voice sounded like an invitation to enter, and in we went. Corporal Trigg ahead.

"Morning, Superintendent," I said gravely. "This is Superintendent Wharton of New Scotland Yard."

"Scotland Yard!" There was no grin on Trigg's face now and his eyes were bulging.

"That's it," I said, and turned once more to Wharton.

"This is Corporal Trigg who's kindly come here to tell us how he discovered Sir William's body."

George didn't turn a hair.

"Very good of him," he said, and began adjusting his antiquated spectacles. I passed him a paper on which I'd written, "Let me handle him, and you come in later." George read that slip, and then unpursed his lips, and looked at me over the top of his glasses.

"What the Corporal's got to realize," I went on, "is that that we are his friends. We've brought him here for his own good. Not a single word that's spoken here will ever come out."

"That's right," said Wharton emphatically. "Just a night among the three of us."

"Take your O.C. Depot," I said to Trigg. "He knew you were coming here this morning, whatever he told you. But he didn't know what you were coming for. He thinks we want you to give us information about a man who was billeted with you at Colchester, so you'll only have to keep your mouth shut and you'll be all right. But you've got to open your mouth wide—very wide—with us. If not you'll lose those stripes of yours for one thing and you'll probably land in jail for another."

"Tell the truth and fear no man," Wharton told him. "And everything in the strictest confidence."

Trigg shuffled in his seat, got out an unintelligible something, and then shook his head.

"All right," I said. "Let me tell you what I think happened and you can correct me if I go wrong. I begin at last Monday week. Sutton, the gardener at Kalpoor, wanted you to help him with the Sten gun. You said you would, and you also knew that Sutton's daughter would be home that afternoon and evening. Tea was at five o'clock and that's when you'd promised to come. The problem for you was how to get there from Manwood Junction. You didn't feel like pushing a bike, even if you could have borrowed one, so you either squared it with your sergeant or chanced your arm, and then took a small ration truck. It was a small one, wasn't it?"

"That's right, sir?"

"Well, now you've found your tongue, why not go on from there?" I said.

"Well, sir," he said. "I was there about an hour."

"Just one minute," I cut in. "When you got to Sutton's cottage you drew right in on the verge and switched the lights off?"

"That's right, sir. And then I was there about an hour and then I came out."

"I see. At about six o'clock. But you didn't come out alone?"

He shot me a look at that and his face coloured.

"Don't be nervous, Corporal," Wharton told him jocularly. "We've all done a bit of courting in our time."

"Miss Sutton came out with you," I prompted.

"Yes, sir. She did. And then I said good night and switched my lights on and moved off. And then I got back to the Depot."

"Yes?" said Wharton, and for a moment or two the room had a strange stillness.

"Then I happened to look at the flaps on the back, sir, to see if I'd left all in order, and then I saw . . . well, sir, what I saw."

"Yes?"

"Well, sir, I was sort of struck all of a heap. What I thought of doing was dumping it in another truck and then I thought there might be an inquiry or something. . . . Then I backed out quietly, sir, right against some railway wagons and put him under a tarpaulin."

"Well, we won't go into any more details," I said. "I think what you've told us is true. But was that the only reason why you put the body in the railway wagon? So that it shouldn't be known you'd taken the truck?"

"Well, sir," he said. "There was my leave."

"I get you," Wharton said. "If you'd reported what you'd found and had got clear in the little matter of taking a truck without permission, you'd have lost your leave because you'd have been kept back for an inquiry."

"Well, yes, sir."

Wharton nodded. I cut in again.

"While you and Miss Sutton were at the gate, or when you drove away, did you see anything suspicious?"

He shook his head.

"Did you see anything at all?"

"I don't know that we did, sir. . . . Only a man."

"A man?" said Wharton sharply. "What sort of a man?"

"Well, sir, he was a curious sort of man, if you know what I mean." He shuffled in his seat. "I was just saying good night to Trixie—that's Miss Sutton—she says, 'Listen!' Then we heard footsteps right close and we saw this man come by. Right against the truck, he was. He had on a funny sort of two-peaked cap."

"And a cape?" I said, and tried to sound only mildly interested. "And he had a beard?"

"I couldn't see all that, sir. He had on a coat of some sort. All floppy like, if you know what I mean."

"That'd be the cape, and the wind blowing it," I said. "But what did he do? Go straight past?"

"Yes, sir. He went right past, and he sounded like he was muttering to himself."

"He was going from Kalpoor towards the railway station?"

"That's it, sir. Towards the station."

"I take it you can see pretty well at night," Wharton said.

"Well, perhaps I can, sir. I do a lot of night driving sometimes."

"Ever see Sherlock Holmes on the pictures?"

His eyes opened wide.

"That's just what she said, sir—Miss Sutton said. Just like the hat Sherlock Holmes had on the pictures."

I caught Wharton's eye, and he nodded.

"What we're going to get you to do now, Corporal," he said, "is to go over everything in order while it's being taken down. Nothing to get the wind up about. Everything nice and friendly. Just a formality, you might say." He cast a roguish eye at me. "After that we might pay him something for expenses and then he can enjoy himself for the day."

"Why not?" I said. "We might ring the Depot and say he'll be back some time in the evening. How's that sound, Corporal?"

"Not too bad, sir," he told me, and for the first time since entering that room there was on his face something like a grin.

It was nearer twelve o'clock than eleven when Corporal Trigg departed, and there was no vestige of a grin on the face of Wharton.

"How'd you come to rumble him?" he was asking me.

I told him, and all the thanks I got was a grunt or two.

"A bit of luck for *us*," was his sole comment. "If it doesn't put Dane in the bag, then my name's Robinson. I don't know what the A.C.'s going to think of it."

"Whatever he thinks of it," I said, "you've got enough to pull Dane in for questioning. He might give the Blaketon woman away, or vice versa."

Nothing was said for a moment or two. I think we both felt the imminence of something in the air, like the quick rustle of leaves in a dead calm, and then a sudden coldness and an overcast sky, and in the far distance maybe, the first rumble of thunder.

"I'll see the A.C. at once," Wharton said. His fingers were at the papers on his desk, but he didn't make a move.

"You've heard about Mrs. Allbeck?"

"A bad business," he said. "A bad business."

"No more information?"

"None," he said. "I had a look at her soon after she died and there wasn't a bruise on her body. One on her head where she struck the bottom stair when she fell."

"You mean she wasn't thrown down the stairs. And didn't fall down?"

"She was killed where she was found," he said. "And as soon as she'd closed the door on that caller."

"A powerful thrust, was it?"

"Oh, no," he said. "Anyone could have done it. The knife was razor sharp at the point. Just an ordinary kitchen knife. The old black-handled kind with a triangular blade."

He got to his feet, and I rose too.

"If you do question Dane, I'd like to be there," I said.

"I think you ought to be there," he told me with a touch of reproof. "I doubt if it will be before the late afternoon at the earliest."

"Any time will suit me," I said. "I'll be at the flat from after lunch onwards."

A minute or two later I was making my way towards Kenray's shop. It was Wharton who had put the thought into my mind, for when he had spoken of a bad business, he had echoed the very words that Tom Fulcher had used the previous night. Somehow too, I felt I ought to say something to Kenray. Just what I didn't know. Words may be more than an intrusion in the personal grief of others, and yet I thought that Kenray would understand.

A constable was by the shop and keeping the curious on the move. I went past him to the shop door, but it was locked. Inside I could see Tom Fulcher, and when he saw me he let me in.

"Morning, Tom," I said. "Mr. Kenray in?"

"No, sir," he said, and almost caught my eyes. "He's at the hospital."

I wrote a few words of condolence on the back of a visiting card—and bleak enough they looked—and gave it to Tom to hand to him. All the words I could find for Tom were his own.

"A bad business, Tom."

"It is that, sir," he said. "I daren't think about it, sir, and that's a fact. If I did, I'd . . . well, I reckon I'd sit down and cry like a school kid."

"I know," I said. "And Mr. Kenray, how's he taking it?"

"He don't say much, sir, but I reckon it's finished him."

"How?"

"Reckon he'll give up the business, sir. That's what he says. Besides, sir, we can't carry on without her. I can't run this shop and Mr. Kenray he have to be away."

"He didn't say what he was going to do?"

"Well, sir, he did and he didn't. I reckon he mean goin' back to the old home, sir."

"And you'd go with him?"

"Yes, sir. I'd go with him," He drew himself up with a queer natural dignity. "I've been with him all these years and I reckon I'll be with him as long as he wants me."

"Even down there you won't forget her," I said, and then knew I should have kept my foolish mouth shut. "She was a fine character," I went hastily on. "You couldn't be in her company without feeling that at once."

"You never really knew her," he said. "Ever since Master Hugh got killed, she was never the same. Picked up a bit for a month or two and then she let it get right a hold of her. Used to snap my head off sometimes—not that I didn't deserve it. Then she'd apologize. Sometimes after a day or two it would be."

Then he was suddenly looking up at me.

"Wait a minute, sir, and I'll show you something."

I heard him going up the shop stairs and into the room above. It was his own room that he must have gone to, for it was a matter of minutes before he came down, and he was handing me a photograph.

"There you are, sir! That's how she was when she'd just left school and reckoned she was goin' in for paintin'. I found it some little time ago in some stuff she'd thrown away."

It was a picture of a radiant girl, and taken in full summer. A man had his arm in hers and a hand on one of the balustrades of the fountains of the Eiffel Tower, and the Tower itself was the immediate background.

"In Gay Paree, that's where that was taken," Tom said.

"You don't know who the man is?"

"One o' them painters, I wouldn't be surprised." But it was a thought of his own and he was busy with it, rather than my question.

"Gay Paree," he said. "She was a gay one too. Up to all manner o' tricks when she was home." He gave me a sideways nod and then looked up at me again. "Regular fooled her old father once, she did. I know the old Reverend was a bit short-sighted, and his hearin' wasn't what it was, but she fooled him real proper. April Fools' Day it was, and what must she do but get hold of some curate's clothes from somewhere and put her hair up and so on and knock at the door, bold as brass. I reckon the maid was in the know, but howsomever she showed her in and darn me if the old Reverend didn't talk with her for quite a time till she give herself away by bustin' out laughin'."

"And how did her father take it?"

"They reckon he was pretty riled at first. Then he had to laugh." He gave that sideways nod again. "Don't reckon anyone could be angry with her very long."

It was a happy note and I knew that it was on that that I should leave him. I was smiling as I held out my hand.

"Well, I must be getting along, Tom. I shall see you again soon, I hope."

"I hope so, sir," he told me.

"Good," I said, and at the door: "Don't forget to give Mr. Kenray my card."

"I won't forget, sir," he told me.

I stood for a moment or two on the pavement, wondering whether to lunch in or out. Then I decided to lunch at the flat, and, if Wharton hadn't rung, to spend the afternoon on a long letter to my wife. The wind cut chill as I moved away, and as I thrust my hands deep into the pockets of my overcoat, there was a something strange that I felt. I pulled it out, and it was that photograph of Tom Fulcher's.

Chapter XVI
OUT OF THE DARK

It was getting on for five o'clock when Wharton rang me, and he was afraid he'd still have to keep me hanging around. There had been complications, he said, and it mightn't be till eight o'clock or so that we'd be able to see Bertram Dane.

"What's happened to Leverton?" I asked. "Has he done any talking?"

"Not he," Wharton said. "He'll be out on bail tomorrow. I don't think we'll be able to hold him longer."

"And Mrs. B.?"

"Funny thing about her," he said. "She shut that office of hers at midday and went home. She was still there when I last heard."

"What's the idea? Going to try a getaway?"

"Where can she get to?" George said and snorted.

"What about watching her?" I said. "Is that possible in the black-out?"

"It can't be done," he told me. "All we could do was to get hold of the manager. The first sign of her clearing out and he'll let us know."

I went out then for a breath of air, just a short walk before the black-out. When I came back I ordered dinner and then looked through the evening paper I'd bought. There was only a brief paragraph about Grace Allbeck. It said she had died in the early hours of the morning and that the police had new and vital information. Developments were to be expected at any hour.

That afternoon I had been very much of a fool. I should have rid my mind of the case by going to a cinema, and instead I had written that long letter to my wife, and, as requested, I had told her about Grace Allbeck; and so, what with that and reading that paragraph in the paper, my mind was filled with the very things which I should have done better to avoid. For there comes a time in every case —and I'm told it comes to a novelist near the end of his book—when one sees so far ahead that the mind is filled with an intolerable anticipation. The novelist eats his book, drinks it and sleeps it, and until the last word is written, he is beset with the very frenzy of work.

That was how I was feeling about the case. It was true that I could not foresee the very last word, but at least I was out of my private tunnel and there was light ahead. I knew too that George and I were working on parallel lines, and that sooner or later a tremendous divergence must come. And as I realized that, I suddenly made up my mind that I would see just where I stood. So I took a sheet of paper and began jotting down the things that had occurred to me since that curious moment when I had remembered George's theory that Mavin had intended to put a sleeping draught in Pelle's coffee.

By the time I had finished, dinner was brought up. You may not see much point in all the things I had done. I had studied carefully, for instance, the trains from Charing Cross and Pangley; I had read the article on Jewellery in the *Encyclopedia Britannica*, and under a strong glass I had studied that photograph which I had found in my overcoat pocket. I had even rung up an acquaintance at a private detective agency and, not trusting George's opinion, had asked his views about tailing a suspect in the black-out.

On my sheet of paper was a jumble of oddments and I propped it against the half-empty beer-bottle and began trying to sort the vital from the irrelevant. Then the telephone went. It was a message from George. I was to meet him at a quarter to nine outside St. John's Wood Station.

I hurriedly finished my meal and calculated that I had ten minutes before I need start. The very knowledge brought an urgency, and then a slow anger began to take its place. Laverton out on bail, and fixing things, for a clean bill of health. Complications, George had said, about Bertram Dane, and it looked as if he too was going to wriggle clear. Marion Blaketon at her flat since midday, and the black-out making a getaway the easiest thing in the world. And even if she stayed put, in the morning she and Leverton would be putting their heads together and forging a series of steel-clad alibis.

But, my God! I told myself, whoever got clear, she should not. And then I began to think, and as I stood there with my glasses in my hands, thought had never been more clear. There was not even a word to write down of the things I must say, or the order in which they should be said.

Another moment or two and I was dialling a number. So furious had been that sudden gust of anger that now, in the few seconds of waiting, an even cooler iciness of thought had come and my pulse had never a quickness of beat. Three minutes later, when I laid the receiver down, it was racing like a mad thing.

The night was clear. The stars were shining and a young moon was in the sky. I turned over my loose change for luck and then, just as I went into Leicester Square Station, I heard a siren.

It must have been the first, for there were no signs of a raid as I made my way down the escalator, and the train I took seemed more than half empty. It was about five minutes short of the rendezvous time when I came out at St. John's Wood, and then there wasn't much doubt about a raid being on. Away to the east the barrage was terrific and while I stood there waiting for George, it began to the south-west. There was no shrapnel falling at the moment, but I wished I'd had the sense to bring a tin hat.

A dark saloon car drew in and George stepped out.

"There you are then," he said and in his voice was a considerable relief. "I was just going to look for you. What do you think we'd better do? Take the car or leave it here?"

"I don't mind," I said, and then heard the first patter of falling shrapnel. George grabbed my arm and fairly hustled me in.

"Push on" he told the driver. "When you get inside the gate, draw in under those trees."

I gathered he'd been reconnoitring, and I asked him bluntly if he'd come by car because he was expecting to take Dane back.

"No, worse luck," he said. "All we've got to do is give him a thorough questioning. If he won't talk or explain his movements that night, then he'll be asked to come to the Yard to-morrow. While he's there we may have a search of his house."

"Getting a bit thick, isn't it?" he said, and told the driver to pull in for a moment. Even while he was talking there was a heavy crump not too far off to the east, and our car felt the blast. Somewhere in the darkness beyond the kerb a voice said, "Look!" and there almost above us was a plane held in a cone of lights. The noise around was deafening and not too far off I heard the whine of a falling bomb, and I shot my head in and cringed to my corner. Once more the car shuddered, though the bomb had been farther than I'd thought.

"Just the night there would be a raid," George said peevishly.

"Don't worry about me," I said, about fifty times more bravely than I felt. "If my name's on one, it'll get me."

"Push on," Wharton told the driver, and on we moved. We must have been fairly close to the house for it was no more than a minute before we turned into the open gateway. The driver flashed on his lights for a split second and then nosed the car under the trees. A voice called, "Put out those lights!" and a warden was making his way across.

"Oh, it's you, sir," he said to Wharton. "Thickened up a bit since you left."

He said no more, for barely a quarter of a mile away was a crump and a crash.

"Getting a bit too near," Wharton said, and as he told me to come on he must have nodded back to me in the dark.

"Keep in close," he told me. "There's a short cut round by this wall."

"Has Dane got a shelter?" I whispered.

"Not he," he said. "He's a fatalist, like some more I know."

I swallowed the implied reproof and reached out to feel him in the pitch black by that shrubbery wall. Then right on us, so it seemed, was the first whine of a falling bomb. It seemed to gather momentum as we threw ourselves to the ground, and suddenly there was the flash and the roar, and the sound of falling glass.

"Better get under the end of the house," George growled at me. "A bit too close for my liking."

My knees and elbows felt sodden and chill as I moved on after him, and it was then that we heard the whistle of bombs again. Things happened so quickly that they had no real sequence. I seem to remember that I was about to throw myself flat again. The crescendo whine of a bomb seemed on the very top of my skull and then just ahead was a tremendous flash and in the sudden glare was a kind of general disintegration. I didn't even feel what hit me. It was like that time in 1915 when at one moment I was talking to my sergeant and at the next I was opening my eyes in a clearing station. Now when I opened my eyes I knew I was somewhere in bed. My glasses must have been smashed for what I could see was a blur of light out of which there moved a figure.

"What's happened," I said, and as I moved I felt a pain like a red-hot needle piercing my skull. My hand went up and I touched a bandage. Something closed round my hand and drew it away.

"Drink this," a voice said gently, and I felt an arm beneath my neck and something cold on my lips. It tasted bitter, and all at once I was beginning to remember.

"What happened?" I said again. "What happened to Wharton?"

"Just lie quietly," she said and the arm drew gently away. That pain shot through my skull again and then it seemed that the blur of light went away.

When I opened my eyes again I knew it was daylight. A sister must have been watching me, for as I stirred she moved away. A moment or two and I heard a Voice that I seemed to recognize, and as I tried to raise myself on my elbows, there was the same old pain in my skull.

"Well, how are we now?" the voice said.

"Wroce, isn't it?"

"That's right," he said, and his fingers closed about my pulse. "How're you feeling in yourself?"

"Not too bad," I said. "In fact I think I'm devilish hungry." I stirred in the bed as things came back. "What happened exactly?"

"You got knocked over by blast," he said. "There're twelve stitches in your skull. Nothing to worry about at all."

"And Wharton?" I said. "Superintendent Wharton?"

"He's all right," he said. "He was ringing only a few minutes ago to ask how you were." He tucked my arm in again. "Now we might see about a little something to eat."

"How long before I can get out of here?" I wanted to know.

"Two or three days—with luck," he said, and then I had a sudden alarm.

"My eyes are all right?"

"Why not?" he said. "Your glasses were smashed and your eyebrows cut a bit, that's all."

Before my meal came they had got me my spare glasses from the flat. Maybe I'd have had more sense not to have seen that meal, for I loathe boiled cod and have no great passion for rice-pudding—not that there was much of either. But after it I did feel a tremendous urge to sleep, and though I woke once or twice in the night, when I really awoke was at about ten o'clock on the Thursday morning. There was no particular twinge when I moved my head, and when Wroce came the first thing I asked him was when I could go home.

"Maybe to-morrow," he told me airily. "Your visitor's coming this afternoon."

"Wharton?"

He nodded. "But only for ten minutes. The first sign of a temperature and in here you stay."

Perhaps that was why the sister tucked me in and told me to stay put just before George arrived.

"Well, well, well," he said, and looked down at me. "And how are you feeling?"

"Very much of a fool," I told him.

"The doctors know best," he told me oracularly, and drew his chair in. "Got your bandages off, I see. A nasty crack that was."

He gave me a whimsical look and I knew he was itching to tell me that only a skull as thick as mine could have survived. I told him so.

"Well, you had a lucky squeak," he said. "An inch lower and you mightn't have been here. I was luckier still. Got blown into one of those laurel bushes. Tore my overcoat a bit, and that's all."

"And if I know you," I said, "the Government will be paying for a new one."

"That's more like your old self," he told me delightedly. "And now would you like to hear some news? Or have they told you."

"Don't tell me you've gone and frightened the life out of Bernice!"

"I did think of letting her know," he said, "and then they told me you'd be about again in a day or two. What I thought you might like to know was about Dane." His voice lowered as he drew in his chair. "That last bomb went plumb on the back of the house."

"And he's dead?"

"Blown to smithereens," he said. "No one else hurt. That man of his was down in the front with the wardens and never got a scratch. I've been round there this morning watching them sift the ruins."

"Sift?" I said.

"That's it," he said. "Sift's the word. Hoping to find that missing ring."

I said nothing. There was something else I wanted to know and yet I was afraid to put the question. And while I was trying to think of some roundabout approach, George gave the information himself.

"Another old friend of yours has slipped through the meshes."

"Leverton?"

"Leverton!" He gave a little snort. "He's where we want him—thank God. I meant our friend Mrs. B. You haven't heard about her?"

I shook my head and I could feel my heart beginning to race.

"Took an overdose of sleeping tablets that very same evening"—it would be the Tuesday that he meant—"and wasn't found till late the same night."

"Dead, was she?"

"Dead as a door-nail," Wharton said, and was looking guiltily round. Wroce had come up on the blind side.

"What's this about dead," he said. "Nice cheerful subject to talk about?"

George chuckled as he got to his feet.

"Time's up in any case," Wroce told him. "To-morrow you can talk death and bloody murder to your heart's content."

"You're letting me out?" I said.

"Kicking you out," he said, and George guffawed. "What do you think this is? A hotel?"

I got back to the flat the following afternoon. George rang me after tea and said he'd come round for an hour, if it wouldn't tire me too much. I told him to come before seven o'clock and stay for a meal, but he wouldn't make any promise.

As a matter of fact it was just after six when he turned up. I told him I was feeling fine and that it was damned nonsense about taking things steady. The head was a bit sore but for the rest I'd never felt more fit.

"You're looking pretty pleased with yourself too," I said.

"I don't know that I won't take a little holiday when Leverton's case is over," he told me.

"You mean all the other business is settled to your satisfaction?"

"Signed, sealed and delivered," he told me, and was feeling in his waistcoat pocket. "What do you think of that?"

What he gave me was a tiny circular piece of gold. I stared for a moment, then fetched my glasses. Just visible inside that back section of the ring a letter or two could be made out:

. . . y to . . . ide

"He had that ring then?" I asked.

"Of course he had it! Wasn't that what we were sifting that rubble for?" He wrapped the piece of gold in paper and put it back in his waistcoat pocket. "Signed, sealed and delivered; that's what it is. The Blaketon woman kept him informed. She pumped that little chit of a Chaddon, and young Mavin. She made Pelle miss his train and then Dane cracked him on the skull. Clear as crystal, that's how everything is."

"But if the bomb hadn't caught him, you'd probably have never brought it home."

"I'm not so sure," he said. "That Blaketon woman was beginning to weaken. If I'd caught her that evening before she did herself in, I think she'd have talked."

"There is just one little thing I'd like you to enlighten me on," I said. "I can understand his sending back the balance of the jewellery after he'd got the ring, but wouldn't you have thought that Marion Blaketon would have insisted beforehand on the rest of that jewellery as her perquisite?"

"Have you ever tried to argue with Dane?" he told me, and I thought he was begging the question uncommonly badly. "Unscrupulous, that's what he was. Even if he'd promised the balance of the jewellery to her, he'd have changed his mind if he thought fit. And he did think fit. Wasn't there an enormous risk in letting a woman like her have all that stuff to dispose of? Far safer to send it back. And maybe he gave her a cash payment instead."

"And what about Grace Allbeck?"

"Who killed her?" He waved a quick airy hand. "Who could have killed her but Dane. You ought to know that. You saw him that morning just leaving Kenray's shop. He'd taken that ring there to ask her opinion on it. It wasn't common property, if you remember, that Kenray was advising on that jewellery. Grace Allbeck had suspicions and wouldn't have anything to do with it, and that's why he was shaking his fist at her. Then later he learned through Marion just what kind of brick he'd dropped. It was when that Leverton business broke and the Blaketon woman was scared stiff."

"But suppose Grace Allbeck had mentioned the ring to her brother."

"The answer's that she didn't," he said with a shrug of the shoulders. "If she had, then he'd have told us. Or wouldn't he? People in their high-class line of work have to be very careful of making disclosures about customers."

"Well, everything looks good to me," I said, and never had I felt so much of a hypocrite as I filled his glass. "Another case finished, George. Here's to it, and the next."

He gave me a nod and then took a swig.

"Between you and me," he said, and swept that hand-kerchief of his across his vast moustache, "I'm saying goodbye to that case with devilish few regrets. One or two things still don't satisfy me, but since they satisfy the Powers-that-Be why should I worry? Hush-hush cases never were in my line, and never will be."

"Then here's hoping this will be the last of them," I said, and finished off my tot. "And where did you think of going for this holiday of yours?"

We talked about that and other things for another quarter of an hour and then George got up to go.

"Well, we've pulled it off again," he told me at the door, and it took me a second or two before I realized he was harking back to the case.

"I don't seem to have contributed much," I told him, and I really meant it.

"What about Corporal Trigg?" he said. "Wasn't he just the little bit of something extra we needed when things didn't look any too good?"

"That's rather generous of you, George," I said. "You might as well say the case wouldn't have been solved if Corporal Trigg hadn't been going on leave."

He gave a shake of the head that meant nothing in particular and then held out his hand. He'd be seeing me before that holiday, he said—if it eventuated—and would I remember him to Bernice when I wrote. And didn't I think I'd be sensible if I told her about that raid and got her to come to town for a few days.

I gave a smile as good as any of his non-committal best, and watched till the lift had gone. Then I went back to the room. But when I came to analyse myself I couldn't make up my mind. What was I? Merely a liar out-and-out, or a liar through lack of moral courage? And then by the time the evening meal had come in, I could almost tell myself I was neither. How could I possibly have said to George, "George, you're all wrong. Dane didn't kill Grace Allbeck. Dane had nothing to do with Marion Blaketon. It wasn't Dane who cracked old Pelle on the skull."

I repeat, how could I have told George that? And why should I have told him? What was it that Theseus had said to the Athenian clown?

Never excuse, for when the players are all dead, there need none to be blamed.

That was it—the players all dead and none to be blamed. And why drag in Francis Kenray, far from blameless though he too had been? And old Tom Fulcher too.

So I shook my head and told myself that I'd done right to leave Wharton with his solution of the case. And then a night or so later I changed my mind.

<h1 style="text-align:center">Chapter XVII
WHARTON LISTENS</h1>

ON THE SATURDAY MORNING I took my first walk. I wasn't so full of beans as I'd boasted to Wharton and there was a faint humming in my ears but the walk wasn't long. No farther than Kenray's shop, in fact, and the excuse was the returning of that photograph. But before I set out I rang the shop to make sure Kenray wouldn't be there.

"Thank you, sir," Tom said, pocketing the photograph. "I'd been lookin' for it everywhere."

"Did you say Mrs. Allbeck had thrown it away?" I asked. "I found it among some old paper for salvage," Tom said. "I reckon she might have made a mistake, though."

"And you've no idea when Mr. Kenray will be back?"

Tom said he thought he'd be in at midday.

"Must be trying, that daily travelling," I said. "Pangley isn't too far, but I shouldn't like to have that journey each way every day. Has he always lived down there?"

"Bless you no, sir," Tom said. "Only about fifteen year or so. When I first come up here we was livin' at Faversham Square. Why we moved out to Pangley was because he thought the country would do Mrs. Kenray good. And then there was Miss Grace. She allust had a hankerin' after a flat, as they say, so we give up the Dover Street shop and took this place here. And a rare good change it turned out to be."

Those were the last inquiries I was to make and I could tell myself that what I had learned I would keep to myself. Wharton had said that the case was over. He was satisfied, and, what was more to the point, the Powers-that-Be were satisfied too. Who then was I to go raking things up?

But there I reckoned without myself. I mentioned how cases and books can so work on the minds of those immediately concerned that the work in hand becomes an obsession and the mind has no rest till it is rid of it. By the Sunday afternoon I had worked myself up to just such a pitch. Either I had to confide in Wharton or I would have no freedom from its haunting. And then I made a sudden decision. I guessed that George would be at home, and I rang him there. I was feeling a bit lonely, I said, and would he drop in some time and share my evening meal. He said he'd be delighted and we agreed on half-past six.

When I hung up I hardly knew what I was feeling. In a way I had wished him to refuse, for in the very depth of me I was scared stiff. How could I, the apprentice, have the effrontery to criticize the old master? How could I do it without causing some reopening of the case? And yet in a way I was pleased that I'd committed myself. It was like being scared of a visit to the dentist and then the subsequent relief when one has forced one's self to the step of making an appointment.

George arrived on time and as I took his hat and coat I thought I knew my opening questions. But I deferred them till we were comfortably at the fire and the two tots of beer had been poured.

"Well, here's to another case over, George," I said again. "I take it *is* now very definitely over?"

"Oh, yes," he said, and raised his glass before he took a swig.

"Even if anything else came out, it wouldn't be re-opened?"

"What else *could* come out?" he said, and settled snugly into his chair. Then he was giving me a look. "What's behind all this? You're not getting at anything, are you?"

"Well, yes and no," I said. "But one does have ideas, you know. Do you think any conscientious author, for instance, ever wrote a book without realizing afterwards that he might have made a better hand of it? The same surely with a case."

"That wouldn't pay in our line," he told me. "Done's done, and the motto is, get on with the next." Then came another suspicious look. "Mind you, I think we might have handled that case differently. Still, why worry now?"

"That's how things strike me," I said. "I think if we'd had the wisdom of both men and angels, we'd have handled it differently, and we mightn't have arrived at the same end. Wait a minute," I said hastily. "That statement wasn't quite right. I should have said that *I* might have handled my side of things differently, and *I* might have arrived at different conclusions."

"Such as what?"

I fortified myself with a pull at my glass and then freshened up both before I spoke.

"I'll be perfectly frank, George. There's something on my mind and I'd regard it as a favour if you'd listen patiently while I get it off."

"Why not?" he said, and tried to make the remark humorous.

"That's very good of you, George," I said. "Honestly I'm regarding it as a favour. But I do have to say that I want you to be fair to me, and I'm certainly going to try to be implicitly fair to you. For example, I own that there were things which Tom Fulcher told me which I thought at the time had no bearing on the case, and which I never, therefore, mentioned to you. There were things about Kenray which didn't strike me as important at the time, but which have certainly done so since. There were things I noticed about Grace Allbeck and to which I saw no reason to attach importance. There were things in Pelle's autobiography which struck me as curious and no more. Then when it was too late they acquired a significance.

"In fact," I went on, "I probably shan't be talking for a minute before you'll be saying, 'You didn't tell me that,' or 'That's the first time I ever heard of it.' Also I may mention things that I did tell you, and you didn't attach any special significance to them, perhaps because I hadn't done so myself.

"As to your being fair to me, I ought to remind you that there's nobody now who can be questioned and so I have to rely on such past impressions as I've already mentioned. And if I'm to speak impartially, then I have to admit here and now that I can't recall every tone of voice and every gesture, and so certain words and statements may still sound bald and unconvincing to you."

"A hell of a long prologue, isn't it?" He was trying to make his tone whimsical. "And what's it all lead to?"

"If you'll be patient with me, you'll see," I said. "It may be a longish story but dinner isn't till a quarter-past seven and it'll be over by then. All you've got to do George, is to keep your glass filled and listen to me."

"Won't be the first time," he told me.

But that long preamble of a tale had cleared my mental air. Something told me to discard apologies and get down to facts and let recriminations and minor inquests look after themselves.

"Well, I'd like to begin with Grace Crowner," I said.

"Who's she?"

I explained all that, and then made a fresh start.

"In 1911 Grace Crowner had just left finishing school in Paris and was announcing that she wanted to take up painting. She was a high-spirited girl who was quite capable of looking after herself, and I think her family had to agree to her proposal. And then almost at once she was writing home that she might be getting married. The old Vicar, her father, went to Paris in considerable alarm, and what happened I don't know. I can only judge that he was too late to see the man in question, and I'm fairly sure his name never came out publicly. Tom Fulcher showed me, however, a photograph of her with that man, and I had no great difficulty in identifying him as Pelle."

"No!" he said, and sat up in his chair.

"It's beyond question," I said. "And in that photograph she looks brimming with happiness and he's holding her arm with an air of satisfied possession. And yet—and that almost as soon as he got back to India—he was marrying another girl.

"He was on leave in Paris, where his father lived, in 1911, you may not remember, and in his autobiography he gives no account whatever of how he spent that leave. And why? Because his time was all taken up with Grace, and because he must have known all his life that the whole episode and what followed was as near despicable as could be.

"Why did he marry, for instance? I think we can believe Marion Blaketon for once. It was for the purpose of advancement, and he certainly did uncommonly well out of it. But I wonder what lies and subterfuges he had to resort to when he had to write to Grace Crowner. I know the effect his letter had on her. She had a nervous breakdown, and nervous breakdowns aren't easily forgotten, nor are the causes that led to them.

"At any rate she came home and she recovered sufficiently to be marrying in a few years' time an artist named Allbeck. My own view is that it was a kind of rebound marriage, though that doesn't affect the argument. He joined the Artists' Rifles and was killed in France at the very end of the last war. Her son, I gather, was posthumously born."

"But why wasn't I told about that photograph?" George was asking and not without cause.

"Because it didn't come into my possession till too late," I said. "But to go on with Grace Allbeck's story. She must have heard news of Pelle from time to time, if only the snippets one sees in the Press. He had a son and doubtless she was aware of his doings in the days when athletics made splash headlines. Her own boy went to Cranwell and then to an Indian station. Later he came back and was killed in action over Dieppe. That was the final and culminating tragedy of her life, and yet she began slowly to get over it. Then she began really to change, and my evidence is what Tom Fulcher told me. I think the change was due to two things. I think she saw about six months ago a picture of young Pelle when he was home on leave and having a good time at Newmarket. Mavin showed me that picture which Sir William had cut from *Society News*. The second thing that happened was, I think, a much later reading of that paragraph in the *Clarion*. Tom Fulcher took the *Clarion*, though we didn't know that at the time.

"Now take the concentrated effects of seeing that photograph and reading that gossip paragraph. I claim that all her life she'd nourished a bitter hatred of Pelle, and now what did she read? That he was to be in charge of jewellery—a small point and one that made only a small rankling. But he with his sheltered and prosperous life and his knighthood and her husband dead in France. His son, sleek and safe and basking in cheap publicity, and her boy dead in the sea by Dieppe. Was there justice in the world, or right? What else had life to give Pelle, and what pitiful little was left for it to take from *her*?

"I won't labour that, George, but I think that from then on her life was one of concentrated bitterness and brooding hatred of Pelle. But there was nothing she could do except think. And then came the queer twist when Kenray was called in as consultant to Pelle. If Pelle had ever heard his name from Grace Crowner he had long since forgotten it, and the association meant no contact with a Grace Allbeck, even if he knew that second name. But to her the whole business of that association must have been a torture. A point I would make, by the way, is that I'm sure Kenray never knew the name of the man who'd caused her breakdown all those years before. He was in London at the time, for one thing, and Crowner was only his stepfather.

"And then came the day when Kenray told her about Pelle's madness, or obstinacy, in talking of taking that jewellery personally to Kalpoor. Whatever Kenray may have suggested to the contrary—and I think later you'll see he had reasons—there's no doubt in my mind that he told Grace Allbeck all his business affairs. She was his partner and a supremely capable one. I think she asked him, as I did you, what would be Pelle's responsibility if anything happened to the jewellery in transit, and he doubtless gave the opinion that you gave me—that he'd be held guilty of gross negligence and responsible in law for the value of the stolen articles.

"From then on she began making plans to ruin Pelle. She sent him on that wild-goose chase that afternoon, for she'd lived in Faversham Square and knew the numbers of the houses. She even thought of a suitable suspect on whom the police might waste considerable time; a man for whom she'd neither liking nor sympathy—I mean, Bertram Dane. I suggest she rang him up under an assumed name, and altering her voice. I can tell you an episode that Tom Fulcher told me which made that well within her possibilities. Probably she said she had a papal ring of great age and value and he could see it at a certain time—she named the train from Charing Cross—and at that time only, as she was going away that night. I'd say the fictitious address was in Manwood Lane and she was careful to tell him to go just into the town and there he'd get a bus to drop him at her door. When Dane asked how she knew the ring was genuine and valuable, she said she'd consulted Kenray."

"The devil of a lot of suppositions, aren't there?"

"I don't think that's entirely supposition, George," I said. "When I asked Grace Allbeck why Dane had shaken his fist at her that morning, she told me, and she could tell me only the truth, for if we questioned Dane, then his tale would have to agree with hers. Remember, George, that in Grace Allbeck we have a woman of more than ordinary intelligence who could drive a purpose remorselessly through. What she told me was that he was accusing her of double-crossing him in the matter of a ring by trying to buy it from a client. That means he put down the failure to find that client to some fault of his own and he was intending to go to Pangley again when the lady returned and have the matter out with her. Later on I'll try to show why he didn't go to Pangley again."

"Just a minute before you go any further," George said, "I'm not so blind that I can't see out of one eye at least. Are you going to tell me that she killed Pelle? What about her alibi?"

"That's what I'm coming to," I said. "You put the idea into my head when you suggested that Mavin had thought of doping

Pelle's coffee. But that's rushing on ahead. What she did first, I'd say, was to tell Kenray when he went off to that sale that Monday that he wasn't to tire himself but get back early to the shop and have some tea before getting on with that office work he'd mentioned. That gives us two eventualities to face.

"Suppose first that he came back late, so late that she'd have had to take the four-fifty. Then I think she'd have left a note saying the kettle was on the boil and she'd had to slip out for something and he was to make himself a cup of tea. In that case the dope would have been in the milk.

"But that didn't happen, so we needn't go into it further. What we'll do is look at his own evidence. He says he got in at about five—"

"But she was there!"

"I know she was. I repeat, he says he got in at about five. Is there a clock around there where he could have seen the time as he came in? There isn't. And it was a filthy afternoon, wet and heavily overcast. Analyse his own evidence again and you'll be of the opinion that he came in dog-tired, and he said to her, 'What's the time?' She said it was nearly five, when as a matter of fact it might have been no more than half-past four. Then she said how dreadfully tired he looked, and into the office came the tea and a sleeping powder in it. It was, 'Drink this and then lie back for a bit. There'll be plenty of time to do your work.' Then in a matter of minutes he was asleep, and she could catch that four-fifty. Fulcher had been conveniently got rid of, and I expect she'd bought her ticket beforehand and it would take just five minutes from door to train.

"Perhaps she wore a veil. In any case she had only old Dane to dodge, and when she got out at Pangley she would expect him to take the left fork to the town. She hurried on ahead of Pelle and waited for him just short of Sutton's cottage. Remember how Kenray let slip that she could see in the dark like a cat? And undoubtedly she never meant to kill. All she wanted was to snatch that case, but when she struck, the blow must have had in it the hatred of years. But she wouldn't be worrying about him when he fell. She'd have been listening for steps, and drawing back to the hedge to empty that case into capacious pockets. Then she threw the case into the gorse of the common, for it would have been too dangerous to take. I think she must have gone partly through a gap in the hedge to throw the case and that when she came back to the road she was just near enough to Trigg's truck to see it. All I can think of then is that she had a kind of womanly softening. She didn't know Pelle was dead but she'd accomplished what she'd set out to do, and by putting him in the back of that low truck she may have had an idea that he'd get attended to wherever it was that truck was going."

"You think she could have lifted him? The body was limp, remember."

"I saw her lift something just as heavy as he," I said. "A box that made Tom Fulcher stagger and wheeze, and that was the first time I saw her. But as I was saying she had to hurry back to the station to dodge Dane. When she got back home, it couldn't have been more than a minute or two before a quarter-past six. The meal had been prepared beforehand and all she had to do was to warm it while she tidied herself and hid the jewellery away. Then she woke Kenray up. 'What time is it? Not much after six. You've had a lovely sleep and I hadn't the heart to wake you. And you'd better get yourself ready now because dinner will be on in five minutes."

"As for what she intended to do with that jewellery, I can't say. Kenray was due to leave for the States in about ten days and then she might have taken it out to the country and buried it somewhere. What I do believe is that she'd never have profited a penny from it. But what she did do that night when Kenray had gone was to send that ring to Dane, posting it, of course, in the morning. That was for verisimilitude. In it was a letter with the address simply London, and saying that as Dane hadn't called as requested or arranged, and the owner had been on her way through town, she was sending the ring for inspection, and at some convenient time she'd expect to hear from him."

"But that ring wasn't a papal ring," protested George.

"I know it wasn't. But wouldn't he expect a silly bletherer like that woman to make a mistake? Hadn't she already bitched him up about her address?"

"You're too ingenious for me," he said. "But go on. Let's hear the rest."

"Well, what we come to is a general proof," I said. "I claimed that Grace Allbeck wouldn't have profited by taking that jewellery, and yet she virtually stole that ring. But did she? Or did she give a *quid pro quo*?"

"I don't get it," George said.

"This is what she did," I told him. "She valued that ring at a thousand pounds, and so she gave something else worth a thousand pounds to make up for it."

I waited for him to say what I knew he'd say.

"But she'd given that piece of jewellery long before that!"

"Had she? Just think. What proof is there?"

"The proof of the lists that Pelle made."

"Do you know if they showed an anonymous piece of jewellery?"

"Well, I can't say I do. As far as I remember they showed several anonymous pieces."

"Exactly. And who was checking the lists at Kalpoor that morning when the jewellery was returned?"

"Kenray was."

"Exactly!" I said. "And there we are. All he had to do in his own good time was to slip that piece of jewellery in with the rest. Substitute it, if you like, for another anonymous piece that wasn't worth much."

"Here! Just a minute," and he held up a hand. "What's this you're getting at? Are you making Kenray a confederate?"

"Yes and no," I said. "What made him suspicious about his stepsister I can't say, but it might have been any number of things. Maybe something went wrong with the sleeping powder and he woke up too soon. He found she was out and then went off to sleep again, and later wondered why she'd said she'd been in all the time, looking after the meal. Then he began next morning to wonder a whole lot of things. Where had she been?

Why had she always seemed so interested in Pelle? Why had she asked for the telephone number of his office? And so on and so on, George, and yet the proof doesn't lie in that. I'd say he found her very strange the next morning and that's when he got the whole story out of her. The ring couldn't be recovered for it had been posted to Dane that morning, so it was he who suggested the gift in its place. There always seemed something curious to me about that gift, and I think there did to you. And now you also know the answer to something else that puzzled you at the time. Your instincts were right, George. There *was* something fishy about Kenray's coming to see you that morning. What he came for was to see how much you knew, and to spike your guns. Another awkward thing he had to do later on was to go to Pangley and find that attaché-case, and he did that on the night when I went to see Mavin, and though I wondered why he'd come to see Mavin, all I thought was that it was about the jewellery."

Once more George raised a pontifical hand.

"Mind you, I'm not agreeing with all you've said, though some of it sounds mightily suspicious. But what you're saying about Kenray—well, that hasn't got so much proof as you said."

"Then here's some news for you," I said. "Kenray changed his mind about going to the States. He was sending her instead. Now do you see how he was shielding her? She'd never been there on business before. And another thing. Kenray's giving up his business and retiring to the country. He wants to get the thing out of his sight even if it'll be harder to get it from his mind. And I could tell you all sorts of little things about her. That morning when I saw her lift that heavy box, for instance. She didn't see me but when she did she was scared. Wondered who I was, and her eyes kept probing me. Knew she'd made a blunder in letting a stranger see her lift that box. It reminded her of what she'd lifted the previous night, and so she had to tell me—a stranger—that she hadn't really the strength to do what she'd already done. Then she pretended Tom Fulcher wasn't a countryman because she didn't want him questioned about herself, and where he'd been the previous night. And then that night when you and I went round she'd had a headache and I asked how the head felt. She was just about to say, 'As if I'd been clubbed,' and then she remembered in time. I said it myself and I saw her wince."

"Well, I won't commit myself," George said. "But why did she dare to send Dane that ring? Suppose it had come out that it had been taken from Pelle's dead body?"

"Tell me something," I said. "Did Dane have that ring on him when he was killed?"

"As a matter of fact, he did."

"That's what I thought. What would a collector as unscrupulous as he was worry about the origin of that ring? True he daren't put it in his collection, but he could carry it about with him and take it out of his pocket every now and again and gloat over it. But about your general incredulity George, or your lack of credulity. Perhaps I haven't sufficiently accentuated her feelings and motive. Not the motive for *killing* him, George. Don't forget that. The motive for ruining him financially and making him publicly ridiculous. And I do think even in our little way, George, you and I have had our own small indignations during this case—the simonism and nepotism, for instance, and strapping young men like Bill ('Skittles') Pelle being far too valuable for machine-gun fodder, and war-time cushy jobs and rackets."

"I know," George said, and pursed his lips reflectively. "The motive's there all right. But doesn't what you've been saying upset our theories about Dane and Marion Blaketon?"

"They do more than that," I said. "They knock them cock-eyed. I don't think now that there was any more between Dane and the Blaketon woman than there is between you and Lady Omnium. I doubt if either knew the other's name."

"Then why did she ring that Chaddon girl that Monday afternoon?"

"For the reason she gave," I said. "To ask her to a party. And the reason she asked me to that party was, as you said, to prove there had been a party in her mind. And also possibly to prove to me how well-conducted her parties were. I think she may also have wanted me to have a good impression of her generally."

"Why? The Leverton business hadn't broken then."

"But she had something else on her conscience, George. I'm pretty sure it was a man of hers who tried that burglary that Mavin circumvented at Kalpoor. Probably Leverton provided the burglar. I think she was trying to cultivate me just as she cultivated any likely person. Doris Chaddon, for instance, to learn all about the jewellery, and Mavin to learn about the autobiography, and me to learn how things were going at the Yard."

"I can get the rough hang of all that," George said, "but there's something else that's gone a bit cock-eyed, as you put it. You say Dane had that ring sent to him anonymously. Very well then, he didn't kill Grace Allbeck because he knew she knew he had it. Why did he kill her then?"

"The answer is that he didn't," I said, and he sat up and stared.

"Dane didn't kill her! Then who did?"

"Marion Blaketon did," I said, and then after a moment or two: "And I killed Marion Blaketon."

There was a tap at the outer door. I hopped up at once and in came the waiter and a boy with a couple of trays. Then we had to leave the door open for the room to clear of smoke and in the cloak-room we had a quick clean up. Neither of us said a word, unless it was that I remarked that the water wasn't very hot. George made noises like a trumpeting elephant while he laved his face and spluttered in the bowl, and I could guess what he was wondering. Then we went back to the warm room again. There was hot soup on the table; cold galantine and salad and potatoes and some apple pie and custard. I fetched a bottle from the back room.

"Some of that port you always liked, George," I said. "If you don't mind drinking with a murderer."

"You're pulling my leg," he told me, but he glanced at that stitched skull of mine all the same.

"Oh, I'm sane enough," I said. "Exaggerating a bit perhaps. Maybe you won't think it murder after all."

I kept him off till he had finished his soup and then he simply sat back and waited.

"Here's how it was then, George," I said. "Go on eating, and I'll talk and eat. About who killed Grace Allbeck. Remember how we discovered that Marion Blaketon had tried to sell her a piece of stolen jewellery? And how Grace Allbeck had taken her name and address? Well, let's go back a bit.

"That Saturday night at her house I did some fake fortune-telling, as I told you. I don't know a thing about it so I extemporized. The Queen of Clubs turned up and somewhere or other I'd read that she represented a dark or darkish woman of middle age, so I told Marion Blaketon to beware of a dark woman. I told her other things but that's the one that matters, and the fact that I obviously convinced her I was the genuine thing in fortune-tellers.

"Go on to the last time you saw her. The Leverton business had broken and you'd scared her stiff. And most of all with that bluff of yours, that you had certain sources of information that she wouldn't suspect. But she did suspect. She remembered what I'd told her about a dark woman. She remembered—and I'll bet a cold shudder went down her spine—how Grace Allbeck had her name and address and suspected her of trying to dispose of stolen property. When she got home she began working out how she stood, and it was a hell of a prospect. Whereas she might or might not swing clear in the matter of Leverton, she knew no reason why Grace Allbeck shouldn't give her away—and Grace Allbeck was the sister of the man intimately concerned with that jewellery. That made her think of the burglary and if we knew the man who'd tried to make an entry. And my conclusion is that it all added up to the one thing—that Grace Allbeck was the immediate danger.

"I think she rang her and recalled herself, and made an appointment. Maybe as soon as she was in that side door she asked a question. 'I suppose you never told anyone about that piece of jewellery I brought here and asked you to buy? I mention it because I discovered later that it had been stolen.' Maybe Grace Allbeck told her—either then or in the original telephone conversation—that she'd said nothing, not even to her brother.

Then Grace turned to show her upstairs and Marion Blaketon struck her with the knife."

"There may be something in it," said George. "But anything else?"

"Yes," I said. "We move on to the Tuesday night when I was waiting to go to St. John's Wood. I began thinking about some of the things I've been telling you, and something suddenly told me that Marion Blaketon would wriggle clear of that murder. I had nothing but suspicion and flimsy circumstantial evidence to go on, and I couldn't see how the murder could be pinned on her, and then all at once I got blazing mad. I told myself I'd be damned if she'd swing clear. So I grabbed the telephone and rang her up. I wrote down this afternoon every word of the short conversation. Here it is if you'd like to read it."

George gulped down his mouthful, adjusted his spectacles and read.

T. That you, Mrs. Blaketon?

B. Yes?

T. Do you recognize my voice?

B. But of course! It's Ludovic.

T. Forget it. And listen, Mrs. Blaketon, and don't interrupt. I'm taking a hell of a risk to give you a warning. Inside a couple of hours at the most you'll be arrested.

B. Me!

T. Yes, you. And for murder. MURDER. Haven't you read the evening papers? Grace Allbeck left a statement about everything. Everything! Does that convey anything to you? And Wharton's now with the Public Prosecutor and I happen to know what's been decided. Put your nose out of your door and you'll find you're being watched.

B. (After a pause.) It can't be. It isn't true!

T. Mrs. Blaketon, I beg of you. Didn't I try to give you a tip about Grace Allbeck last Saturday night? We knew a good deal then. You know what murder means, and they've got you.

"That's all, George," I said, when I'd taken that paper back. And as I held a corner to the fire and watched it burn: "And you know the result. She didn't kill herself because of the Leverton business. You and I know she might have wriggled clear from that, even if she might have had to give up the secretaryship of that Society. What she killed herself for was the killing of Grace Allbeck."

He grunted as he began again on his meal.

"A risky thing to do, wasn't it?"

"It was," I said. "But I liked Grace Allbeck. As you told me, George, I have my likes and dislikes. I didn't like Grace Allbeck less because she'd felt herself driven to ruining that old fool Pelle. And I don't think the less of Kenray because he tried to cover Grace up."

"A detective's no right to be a Jekyll and Hyde," George said doggedly.

"But I'm not a detective," I told him. "Aren't you always telling me so!"

He shook his head and said nothing, and for a minute or two we got on with our meal. Then he pushed his empty plate aside and I took it away with my own, though I hadn't finished.

"A most extraordinary story," he said heavily, even if his eyes were regarding with interest the slab of pie on his plate. "What I reckon is that we'd better say no more about it."

"I'm with you there," I said. "I've got it off my chest and I feel better. And supposing the case were reopened, what good would it do? The principals are dead, and if they weren't then everything I've been telling you is so fantastically circumstantial that it wouldn't convince a jury of nitwits."

"You're right enough there," he said, and went on with his pie. Then in a minute or so he was asking what was amusing me.

"I wasn't amused," I said. "I was merely thinking of something. I know this case is over and done with and your own solution is officially correct. But suppose it were reopened. Who'd get the blame for any slip-ups? The apprentice or the old master?"

He paused in the middle of his final mouthful of pie.

"What's the idea? Trying to blackmail me?"

"God forbid, George," I told him hastily.

Then I was fetching a couple of port glasses and passing a full one to him.

"Here's to forgetfulness then, George."

He nodded a good health, took a drink and smacked his lips. George would have been popular with the Arabs. A belch to show appreciation would have been right up his alley.

"A drop of good stuff this."

"A cigar?" I said, and handed him the box.

"Trying that blackmail stunt?" he said, but there was definitely a twinkle in his eyes as he peered at me over those spectacles he was still wearing.

"Not a bit of it," I said, and drew his chair towards the fire. "Just a celebration on account of my being blown back from hell's gates instead of through."

He gave a little sigh of content as he stretched his feet towards the fire.

"Just one little question," I said coaxingly, "and then we'll forget all that damned silly theorizing of mine. Just suppose I'd come to you a week ago with what I've told you to-night. What do you think you'd have said?" George drew in a steady breath of smoke, then blew it slowly out. Then he peered at me, and I was practically sure that he winked.

"What would I have said? I reckon I'd have said we'd got something there, or my name was Robinson."

THE END

www.ingramcontent.com/pod-product-compliance
Lightning Source LLC
Chambersburg PA
CBHW070944190726
48292CB00004B/1334